AN UNEXPECTED KISS

A shiver of awareness ran through Felicity as his warm breath whispered past her ear. She was in the arms of a man, and she quite liked everything about the feel. Shock raced through her. This led to dangerous thoughts. She pushed her emotions aside and concentrated on the lads.

She drew back and gazed up at the earl. "You will make certain that they are well taken care of after they return to school? That this man will be dismissed if he's been mistreating the boys."

Fennerly looked down into her beautiful tearstained face, and something seemed to clamp around his heart. She was the most desirable woman he'd ever known and it wasn't merely that beautiful face. It was that vulnerability he'd seen. Over the last few days he'd also seen a goodness deep inside that was rare in a woman of their class. She truly cared about others, but especially the less fortunate. In a husky voice, he said, "I promise."

Time seemed to freeze as she gazed up at him so trustingly. He suddenly realized he wanted to kiss Miss Newman. As they stood alone in the hall, the only light was that from the open nursery door and the gentleman threw caution to the wind. He lowered his head and tasted those lovely lips. . . .

—from "Father and the Notorious Miss Newman,"
by Lynn Collum

BOOK YOUR PLACE ON OUR WEBSITE AND MAKE THE READING CONNECTION!

We've created a customized website just for our very special readers, where you can get the inside scoop on everything that's going on with Zebra, Pinnacle and Kensington books.

When you come online, you'll have the exciting opportunity to:

- View covers of upcoming books
- Read sample chapters
- Learn about our future publishing schedule (listed by publication month *and author*)
- Find out when your favorite authors will be visiting a city near you
- Search for and order backlist books from our online catalog
- Check out author bios and background information
- Send e-mail to your favorite authors
- Meet the Kensington staff online
- Join us in weekly chats with authors, readers and other guests
- Get writing guidelines
- AND MUCH MORE!

Visit our website at
http://www.kensingtonbooks.com

A WIFE
FOR PAPA

Lynn Collum

Laura Paquet

Hayley Ann Solomon

ZEBRA BOOKS
Kensington Publishing Corp.
http://www.kensingtonbooks.com

Contents

Father and the Notorious Miss Newman

Lynn Collum

Chapter One

A good father always worries about his son's welfare no matter the young man's age. Especially a father who committed a dreadful folly in his own youth. Hugh Holmes, Ninth Earl of Fennerly, was just such a man. He'd spent the better part of his adult life determined to protect his son from making the kind of foolish mistake he'd made at eighteen.

At Oxford at the time of his life-changing blunder and patently unaware of all the dangers the world held for a wealthy young man of good family, Lord Fennerly had gone on holiday with a school friend. In Brighton the naive earl met the beautiful Lady Cassandra Lawrence. His youthful inexperience with women allowed him to see only her beautiful face and lithe figure, not the impulsive and temperamental traits that surfaced when her wishes were thwarted.

Without the wisdom of his long-dead father to urge restraint, Hugh had rashly made an offer for the lady at the end of three short weeks, despite his friend's warnings to proceed slowly. The lady's father, the Marquess of Burnfield, had gladly accepted the earl, happy to have his willful child off his hands before she created some scandal. The pair were married within the month, and a besotted Hugh had brought his bride to London to meet his mother. It took Lady Cassandra a scant two weeks of living under the same roof to show her true nature to her husband and mother-in-law. By the time

Hugh fully understood that the lady was utterly spoiled and selfish, it was too late.

He endured two years of misery, the only bright spot throughout was the birth of his son and heir, Barclay. The earl's reprieve from his disastrous marriage came a year after his child's birth when Lady Cass developed an inflammation of the lungs after a drenching while out with her raffish friends. Despite the doctor's best efforts, the lady expired. The Earl of Fennerly, widowed at twenty, retired with his son to Kent, having learned a cruel lesson about life and love.

With the help of the dowager countess, Hugh raised his son to be a responsible young man. Over the years her ladyship had periodically encouraged the earl to find a new wife, but Lord Fennerly had adamantly refused, convinced that love was an illusion perpetuated by poets and writers. He contented himself with adding to his wealth and taking care of his estate and family while dabbling in local politics. If he felt any loneliness he was able to keep his suffering from others. Yet while he showed no inclination to again marry, he encouraged his son's budding romance with the daughter of their nearest neighbor. The Honorable Miss Mary Camp was everything Lady Cass was not, which suited the earl and his mother perfectly. After all, his son would need to produce an heir in time.

At eighteen, Barclay duly went up to Oxford with all kinds of warning to be careful of strangers. Hugh and Lady Fennerly visited the young man at regular intervals and were convinced he was prospering in his studies, making respectable friends, and growing into a dependable young gentleman.

With most things in life, however, when one thinks things are going smoothly something comes along to upset the applecart. That something for Hugh proved to be the Notorious Newmans, a family whose infamous exploits were only equaled in notoriety by their good looks.

The earl had little idea when he opened the weekly letter from his son that morning that the missive would turn his life upside down. Having just sat down at the breakfast table with his mother, he poured himself a cup of coffee, then broke the seal and began to read..

"Clay sends his best." The earl smiled at his mother, who was looking quite lovely with her silver hair hidden beneath a new lace cap she'd had her maid copy from the latest *La Belle Assemblè*.

"Does he mention his cold? Did he take my advice to take a bit of whiskey, honey, and lemon juice for his cough?" Her ladyship pushed aside the *Morning Post*, having finished perusing the Society columns, eager to hear of her grandson's doings at university.

A frown appeared on Hugh's mildly lined brow. At nine-and-thirty, he was a handsome man who still turned female heads. But most of the local ladies had learned long ago that casting out lures was a waste of time where Fennerly was concerned. He seemed determined to remain a single widower.

The gentleman looked up at his mother, his gray eyes filled with worry. "There's been an outbreak of measles at Oxford. They are sending all the young men away for three weeks."

"Measles! Thank heavens Clay had a case back when he was seven. We have nothing to fear. I should enjoy having our young scholar home for a few days." Lady Fennerly drew the sugar dish toward her and added an extra lump to her coffee—what would one more hurt at her age after all?

"He's not coming home. The boy is going to London to stay with his new friend , Aaron Newman, until university is reopened."

Not being daily involved in London Society, the dowager grew thoughtful as she pondered who this young man her grandchild had befriended might be. Then her eyes widened. "Do not say that is one of Viscount Newley's sons."

"I fear it so. They are to stay at the viscount's town house."

"I have heard that the only thing more handsome than Newley's sons are his daughters."

An icy feeling crept into Hugh's gut. "Is the eldest Miss Newman not the lady whose name has been linked to several of the most wealthy young men of Society? Never able to bring a single one up to scratch, or so I hear."

"No doubt they were frightened off by her father's reputation and his low companions, not to mention his ever-present debt. But surely that girl must be nearing thirty, a positive ape leader."

The earl laid his son's letter on the table. "True, but Harlin's heir was scarcely out of the schoolroom when he became ensnared by her last year. I spoke to the marquess in the House of Lords, just after he'd sent the boy off to Greece. Swore the girl was a gazetted fortune huntress. Lord Huntley's heir had an equally close escape several years earlier, or so he swears."

Mother and son grew silent as they pondered the situation. Lady Fennerly finally said, "This is Clay we are speaking about. You have raised a sensible young man. There is no need to worry that he will fall under such a female's spell. Why, he is completely in love with Miss Camp."

"Yes, to be certain." The earl nervously tapped the tablecloth with his fingertips. His son had the advantage of a father's advice, and Hugh must trust that Clay wouldn't fall prey to just any pretty face.

Her ladyship patted the Society column of the folded newspaper. "No doubt, the young men will be out on the town and rarely see the viscount's daughters." A glimmer of confidence glistened in her brown eyes.

"Yes, to be certain." Hugh had never seen Lord Newley's eldest daughter, but even in the country her string of admirers was the subject of gossip.

"He could use a bit of Town Bronze." The countess nodded her head then continued her breakfast.

"Still, I cannot like him rattling around with such an infamous set." The earl picked up the letter and eyed it thoughtfully.

After a bite of Cook's famous sweet rolls, the lady patted

her mouth. "We mustn't coddle the boy too much, Hugh. Besides, it is only for three weeks."

The earl nodded, but his features were still creased with worry lines, as all the possibilities flashed in the gentleman's mind. After several moments of silence, he softly recalled, "I was so besotted at the end of the first week I would have married Cassandra then if we'd been in London where I could have procured a special license."

They stared at each. The dowager sensed her son would not rest until he saw his son safe. She put her napkin on the table. "Well, I don't suppose it would hurt if we traveled to London, if only to reassure you Clay is not one of those silly, empty-headed lads who falls into every kind of scrape ."

Lord Fennerly rose. "I shall have the carriage ready to go in thirty minutes."

A Greek once observed that the gods visited the sins of the father on the sons, and Viscount Newley's offspring could verify the truth of the maxim. Their father's reputation for gaming, wenching and drinking had been long established before the first of his four children was even old enough to visit London. He'd managed to marry twice and squander both ladie's fortunes before he was five-and-thirty. His reputation as a wastrel barely allowed him to move on the fringes of the *ton*. Much of his time was spent in low gaming hells, mixing with the riffraff of London's seamier population. This fact greatly affected his children's chances of making good alliances. Yet his addiction to vices was such that he'd paid little heed to that fact. His deteriorating finances at last penetrated his world.

Early on the same morning that Lord Fennerly would read the alarming letter from his son, Lord Newley wandered out of his favorite gaming hell into the damp dawn air. He had strolled only half the distance to his town house, lacking suf-

ficient funds for a hack, when he was accosted by two ruffi-
ans. After a pummeling to his face and body, the gentleman
was issued a warning to pay what he owed a certain man on
Oxford Street or something bad might happen to one of his
pretty golden-haired daughters. He managed to stagger home
and collapse in the front hall of his town house, which created
a stir among the servants just up to begin their morning duties. In the ensuing chatter of moving the man to his bed, the
entire household was awakened.

Felicity Newman, golden curls spilling from her lacy
nightcap, stepped from her bedchamber as she tied the sash
to her wrapper. Seeing the upstairs maid, the first and second
footmen, as well as the scullery maid and cook huddled outside her father's door, she made her way down the hall, a
tingle of fear in the pit of her stomach. As she drew near the
huddled servants, the butler stepped from the room and
barked orders. The small group scurried in different directions, a look of pity in their quickly averted eyes as they
passed Miss Felicity.

"Carson, what has happened?" She tried to peer into the
room, but the butler pulled the door three-quarters shut, so
that all she saw was her father's black evening coat tossed
over a chair. She could hear Lowe, her father's valet, mutter-
ing under his breath as he hurried about the room.

The gray-haired butler, with the family since before Felicity was born, spoke in a low voice. "Your father's been
injured, miss."

Several other doors opened along the hall almost simultaneously. Aaron, along with his friend Barclay, both just
arrived a day earlier from Oxford, and the youngest Newman
offspring, Hope, wandered into the hall, everyone disheveled
from a night of slumber. The fourteen-year-old rubbed her
eyes. "What has happened, Felicity?"

"Go back to bed, all. I was only speaking with Carson."

Hope, on hearing a groan emanate from her father's chamber, marched to her sister's side. "I am no longer a child. I want to know." The young girl's chin jutted defiantly.

Felicity sighed and realized her sister would have to learn of their father's injury sooner or later. "Very well, you may stay." She returned her attention to the butler. "What happened to Papa?"

"Felicity!" her father bellowed from his bedchamber. "Is that you I hear? I must speak with you at once."

"Yes, Papa." She put a hand on her sister's shoulder. "Wait here." She hurried into her father's room and gasped at the sight of his bloodied face. "Lowe, have you sent for the doctor?"

Lord Newley roared, "I don't need to waste money on some cursed sawbones. My man can handle this." He jumped as the valet patted at one of the cuts, then the viscount gestured his man away.

Felicity frowned, *but you waste money on the gaming tables all the time, what is a little more*? Instead of voicing such a thought, she merely said, "How did this happen, sir?"

Before the viscount spoke, he saw his younger son standing in the doorway, flanked by Hope and the boy's school friend. "Come in, Aaron, you will be involved in this as well. This does not concern the rest of you."

Felicity's cheeks burned at her father's rudeness to her brother's friend. Lord Barclay was a delightful young man and seemed to be a good influence on Aaron. The young men had stayed home the night before, determined to entertain the ladies. She didn't want him to be so shabbily treated. She smiled at her brother's guest. "Would you be so kind as to see Hope back to her room, sir?"

The young man nodded. He put a comforting hand on Hope's shoulder and urged her back down the hall

Aaron came into the room and closed the door. "What can I do, sir?"

"You must escort your sisters to Newley Manor this very day. Perry is there rusticating again. When you get there inform him that he must take the girls up to Walham Castle to stay."

"Walham!" Felicity protested. "But, Papa, that is all the way in north Yorkshire and winter is coming. It is dreadfully bleak this time of year. Why can we not stay at home in Fenton?" Then her eyes widened as a fear that had long haunted her dreams came to her. "Do not say you have lost Newley Manor."

"Don't be pert, girl. The manor is entailed and I cannot mortgage it."

Felicity sent up a prayer of thanks that her grandfather had had the forethought to do them such a favor. No doubt he saw his son's penchant for vice early on and had put the entail in place.

The viscount gingerly touched a finger to his swollen black eye, then winced. "It's not safe here or at Newley Manor. They might look for you there."

Aaron frowned. "Who is *they,* Papa?"

"The men who did this to me." The viscount closed his eyes a moment, then his voice grew shaky. "I've had a cursed streak of bad luck recently. I owe a cent-percenter a great deal of money. He's threatened to hurt the girls unless I pay."

Brother and sister gazed at one another across the four-poster bed for a moment. Aaron took a step toward where his father lay. "You can have what's left of my quarterly allowance, Father." Another thing the Newmans could thank their grandfather for, since he'd set up small stipends for each of his grandchildren before he died that their father could not touch.

The viscount laughed rather hysterically. "And have you twenty thousand pounds in pocket change?"

Felicity gasped. She knew her father stayed under the hatches, but nothing like this kind of debt. Newley Manor, once a productive estate under her grandfather, had been bled dry by his son. But Perry, the eldest, had taken to overseeing the day-to-day workings of Newley Manor, and it was showing progress. Their father always thought his heir was rusticating, but Felicity knew that Perry much preferred the country, a fact the viscount would never understand. She'd known her father's penchant for gaming was extraordinary, but thought his wins had kept them from falling too far into debt. Shocked, she said, "Papa, when did you borrow so much money?"

"What does that matter? I owe this man twenty thousand pounds and haven't the funds to pay him."

Something about the way her father avoided her eye made Felicity suspicious. Then it dawned on her that he'd taken advantage of the rumors regarding her and Randall Harwood, the Marquess of Harlin's heir. She'd done her best to discourage the young cub, but he'd gone so far as to ask her father if he might pay his addresses, which had sent the viscount into a paroxysm of delight. She'd informed him in no-uncertain terms that she wouldn't marry a lad who was wet behind the ears just to please him. She glared at her parent. "Papa, how could you?"

The room fell silent. Then to her brother she said one word, "Harlin." A dawning comprehension came to Aaron's face. The family had always been short of money, but Felicity assumed her father won as much as he lost. Besides, he possessed the dowries from Perry and her mother, along with Aaron and Hope's mother. Despite her fears that one day he might do something foolish, she had always believed that he would never go beyond the pale—beyond what he could pay back. Now he was deeply in debt and unable to pay. Had he not done enough to harm their reputations? Now their very lives were in danger.

What a fool she'd been not to see this coming. It wasn't like all the indications hadn't been there, but she always believed her father would never intentionally harm them. Felicity had made her bow to Society ten years earlier under the guidance of her stepmother, who'd been alive then. They had scarcely been in London a week when Felicity realized her father's standing in Town was tainted by his tendency to engage in shady games of chance, associate with low types, and flaunt nearly every rule of polite Society. Few were willing to align themselves with a Newman for fear the bad blood had been inherited. Even worse was the possibility her father would forever be a weight around their neck, always pockets to let and in debt.

Hurt by the numerous snubs and improper proposals she'd received her first year, Felicity realized that the only men likely to make her an offer were wastrels of her father's ilk or rich Cits hoping to buy their way into Society. Determined to have neither, she had made up her mind to embrace those things that interested her. After she dwindled into spinsterhood, she at least would have enjoyed her years in London. She took up with a raffish set of young ladies who drove phaetons in the park, raced their horses against their equally raffish male counterparts, attended masquerades, and perhaps worst of all espoused the ideas of Mary Wollstonecraft. Such antics had brought her a great deal of attention. Her stepmother had pleaded with her to think of her reputation, but Felicity had always been too headstrong for her own good.

Soon she'd become the darling of every rebel bent on defying their parents' wishes. Some of the fools had claimed to be bewitched by her beauty, and offered for her. But Felicity never once was tempted to marry. Not even the ones who could have ended her father's constant shortfall of money. She simply wouldn't feel right drawing an innocent person into her family circle.

Over the years, her father occasionally urged her to consider marriage when his funds grew low, but often a lucky streak made him forget the issue. Felicity now understood why her father only last week had pushed her to be nice to Mr. Gilbert Barbour, a wealthy shipwright some twenty years her senior.

Twenty thousand pounds owed! Their very lives in danger!

There was nothing for it, but they must leave. "Papa, you must come with us. If they cannot find your children, they are likely to hurt you again."

"Spend the winter at Walham? I'd likely die of boredom or worse." The viscount shuddered. "No, I shall stay in Town and see what I can do to turn my luck around."

Felicity protested, "But, Papa, you only risk—"

"I won't leave, girl. Don't argue with me. Go help your sister pack. I shall have the carriage out front by nine. I want you at the Hall by nightfall." He glared at her as best he could with his injuries. With a frustrated sigh, she turned to leave, well aware that he wouldn't listen to her protest.

Aaron followed her to the door, but his father called him back. "I must have a word with you, boy."

Felicity left to do as she was bid and as the door closed, Lord Newley grabbed his son's arm. "I need you to hurry to Armistead's house in Cavendish Square." The gentleman pointed at his coat and Aaron picked it up, handing it to his father. Newley rummaged in the pockets and at last pulled out a stack of vowels, which he handed to his son. He grinned. "Had a bit of luck rolling the bones at Tanner's last night. Collect the debt and bring it to me before you leave."

His son looked at the vowels with distaste. Dicing was such a vulgar sport in his opinion. "Very well, Father."

Aaron returned to his room to dress while Felicity helped Hope pack for a trip neither wanted to take. By eight o'clock both girls were packed and dressed, so they went down to breakfast, where Lord Barclay was already busily making inroads on a large plate of ham and eggs. He rose and greeted the ladies. After they were served and had eaten, Hope immediately began to urge him to come to Huntingdon. Felicity mused that her sister had developed a crush on the blue-eyed, black-haired sprig of manhood.

When he demurred, saying he didn't want to intrude, Felicity added her voice to the invitation, not so much to please her sister, but fearful that while staying at their town house Lord Barclay might be mistaken for a family member by this man who was threatening violence. "There is excellent hunting this time of year and Perry is trying to breed the next Ascot champion, so there will be much to keep you and Aaron entertained should you decide not to return to Town."

Before Lord Barclay could respond, a ruckus sounded in the hall, and everyone went to see what had happened. To their horror they found Aaron prostrate on the hall floor as Carson held his head. Blood trickled from a cut on the boy's chin, one eye was blackened, and his lip had swelled to twice its normal size. He was holding his ribs as well.

Felicity flew to him, Hope and Lord Barclay on her heels. "Oh, dear Lord, those men found you, did they not?"

Aaron nodded, which caused a sandy blond curl to tumble onto his sweat-beaded forehead. Through clenched teeth he got out, "They took Papa's money that I had just collected and drew my cork. They told me to tell him that he had until the end of the week to pay."

Felicity ordered the butler to send for the doctor and asked Aaron's friend to help the footman get her brother up to his room. Some thirty minutes later, the doctor arrived to minister to the boy. After some twenty minutes, he came out of Aaron's room, where the others were anxiously waiting. He pronounced that nothing was broken but that the boy would need to stay in bed for a few days. Lord Newley, who'd limped to his son's room, said, "Impossible. He must take his sisters home this morning."

The doctor frowned. "I would not recommend he travel for several days, my lord. It would be very painful, not to mention dangerous, if he has cracked one of his ribs."

"But it's not safe here for them here. I must send them out of Town today." Lord Newley swayed and had to grab the wall to keep from falling.

The doctor ordered him back to bed. "I don't think you need to be up and about yet either, sir."

But his lordship refused to go to his room until the matter was settled. "I won't rest until I see my girls safely on their way and it would seem that my sons are not safe either."

Felicity put a hand on her father's shoulder. "What harm will it do if we wait a few days until Aaron is better and can travel? We shall all stay indoors."

The viscount looked from Hope to Felicity. "These men are bolder than I dare think. I fear what might happen if you remain another day."

Hope stepped closer and hugged her father. "We will be safe, sir."

Lord Barclay cleared his throat, almost hesitant to intrude. "Lord Newley, if you would be willing to trust me, I shall gladly escort your daughters to the safety of Huntingdon. It would be my great pleasure."

Lord Newley frowned as he looked at the boy, who was practically a stranger. "You're Fennerly's heir, are you not?"

"Yes, sir."

"Don't know the man myself, but he has an honorable reputation. I'd greatly be in your debt if you would see them safe, my boy. Are you prepared to go at once?"

"I only need a moment to pack and write a quick message to my father about where I'm going."

The viscount frowned. "Your destination must be a secret. Don't want any word to leak out about where my girls are headed. Just inform him you've gone to visit friends in the country."

"Very well, sir." Lord Barclay hurried off, and the doctor, along with his daughters, helped the viscount back to bed. Some twenty minutes later, after bidding their father and brother good-bye, Felicity and Hope Newman climbed into the family carriage along with Lord Barclay Holmes and headed out of London.

From the shadows of a nearby doorway, a scruffy man watched the carriage depart. He hurried to the man who employed him on Oxford Street. The offices of Jacob Whiner were small and cluttered, but the old gentleman knew the name of every man and woman who owed him so much as a copper. He looked up from his ledger as Ruben, a burly ex-fighter whose nose curved to the left, came in and dropped the bag of coins on the desk.

"Got this from the son this morning." The man rubbed his chin. "Game little cub, but he weren't no match for me."

"Why are you back?" Jacob poured out the coins and counted, then clicked his tongue in disapproval at the small amount.

"It's like ye thought, the gent's sent the little ladies out of town."

A nasty smile tipped Whiner's mouth. He picked up a handful of the coins. "Put the fear of God in him, did you? Send Colson to 'is nibs estate. Have 'im steal somethin' what belongs to the Notorious Miss Newman. Tell 'im to bring it to me. That'll show the old viscount we can get to them any time we want."

Mrs. Kitty Tarkington had just spent a dreadful morning with her mother-in-law, hearing a litany of complaints about her children's conduct. Her head was beginning to ache and she wanted to be in her own parlor with a warm fire, but unfortunately Islington traffic was dreadful that morning. There seemed to be some kind of accident that was delaying her coachman. Impatient to be home, she lowered the window to take a look. At the exact moment she poked her head out the window, a carriage came slowly past. As was her habit, she peered into the recesses of the vehicle to see if it was one of her friends. Her gaze locked on the beautiful face of Miss Felicity Newman, and the girl politely nodded. Kitty had seen the girl in the park and had her pointed out on more than one occasion. The notorious woman was often the talk of London. The carriage slowed as the coachman tried not to lock wheels with the Tarkington town coach. Kitty noted a young man was seated beside the lovely girl.

What poor lad has the girl lured into her net now? she wondered, then her eyes widened as she recognized the dark hair and blue eyes of her cousin's only son, Lord Barclay Holmes. By the time she realized she knew the boy, the Newman carriage had picked up speed and was heading north. Where the devil was Barclay going with the Notorious Miss Newman?

Mrs. Tarkington shouted, "Take me home at once, John." She must send word to Hugh that Barclay was under the woman's spell. But Kitty had scarcely settled back on the squabs when it occurred to her that what she needed to know was where they were going. She leaned back out and called, "Take me to Newley House in Berkeley Square instead."

When the coach pulled up in front of the viscount's town house, the lady went to the door herself, convinced that her footman would never be able to elicit the information she needed. She lifted the tarnished knocker and rapped it sharply.

A footman appeared, and his brows rose at the sight of a primly respectable female. She was not the usual type who mixed with the Newmans. "Yes, madam."

"I have come to see Miss Felicity Newman." She handed him her card, after bending down the corner.

The servant frowned at the scented vellum with ornate lettering. "Miss Newman is not at home."

Kitty laughed gaily. "Oh, do tell her I am here. I'm certain she will agree to see *me*." The only reason she could claim knowing the girl was that Miss Newman was not at home, for she'd never been formally introduced to the chit.

"But, madam, the lady is truly not in the house and is not

expected to return for some time." He started to close the door.

"Oh dear, but I must speak with her." Kitty put out her hand to stay him. "Can you tell me where she's gone?"

The footman eyed her with suspicion. "My master only wishes me to say she has gone north, madam." With that he closed the door.

Kitty stood on the stoop for a few moments. The servant's words sent a chill down her spine. A handsome young man and a beautiful female, no matter her an ape leader, were heading north. Visions of a marriage over the anvil filled Kitty, and her knees grew weak. She must send word to Hugh at once. His son was in grave danger. If the boy had come to Town, perhaps so had her cousin. She hurried back to the coach, and climbed in, but not before she ordered her coachman to take her to Fennerly House on Park Lane.

Chapter Two

"Eloping, I tell you."

Hugh heard Kitty's words, but he couldn't fathom the concept that his son would behave in such a manner. He and his mother had only just arrived at his town house when his cousin burst in with an incoherent tale about Clay and Miss Newman in a carriage heading for the border.

Lady Fennerly eyed her son's face as she said, "What nonsense! Surely you are mistaken. Clay is staying at Viscount Newley's town house to be sure, but my grandson wouldn't involve himself in a runaway marriage. No doubt they were merely on a visit to friends somewhere in Town."

"Mother is right." But a crease remained on his brow.

Mrs. Tarkington put her hands on her hips. "With piles of luggage atop the coach, besides, the footman told me she was going out of Town, and your son was accompanying her. Have you ever set eyes upon Felicity Newman? The woman has the face of an angel. Half the cubs in Town have been in love with her at one time or another. Even a young man as sensible as Clay can take leave of his senses when a beautiful, sophisticated female turns her charms on him. Need I remind you that all Lady Cass needed was a pretty face and you were clay in her hands."

The earl couldn't deny he'd been an utter fool. But unlike himself, Clay had someone to give him guidance. Would his son not ask permission to wed? Or was this woman's hold so strong he'd agreed to such a marriage? He shook his head. Why, he was becoming as fanciful as an old woman. "Kitty, need I remind you that the footman only said they were going north. That covers a great many towns and it doesn't just mean Scotland."

"I quite agree with Hugh, Kitty," Lady Fennerly said from her position beside the fireplace. "You have allowed your imagination to get the better of you."

Mrs. Tarkington looked from the dowager's disbelieving face to Hugh's, which mirrored his fears. She moved to put a hand on her cousin's arm. "Fennerly, I live in Town and I can tell you the last *on-dit*. The viscount's badly under the hatches this time. Moreover, he's been seen courting Old Money-bags Barbour for his daughter. The girl *must* marry this time to save him from utter ruin. Given the choice do you think a beautiful young woman would want to be married to a rotund old man who smells of ship's tar or a handsome young gentleman who is heir to both money and a title." She arched one brow as she looked up into Hugh's face.

Seen in that light, the earl's eyes narrowed. He knew many women had the gift to get what they wanted and that a young man in love was perhaps the most vulnerable.

"I cannot risk my son's future. I must go after him."

The dowager shook her head. "Hugh, pray consider the matter a bit long before you rush off and do something you regret. Clay would never be so inconsiderate."

Kitty folded her hands in front of her. "My dear madam, is it not better to be safe than sorry? If I am wrong there is no harm done, but if I am correct Hugh will have saved his son from a disaster."

"I heartily agree." The earl kissed his cousin's cheek. "Thank you, Kitty. If I get to them in time, Clay will be indebted to you for the rest of his life."

The countess was still doubtful of the wisdom of dashing off after the young man whom she trusted. "I cannot think that Clay would be so rash even if this female is the conniving creature you think her." Seeing the determined look on her son's face, she sighed and then moved closer to the earl and kissed him. "I know you will go no matter what I think." After a thoughtful moment, she added, "If you *are* too late, and he has married the chit, tread softly, Hugh. The truth is we know nothing of this young woman but gossip. Do not do anything that would alienate your son or he will be utterly in the woman's control."

A steely glint came into the gentleman's eye. "I won't be late. I'll stop this marriage."

The earl hurried from the library to make arrangements to depart. Mrs. Tarkington came to where Lady Fennerly stood. "Would you truly welcome this creature into your family?"

The countess pulled her shawl tighter after a shrug caused the pink silk to slip. "Perhaps she's been unfairly judged, perhaps once away from that ne'er-do-well father she will be all that we would wish, and just perhaps we should give Clay more trust. It may not be as it appears."

Kitty shook her head. "And perhaps fairies will come in the night and steal my mother-in-law but it's very unlikely."

Lady Fennerly chuckled. "Is Lady Tarkington still giving you trouble? Shall I tell you a little about Meg Peters nee Baroness Tarkington and the dancing master at The Albert Academy for Young Ladies of Quality?"

Kitty eyes widened. "I'm all ears."

Newley Manor lay just outside the village of Fenton in County Huntingdon, which made the journey take the better part of the remainder of the day. Once free of London traffic and certain they weren't followed, the trio began to slowly relax. The weather was crisp but sunny, and Lord Barclay did his best to convince his companions there was little need to worry. He would take good care of them.

Hope smiled at him, but there remained a hint of distress in the depths of her golden brown eyes. "I'm certain you will, sir. But I worry so for my brother. In a day or so he will feel better and there will be nothing that will keep him in bed, I do assure you."

Miss Newman nodded. "I have never known anyone who hates being housebound more than Aaron. When he was twelve he fell out of a tree at Newley and hit his head, the doctor ordered him to bed for a week. The second day one of the footmen caught him climbing out his window with the intention of going riding. Still, I should think this time he would remember there is some brute out there wanting to hurt him."

Her sister harrumphed. "He will only see that as a challenge and will try to outwit them by coming and going as he pleases."

Barclay, having known Aaron for the past few months, knew that his friend did love to defy the rules more than anyone he'd met at school. He thought about that for a moment, then said, "If you should like I can return to London and keep an eye on Aaron until he is better. Then I will bring him to Walham Castle to join you."

Hope clasped her hands before her. "We would be forever in your debt."

Miss Newman smiled. "You are a true gentleman, Lord Barclay. Aaron couldn't have a better friend."

The young man's cheeks warmed, and he decided that Miss Newman and her sister were quite the prettiest ladies he'd ever met, Miss Camp not withstanding. The Newman ladies were nice as well. Unfortunately, Aaron had engaged in several bouts of fisticuffs when some of the lads at school had made comments about his eldest sister's reputation. Yet Barclay had seen nothing of this notorious family which seemed to match the rumors. The brothers and sisters were tightly knit and caring. While in Town they had treated him to a very tame day of ices at Gunter's, a walk through Green Park, and then a quiet evening of games at home. Aaron had suggested a night on the Town, but his heart clearly hadn't been in it.

There had been nothing about his visit that even his grandmother could find objectionable. True, their father was all that rumor described, but despite Newley's penchant for gaming, he'd shown himself to care about his children when things had gone awry. Barclay suspected Aaron, Felicity, and Hope were more tainted by association with the old gentleman, than truly bad seeds. On that comforting thought, the young man relaxed back into the worn squabs and began to enjoy the trip, all the while engaging in light banter with Miss Hope.

Their journey continued smoothly. After the city of Cambridge, the carriage left the North Road and began to wind along the back roads toward Fenton. They arrived at the manor just after five o'clock to the surprise of their brother, who was not expecting them to return until December. Lord Barclay was introduced to Perry Newman, a slender young man with a tan and a rugged outdoor look about him. The heir greeted his sisters with pleasure and was full of concern for his little brother and father when told of the incidents and their condition. All he said was, "It was bound to happen eventually. Father runs through money like water."

Perry welcomed Lord Barclay and thanked him for stepping in when Aaron was hurt. "I fear you are not seeing us at our best," he said, then he shrugged and added, "but if you listened to the gossips we have no best." A look shot between the siblings and Barclay sensed a resignation about the trio that made him sad.

Hope broke the dark mood when she dimpled at Aaron's friend. "Lord Barclay has volunteered to bring Aaron to Bowes when he is ready to travel to get him out of harm's way."

A thoughtful look came on Perry's face. "Dare I ask if you would do our family one more favor?"

"Anything to help." Barclay arched a dark brow.

"I think my father must sell the matched set of grays I won

six months ago racing Thunder against Harry Thurgood 's chestnut. Would you drive them back to London? They would go for a handsome price at Tattersall's and Father might be able to buy a little peace from this cent-percenter with their price." He looked sheepishly at his sisters. "I never told Father about winning them for I knew how it would be."

Miss Newman nodded her understanding. "We don't blame you. Neither of us has a single jewel left of our mother's."

Barclay was horrified at what he heard. He had always loved his own father, but had never truly understood what a very good man he was until now. He couldn't help but feel for the Newman offspring and what they must deal with. "I shall gladly drive the team back to Town, sir."

Perry grew silent a moment, then said, "Don't let that ham-handed brother of mine drive them in the Park or Father won't get a sou for them. Everyone will think them plodders."

They all laughed, then the ladies bid the gentlemen good day and went up to rest before dinner. Perry happily took Barclay off to the stables to see his pride and joy, Thunder, a highbred Arab stallion, from which the young man hoped to breed a string of racehorses.

At dinner that evening, Miss Newman begged her brother to be allowed another day to pack more fully for their stay in the climes of northern England. Perry agreed, only making his sisters promise not to leave the house, just in case they might have been followed. With their brother encouraging them to put their worries aside, they spent the rest of the evening in loud and fun- filled games in the parlor. By the time they were ready to retire, Barclay found himself envious of the comradery the brother and sisters shared, making him wish he had siblings of his own. It was a shame his father had refused to remarry . As he went to bed that night, he wondered if his father had gotten his letter.

With an extra day, the young men rose early and rode about the estate. Perry showed Aaron's friend what innovations he'd made since taking over the management from a father who took more out than put back. Barclay was duly impressed with Perry's devotion to the land, especially knowing that the man's father likely didn't appreciate the efforts, only the money it brought. The day passed quickly, and Barclay realized he'd found true friends in the Newmans.

The only sour note for Felicity was that her favorite bonnet turned up missing when the girls had begun to pack for the long stay at Walham that morning. It had belonged to her mother, and she'd worn it on walks round the estate. It was rather old and the black velvet was a bit worn, with several of the yellow flowers missing, but she'd kept it for sentimental reasons. With little time to spare, she promised herself to look for it when they returned.

By seven o'clock the following morning Felicity and Hope were once again in the family coach ready to head north under the watchful eye of Perry. When their brother eyed the size of the trunks strapped on the carriage, he swore they had packed enough to stay a year. Teasingly, Felicity looked at Hope and said, "It seemed we didn't pack nearly enough if he thinks it a year's worth of clothing." Everyone laughed before they climbed into the vehicle. Soon the brother and sisters were rolling down the drive. Hope poked her head out the window, holding on to her bonnet. "We shall see you at Walham soon, sir."

Barclay gave one final wave to the delightful child, then climbed up behind the sweetest set of prads he'd ever seen and set out south, hoping to get to London by early afternoon. Perhaps he might see if he could get his father to spring for the cattle, then he remembered that he had promised his father he would wait a year to bring a team to Oxford.

A frown grew between his brows. His father was the best of gentlemen, but he certainly must be lonely with his only child gone off to school. Was it useless to hope that at his father's age, he would find someone to love? Perhaps Miss

Camp might make some suggestions about an eligible widow in the neighborhood when Barclay went home for the Yule celebrations. With the comforting thought that he would see his family next month, Barclay put his mind to his driving.

He arrived back in Town well before five that evening. Thinking to do his friend a favor, he tooled the team to the Park and joined the line of carriages on parade. He saw several of his friends on horseback, who came to ask about the prime cattle he was driving. He casually mentioned they would soon be for sale at Tattersall's. Convinced he had several interested buyers for Lord Newley, he was about to leave the Park when he saw his father's cousin, Mrs. Tarkington, waving a handkerchief at him from her carriage.

There was no one he wanted to speak with less, but he politely drew the curricle alongside, her barouche. "Good afternoon, cousin. I'm surprised to see you out on such a cold afternoon."

"Never mind the weather, dear boy. Only let me say I am delighted to see your father found you in time." There were tears of joy in the lady's eyes.

"Father? What do you mean found me? Is he in Town?"

A look of horror appeared on the lady's face, and she clutched at the carriage door. "Do not tell me you have married that creature! I feared he would be too late."

Barclay sat baffled a moment before understanding dawned. The only lady he had been with was Aaron's sister. "You think I have married Miss Newman. Whatever gave you such a foolish idea?"

His cousin quickly explained about seeing him with the lady going north in a carriage and having informed his father of such. "I just assumed that he caught you before you got to the border and that these horses were your reward for agreeing not to marry the girl."

The young man's hands tightened on the reins. "Are you

telling me that my father has chased after the Newmans' carriage in order to save me from the lady's clutches?"

Mrs. Tarkington, seeing his anger, nodded her head, then gulped as if she possessed a great lump in her throat. "I—it was an honest mistake knowing that girl's reputation."

Barclay could scarcely be civil. "You have greatly maligned Miss Newman. I must go, madam. Good day."

He went first to his family's town house, where he found his grandmother her usual calm self. She confirmed that his father was on the North Road, looking for Barclay. He explained where he had been, then excused himself, informing her he must warn Aaron what was about to happen. He promised he would visit his grandmother again before he returned to school, then kissed her good-bye.

He tooled the team back to Newley House, where he discovered Aaron much recovered and restless in his room. Embarrassed by the situation his prattling cousin had created, there was little he could do but tell his friend about his father's rash journey north.

Aaron's cheeks flamed red, but he offered his friend no rebuke. He pulled the bell for his valet. "I shall pack and we'll leave this very afternoon. We must find them and warn my sister what she is facing."

"But . . . what about your injuries." Barclay was doubtful he should allow his friend to make the trip so soon.

Aaron grimaced as he tried to shrug into his coat. "They are nothing, I do assure you. I must get to my family at once and warn them."

Despite his reservations about Aaron traveling, Barclay was back on the road some thirty minutes later with a fresh team he hired from the Swan With Two Necks. With his friend at his side, he drove at a speed that was much faster than was his normal pace, but he'd never before had such a reason to hurry. His father was about to make a dreadful mistake, and Barclay hoped he could spare the lady such a scene.

* * *

Hugh kicked the wheel with the broken spoke and swore under his breath. What else could go wrong? He'd gotten caught behind several shepherds just outside Islington the first afternoon and lost nearly two hours' time, then night had fallen. He would have pushed onward, but there was no moon to guide him and he'd almost driven off the road twice. What good would it do his son if he broke his neck? So he'd found a small inn and tried to get some sleep, convinced the eloping pair would do the same. Back on the road by six, the morning traffic of milkmaids and farmers bringing their wares to the market proved as bad as the sheep. Once past Woburn, a deluge had slowed his progress much of the second day. He'd only made it as far as St. Neots on the second night, having to stop and inquire about the runaways at many of the large posting inns. He began to worry when he'd not had a single sighting of the Newmans' carriage since Cambridge. His only hope was that the Newmans' large vehicle would have fared worse than his curricle had in the mud.

The earl looked down at his shattered wheel, then at the wheelwright who eyed him warily. "Forgive me, I know it's not your fault that it will take most of the afternoon to replace the tines and forge a new rim. There's an urgent matter that needs my attention up north."

The wheelwright grinned, exposing a random array of missing teeth. "Elopement, eh?"

The earl did not comment. Instead he looked about. "Would there be someplace I might hire a fast horse?"

The man rubbed his hands on his apron and shook his head. "The Brown Wren has hacks but ain't one that could take ye any faster than a good lope. Only decent horseflesh hereabouts belongs to Squire Hendry."

"And where would I find this squire?" Impatience made his voice sharp.

The wheelwright gave him directions. After hiring a poor specimen of a mount from the Brown Wren, Hugh presented himself at the squire's house. It took some thirty minutes of haggling before a deal was struck for a well-ribbed little chestnut Arab. The earl quickly returned the hack to the inn and informed the wheelwright that he would come for his repaired curricle in a few days, weather permitting. He then set off north once again, riding hard and hoping to make the border before nightfall.

Short on funds, Perry urged the coachman to push hard north so they would only require one night on the road. Luckily for him, his sisters were good travelers. Their first day was uneventful and they broke their journey at a small and inexpensive inn that they often used, much off the beaten path of regular travelers. They were again on the road early the second morning, with a simple basket prepared by the innkeeper's wife. Perry was determined to make it all the way to Walham the second day, even if they had to travel after dark. The skies were ominous during most of the day, and the temperature continued to drop as each new hour ticked past. They discussed the possibility of snow, but each avoided the subject of what would happen should they become stranded at some small inn where they might be forced to stay for days. Instead they concentrated on the fact that they were making good time.

They'd been traveling over the lonely moors of Yorkshire for much of the afternoon. Conversation had grown sporadic, and Hope sat peering out the window, looking for a landmark she recognized. She complained, "I'm hungry."

Felicity reached for the basket. "There is one piece of cheese left and some cider."

Hope wrinkled her nose. "I have had enough." She stopped and looked out the window. "Oh, dear, I do believe it's beginning to snow. Even if we make it to the castle we shall be stranded with Aunt for weeks and weeks." Then her eyes narrowed. "Are we not going rather fast for the conditions?" She reached out to steady herself when she pitched slightly to one side.

Perry and Felicity each stared out at the rapidly passing scenery. Suddenly the communicating door on the roof slid open. John Coachman shouted through the opening, "Sir, we're bein' pursued by a lone rider. He's been gainin' on us since we left Rokeby."

Perry peered out the small oval glass at the rear of the carriage. He could see a rider hunched over his horse, his cape flowing in the wind as he pushed hard—to what? Overtake the coach? Or was the man going somewhere further down the road? Ahead of them was Bowes, a small village with little of interest to any but those who lived there. The surrounding countryside, however, was dotted with schools for young lads who were often an inconvenience for their families or whose parents had died and relatives had sent their unwanted burdens north. They were housed in the wilds of Yorkshire for mere pennies compared to what it would cost near London.

Still, Perry wasn't willing to risk his sister's lives on the off chance that they were being followed by the cent-percenter's henchman. "Spring 'em, John. We cannot be more than five miles from Walham."

The coachman closed the communicating door, and within seconds a whip cracked. The carriage began to move at an alarming rate, its occupants bouncing about like toy sailboats during a storm. They hung on to the straps to avoid being injured. There were no cries of fear, only grim silence while they peered out at the snow, which fell in gentle waves, so at odds with the Newmans' desperate flight.

A soft white coating quickly dusted the countryside, and visibility closed to only a few feet. For the coachman, it was a struggle to pick out the twin ruts that constituted the road that turned toward the castle.

Suddenly the carriage came to a sharp upward curve in the road and the speed was too great for the conditions. The driver reined in the team, but he was too late. A wheel hit a sharp rock which protruded from the roadway, and the carriage careened over onto its side, unable to go forward. The team reared and whinnied, then settled in their traces. Inside, everyone was tossed about, while outside John Coachman was thrown into the gorse and rocks of the hillside. The carriage lay on its side, perfectly intact in its overturned position.

When the commotion died down, Felicity discovered herself lying atop her brother and sister in a heap. A groan emanated from below her. "Perry, Hope, are you hurt?" She struggled to a spot where her feet touched wood again, and she tried to help the others.

Hope sat up, her bonnet askew. She tugged it off and held her hand to her head. "Ouch!"

"Let me see." Felicity inspected her sister's forehead and found a goose-egg-sized lump. "Thankfully it's not serious."

Perry groaned and held his ankle. "I think I've sprained it."

Hope gasped as a trickle of blood oozed from the edge of his scalp. Felicity grabbed her handkerchief and pressed it to the gash atop his head. "It's only a nick, but head wounds always bleed a great deal."

Through clenched teeth, Perry asked, "Blood?" He put his hand up and took the linen compress, then pulled it away from the wound. Seeing it completely soaked, the young man fainted dead away.

Felicity sighed. Her brother could never tolerate the sight of blood. "Here"— she gave a second handkerchief from her reticule to Hope—"keep this pressed on the wound. I'll climb out and see about the coachman."

The carriage was lying at such an angle, Felicity could see nothing. She stood and turned the handle, pushing the door

upward and over. Snowflakes had already begun to settle on
the wrecked vehicle. It took her several minutes to struggle
up through the opening, her blue traveling gown hindering
her movement. At last she climbed down to the roadway and
spied their coachman sitting upright on the side of the hill, the
falling snow clinging to his hat and cape, his face a picture of
pain.

"How badly are you hurt, John?"

"It's me arm, Miss Felicity. I think it's broken."

The sound of hoofbeats made Felicity lean back into the
coach. "Is Father's pistol in the compartment under the seat?"

Hope opened the compartment. She took out the gun and
handed it to her sister. "D-do be careful."

Felicity turned to face the man who was following them.
The snow obscured her view of him, and in the cold and
gloom he appeared a rather sinister dark shape as his mount
drew near. She wasn't sure there was powder and ball in the
gun or if the damp would allow it to fire. She could only hope
the mere sight of the weapon would deter whoever he was, especially if he meant them harm.

To her surprise the man rode straight to her, never taking
his gaze from her face. He reined the nearly spent animal to
a halt. He sat his horse, an expensive well-bred Arab, and
seemed to study her with thoughtful contemplation. She in
turned studied him. He appeared nothing like what she would
have thought such a brigand would look. Did cent-percenters
not employ ex-prizefighters to do their dirty work? Or so
Perry had told her once. This man's face was too unscarred
for him to have ever been in a mill. His dark hair, worn a bit
longer than current fashion, curled beneath a neat black
beaver hat. Gray eyes peered out from a handsome, aristocratic face. A hint of concern seemed to linger in their gray
depths as he looked from her to the wrecked carriage and
back. His clothes were expensive but not the height of fashion, his cravat was elegant but not fussy. Surely this was not

a man hired to harm them, for he looked too much the gentleman.

"Are you Miss Felicity Newman?"

Fear gripped her on hearing her name. She lifted the pistol and saw surprise register on his face. "I am. What do you want, sir?"

He stared at the gun for a moment, then got down from the horse. "Madam, I want my son."

Of all the things he could have said, that one surprised her the most. The only gentleman in their carriage was her brother. "Your son?"

"Do not play the innocent with me, Miss Newman. You were seen leaving London."

Felicity lowered the gun. "I have no doubt I was, sir. I did not slip away in the night. But"—her eyes widened as it dawned on her who the gentleman might be—"Lord Fennerly?"

He gave a nodding acknowledgment, but looked past her at the carriage. "Where is Barclay?"

A sudden rush of horror surged through Felicity as the full import of what the earl suspected dawned on her. She, the evil siren, had lured his innocent son north to have one of those scandalous Scottish marriages. She had been in just this situation scarcely a year ago when Lord Harlin had accused her of seducing that fool of a son of his. As if she would wish a husband who had more hair than wit.

At first, a sense of overwhelming despair come over her. Why did this keep happening to her? She had never cast out lures to a single gentleman. She would never marry. It was a reality she had accepted her first Season ten years ago when she had fully learned how Society viewed her and her family. Yet still people believed that these green cubs who appeared every Season were victims of her wiles, instead of their own folly. As the realization came to her that she would again have to face down an irate and irrational father, her chin came up defiantly. Nothing she could say would convince the man before her that she was not what he thought, so she would merely send him on his way. "You have wasted your time coming all this way, sir."

The cold look that came to the gentleman's eyes frightened Felicity, but she held her ground as he stepped to her and grasped her arm and pulled her to him. "Are you married to my son, madam?"

Anger surged and another strange sensation she had no time to understand. She spoke without thinking. "And what will you do if Lord Barclay is mine?"

A hand came up and grasped her slender neck for a moment, but it was more of a caress than a threat. "You do not want me for an enemy, Miss Newman. I am not some callow youth to be toyed with at your whim."

A strange tingle raced through Felicity as she looked up into the gentleman's angry face. There was something so very masculine about him, it made her knees grow weak. This was nothing like her encounter with the aging Lord Harlin, who had spent too much time at table with too little activity. Lord Barclay's father was an athletic, virile man who was quite used to getting his way. He was a man of command, and she had to resist the urge to do his bidding. She struggled to find the right words.

From behind them, Hope shouted, "Unhand my sister, you brute." The young girl scrambled down from the carriage as Lord Fennerly's hand fell away from Felicity. Perry's head appeared through the open carriage door seconds after his sister climbed down. He still held a handkerchief to the wound.

"W-what is going on here? I say, the snow is falling hard. We need to get to Aunt's soon or we shall be stranded." Perry looked at the surrounding moors, which were quickly turning white.

Ignoring young Newman's babbling, the earl stared at the

beautiful female whose gaze had burned with defiance only to soften into concern at the sight of her injured brother.

A sense of foreboding stirred in the pit of Hugh's stomach. Where was Barclay? "I don't understand. My cousin swore that she saw my son in your carriage."

The younger Miss Newman frowned. "You are Lord Barclay's father?" On seeing her sister's nod of assent, she put her arms akimbo. "Well, sir, you could certainly learn some manners from your son. He was all that was kind to us and you have wrecked our carriage."

Miss Newman bit out. "He thinks I eloped with Lord Barclay."

The Earl of Fennerly was treated to Miss Hope Newman's temper at its worse. "How dare you accuse my sister of such conduct! Of all the outrageous things! Why do you *old* gentleman persist in thinking my sister chases after your addle-brained sons when in truth they pester Felicity to distraction? Not that Lord Barclay was such a one. You, sir, should be ashamed that you think so little of your own son that he would behave like the worse kind of puppy, like Harlin's son. Why, Lord Barclay was a proper gentleman the entire time and never made calf's eyes at Felicity, not once. He even offered to drive us back to Newley Manor when my younger brother was injured and couldn't go. You, my Lord Fennerly, can climb back on your horse and leave us in peace."

"Hope, remember your manners," Felicity Newman warned, then arched one delicate brow as she turned to him. "As you can see, sir, your son is not here. You may leave us."

Hugh looked from Miss Newman's cool disdain at the trimming he'd just received, to Miss Hope's flushed anger, to the injured boy's befuddlement while he stood in the carriage. No doubt he was Newley's heir, but at the moment the confused lad didn't quite seem to comprehend what was happening. Great heavens, not only was his son not with the

Newmans but his foolish pursuit had left them with their carriage wrecked and their brother injured. He drew his hat from his head.

"Pray, Miss Newman, please accept my heartfelt apology. There can be no excuse for my conduct—"

"True." The lady interrupted, not helping him in the least. "Just go back to London, Lord Fennerly. Your son should be safely back in Town by now." She moved back to where her sister stood.

Hugh put his hat back on his head, ignoring the wet snow that clung to his hair. "Madam, as much as I hate to again disoblige you, I will not leave you here, stranded. Your brother is injured as is your coachman. I fear you are going to have to tolerate my presence for a bit longer."

The earl watched the falling snow quickly gathering on the landscape. Unless he did something soon, they would all be stranded out here on the moors. But as his gaze returned to Miss Newman's frigid face, he doubted the lady would accept his help unless he merely took command. Without further argument, he set to doing what was needed. The lady watched in outraged silence, her arm round her sister.

First he examined the coach. It appeared intact; the wheel had merely slid off the side of the roadway, making the vehicle, which was overloaded, tip over. He climbed the hill to the coachman. After several questions, he realized the man would be unable to drive them further.

The earl returned to the ladies. "We must pull your carriage upright, then I will drive you to your destination."

"Go away, sir," Hope snapped. "We shall manage."

Miss Newman eyed their carriage. "My dear, the least he can do is get us back on the road. I don't think you and I can do it by ourselves, not with John and Perry hurt."

Hugh watched the resigned expression on the lady's beautiful face. He could see why the young men of London would be vulnerable to such beauty. Miss Newman's features were perfection, from the delicately arched brows and wide green eyes to the full rosy lips. Several guinea gold curls peeked out from under a blue velvet bonnet that framed that face perfectly. So this was the Notorious Miss Newman.

Hope petulantly snapped, "Very well, Lord Fennerly. You may help us, but once we are at our destination, I want you to leave my sister in peace."

The earl nodded. "I wouldn't have it any other way after my conduct, Miss Hope." He bowed with elegance and moved past the young ladies to help the injured brother from the carriage. Without another word the earl set about pulling the vehicle upright, using the team of horses, which he untethered from the shaft. It took close to an hour to perform the task, then reharness the horses and get everyone and everything back into the coach.

With an arm in a makeshift sling fashioned by Miss Newman, John Coachman sat on the box with the earl, eyeing the gentleman's handling of the ribbons with respect. The snow accumulation measured several inches, so the remainder of the trip to Walham Castle was slow since the rutted road lay fully hidden.

Hugh's mind wandered to Miss Newman, who was inside the carriage. She hadn't been the least flustered by their accident. She had tended to the injuries while he had worked at righting the carriage. She had settled her brother and sister in the carriage and encouraged the coachman to join them. Clearly the lady was not so high in the instep as to not care about others. Strange, but the rumors about her had left him with the impression that she was spoiled and willful, but he had seen none of that. Still, he wouldn't want a woman of her reputation married to his son.

At last their destination appeared on the horizon, a dark looming fortress which didn't look the least bit welcoming. Like many of the castles in the northern parts of England, Walham was a great walled structure designed to repel the invading Scots centuries earlier. Hugh drove the coach through the great open doors of the outer walls into a cobblestone courtyard. There appeared to be no one about, and Hugh looked at the coachman. "Were you expected?"

"No, sir, it was a trip that was on the spur of moment, what with the ladies being in danger and such."

From the carriage steps, Miss Newman called, "John, that is none of his lordship's concern." She stepped to the ground and hurried to rap the knocker of the great studded door. Within minutes a bevy of servants arrived to help the injured from the coach. Lady Walham herself arrived. She was middle-aged and plump, with dusky brown curls crimped under a lacy cap. Her delight at the arrival of her young relatives was dampened by the news of their accident. Hugh expected another trimming for having been the cause, but instead the lady welcomed him graciously, after having the servants take the others to their rooms. He watched Miss Newman depart with one last defiant glance at him over her shoulder. What danger did the coachman mean?

"Why, my dear Lord Fennerly, you must be frozen to the bone what with driving on the box. Do come in and meet my guests and enjoy the hospitality of Walham. My sons are in London at present but I have invited a merry group to stay for the month. I shall have dinner put back a half hour."

Hugh bowed, but shook his head. "I think it best that I return to the nearest inn for the night, madam. I have caused your nieces and nephew enough trouble for one day with my foolish conduct. I shouldn't wish to make them uncomfortable by my presence here." Then he looked down at his attire. "Besides, I brought no evening wear."

Lady Walham laughed. "Oh, my, give no thought to that, sir. Why, Felicity, Hope, and Perry are as goodhearted as they come. They will hold no grudge, I do assure you. Besides"— she gestured toward the moors visible through the castle gates—"I do not think it safe to be sending you five miles in a blizzard to try and find an inn. You are much the size of my late husband. I am sure Hughston will see you properly attired, and one of the footmen can act as your valet." The lady squinted up at the falling snow. " I fear you shall be my guest for some time, sir."

Hugh's stomach tightened as he looked out at the building storm and could scarcely see twenty feet beyond the wall. He would be going nowhere that night.

Chapter Three

Lord Fennerly stood at the window of his bedchamber, staring out into the near darkness at the blizzard which had settled over Walham Castle, his mood as dismal as the weather. He'd made a complete fool of himself this afternoon and the torment was not yet ended. It looked as if he would be required to stay here with the very people he'd insulted until the weather cleared. He should have listened to his mother and had more faith in Clay.

A knock sounded at his door. Hugh turned and noted that the room had grown full of dark shadows. A lone brace of candles flickered in the gloom, providing little light in the oversized chamber, which gave the space a dark and malevolent feel. He smiled, thinking himself a fool and called for his visitor to enter.

A young footman opened the door and peered into the room. "Good evening, my lord." Garments hung over the servant's arm. "I'm Morgan, sir, the second footman, and I'll serve ye while yer at the castle."

Hugh politely greeted the servant. The young man lay the clothes on the bed and bustled about the room, lighting more candles even as he asked several questions about how Lord Fennerly preferred things. Once that was settled in his mind, he ask if the gentleman was ready to dress for dinner. The earl allowed the footman to remove his jacket even as he peppered the young lad with questions about the weather. Hugh wanted to know how long snowstorms lasted in this part of England. Were they often stranded after such storms, and lastly how many guest did Lady Walham have?

The young man was respectfully reserved, answering the gentleman's questions in short, affable responses, taking the gentleman's measure. Hughston had told the housekeeper, who'd told the first footman, who told Morgan that her ladyship had decided that the earl would be perfect for Miss Felicity, if only they could be made to see the advantages of such a match during their stay at the castle. Morgan decided the earl showed no signs of being smitten or wanting to stay and court the young lady, but he certainly wouldn't voice that opinion to his superiors.

Unaware of the speculation swirling round him, Hugh was more concerned with the weather and pressed the servant for information. After hearing the bad news about the snow, he sank into deep thought about what lay ahead of him that evening and paid little heed to the borrowed clothes. The servant helped him undress and don the evening wear. He sighed at the thought he must spend an evening with the very woman he'd just accused of running off with his son. Hopefully, if the footman was correct, Lady Walham had so many guests that he might not have to say another word to Miss Newman or her siblings.

Then a thought occurred to him. Clay had formed a friendship with this family. Hugh thought that perhaps he should make it his purpose to find out if the lady might still pose a danger to the boy. She had certainly managed to bring more than one wealthy young man under her spell. True she was a beauty, but many women in London fit that description. What was it about this particular lady that drew so many young men to her? And was her sister's statement truth? Had those young men pursued a lady who'd shown not the least interest in them? What lay behind that flawless face? Was she a schemer or a maligned victim of gossip? What better opportunity for him to find the truth.

Suddenly Hope's angry words returned to taunt him. She'd called him an *old* gentleman. Was he old at nine-and-thirty? He ran a hand over his face and turned to look at his reflection in the looking glass on the far wall after the footman helped him slip on the borrowed coat. Horror filled him at the reflected sight.

He'd been too distracted to pay much attention, but clearly whoever had owned these clothes had been the worst kind of fop. As his hostess had predicted, they fit well enough. It was the color and style which left him speechless. The breeches were the palest of pink, with silver lacings at the knee. The waistcoat was the requisite white, but tiny pink flowers were worked along the border of the lapels and the coat was a deep purple with oversized buttons the same shade of pink as his breeches. "Saints in heaven," he gasped at the sight of himself. How could he face a roomful of strangers looking like a complete popinjay?

He started to remove the coat when a knock sounded on his door. Before his lordship could protest, the footman opened the portal, and there stood Miss Newman, looking utterly beautiful in a pale blue satin gown with an overskirt of blue spiderweb muslin shot with silver. Her blond curls were dressed high on her head and shimmered in the candlelight. She hadn't a single piece of jewelry about her lovely neck or at her ears, and still looked perfectly lovely.

"Lord Fennerly, my aunt has requested that I show you the way to the Queen's drawing room." As her cool gaze swept over him, Hugh was certain he detected a glint of amusement leap into her beautiful green eyes at the sight of him.

For just a moment, his outraged dignity made him stiffen. Then the memory of what he had inflicted on this young woman and her family flooded his mind. He had no right to be on his high ropes after the mistake he'd made. With resignation, he shrugged and accepted his role in this complete farce he'd set in motion the moment he'd hied off after Clay. He spread out his arms to display his attire and said, "My penance for having behaved like a fool is having to dress like one."

Her eyes widened at his admission of error, but she merely said, "I wouldn't let my aunt hear you decry my late uncle's wardrobe. In their artistic circles, he was thought a Nonpareil."

Hugh swore under his breath at the inadvertent insult. "Miss Newman, I never meant to—"

"No, you never do mean to, do you, sir?" She tilted her chin up and coolly said, "Shall we go? The others are waiting."

He sighed, thinking it would be a very long night. He would never get to know the lady if she kept him at arm's length. He stepped into the hall. "There was no offense intended, Miss Newman. Only this"—he lifted the lapels of the jacket—"is not my usual style."

"I would think not. If temperament is reflected in wardrobe, funereal black is your color."

Hugh didn't take the bait. Instead, he laughed. "I suspect my son will say fool's orange would do best."

Her eyes widened, and her lovely mouth curled upward as if she had forgotten for a moment she was angry with him.

Taking advantage of the softening of her attitude he offered his arm to escort her to the others. "I cannot blame you for such an opinion since you have not seen me at my best. How can I make amends?"

She didn't take his arm; instead she eyed him thoughtfully a moment. "All I would ask is that you treat my aunt and her guests kindly, sir. They are rather eccentric and sensitive to cutting comments." She started down the hall, all pique clearly returned.

Frustrated that little he did seemed to penetrate her icy disdain, Hugh hurried after her and took hold of her arm, then gently turned her to face him. "I would never deliberately give offense to anyone, Miss Newman. I know there is little that will make up for this afternoon, but may I explain my rash actions?"

"There is nothing to explain, Lord Fennerly. I fully understand that you think me a fortune huntress. You are not the first and likely won't be the last." She looked down at his hand and he released her arm.

He drew his hands behind his back and clasped them to resist the urge to shake this obstinate young woman. With a sigh he gave in to his last resort and bared his soul, a thing he'd never done with another female, not even his mother. "I have given my rash actions some thought. Even my own mother thought I was being a fool to think my son would run off and marry. But the events of our lives very often shape the decisions we make. My journey here had little to do with you or your reputation, Miss Newman, and a great deal to do with my own history."

She arched one delicate brow questioningly at him.

"You are too young to have heard the gossip about me." He smiled when her eyes widened. "Yes, I fear I was once fodder for Society's tongues as well. When I was Clay's age I made an ill-fated decision to marry a young woman I scarcely knew." He looked over her head as his thoughts drifted back in time for a moment. Then his gaze dropped back to her face and he continued. "She was a spoiled and destructive woman who was only concerned with her own pleasure. The only good thing to come from my marriage was my son. When I heard he had left London with you, a woman some years his senior and . . ."

"With a reputation for luring young men, your imagination did the rest. The Notorious Miss Newman must be stopped. It is clear you know of my infamous history. It is a favorite topic in Town. But, sir, have you ever met Randall Harwood or Huntley's heir?"

Her question surprised him. "Well, no. I know only their fathers."

"Let me assure you they are nothing like Lord Barclay. They are silly, vain, and utterly spoiled, much as you describe your late wife. I never encouraged either one to pay their addresses to me. In truth, I spurned them both for the buffoons they were. But because they came from 'respectable' families without scandal, in the eyes of Society I was the villainess who tried to lure them into marriage. Ha!" Her green eyes glittered with anger a moment, then a hint of tears pooled in them. "I have refused every offer made despite my father's objections, even the ones that were not known to the gossips. Do you think I don't know what people think of us? Long ago I gave up any plans to be a bride, sir. Despite what you have heard, I have a heart. I would never inflict my father's problems on some innocent man who would forever be dunned to pay the man's ever-mounting debts." She brushed a tear from her cheek with the back of her hand. "But you cannot care about my family's problems, sir. My aunt and her guests are waiting." With that she turned and hurried down the stairs.

Hugh trailed behind her, a strange lump settling in his throat at the sight of the lady so vulnerable. Few in Society had given Newley's children a chance or wondered what it must be like to have a father who gamed away one's hopes and dreams. Hugh had inherited his estate intact as would his son. What a burden the Newmans faced. There was a part of him that wanted to take her in his arms and tell her it would all be well, but it would be a lie. Her father was what he was, and Society would always see him as a wastrel. In turn his children would carry that burden until the day the man died. The least Hugh could do was not stand in the way of his son's friendship with the family, since he believed what she said about those other young men.

He entered the drawing room, where Lady Walham greeted

him with delight. There were nearly thirty guests gathered before him, and none took any particular notice of his arrival, so deep were they into their discussions of topics that ranged from astrology to prose.

As he was taken about and introduced to the lady's guests, Hugh no longer felt quite like a fool in his outlandish attire. Her ladyship had gathered a very picturesque group of people, much involved in the arts and sciences. The gentlemen were a flamboyant mixture of artists, poets, and writers whose creative tastes were reflected in their dress, which ranged from total disregard to current fashion to the brilliant colors of an artist's palette. Hugh's attire was foppish, but positively tame in comparison to some.

On asking, he discovered that young Perry had opted to have a tray in his room. His ankle was swollen, his head throbbing, and he wasn't up to a social evening. However, Miss Hope Newman was there, glaring at Hugh with distrust. He knew he had much to do to make up for his error in that young miss's eyes.

After some twenty minutes of listening to a gentleman from Carlyle speak about the quality of Lord Byron's latest verse compared to Scott's, Lady Walham drew Miss Newman back to Hugh's side. "Since you are a stranger among us, sir, I have put you beside your only acquaintance, Felicity."

Miss Newman appeared not the least nonplussed at the announcement. She put her hand on the arm he offered her without embarrassment. As the group began to file toward the dining room, he remembered her ladyship's words about the kind nature of her young relatives. He would make an effort to put an end to the animosity between them. He whispered, "Can we not start anew, Miss Newman? I will be just another of Lady Walham's guests who is newly met."

Her green eyes held a speculative gleam, then she gave him a half smile. "I cannot think that I would not have liked Lord Barclay's father had I met you under different circumstances, sir. Your son is one of the finest young men Aaron ever befriended. For both their sakes, we shall begin again."

A smile settled on Hugh's face. "I am very proud of Clay, Miss Newman. Do you think your family can be persuaded to forgive me as well?" He looked to where Hope stood watching them.

Before Miss Newman could respond, a sudden knocking echoed in the great hall. Lady Walham urged her guests to continue to the dining room. She remained to see who had arrived unexpectedly and in the middle of a snowstorm. As the others filed in to dinner, Felicity and Hope waited at their aunt's side along with Fennerly.

The butler opened the doors. Two heavily cloaked figures stepped into the great hall, coated in snow. They moved straight to the large fireplace, extending their hands to the warmth. To Hugh's amazement and delight the nearly frozen visitors removed their hats and capes to reveal his son, and from young Hope's exclaims of delight, Aaron Newman.

"Good heavens, my boy," Lady Walham said, as she moved up to embrace her nephew. "What can you be thinking to be trying to travel in such weather?"

Aaron, his nose and cheeks reddened from the cold, laughed, "Lord Barclay here was determined to reach here tonight."

Barclay's gaze darted from Miss Newman to his father. "May I speak with you alone, sir?"

The baroness seemed to sense some undercurrent between father and son. She offered them the use of the library. "I shall have two more places set—"

"Don't bother, Aunt Lily," Aaron called from where he still had his hands out to the heat of the flames, "Join your guests. We shall take a tray in the library after he speaks with his father. We haven't time to change and are very sharp-set."

Felicity watched the earl follow his son as a footman led them to the library. Her ladyship gave the butler orders for meals and warm spiced brandy to be delivered once the gentlemen were finished, then called to her nieces to join her in the dining room. Hope hurried after her aunt while Felicity lingered by her brother.

"How are you? Should you not be in bed?"

"You needn't worry about me. I'm just tired. Go ahead and have your dinner." Aaron settled into a nearby chair and closed his tired eyes.

Felicity looked from her brother to the library door. She hated the idea there might be a row between father and son about her. True, Lord Fennerly had behaved foolishly, but somehow after hearing his story she had it in her heart to understand his fears and concerns.

Perhaps she might be able to stop any possible disagreement. She hurried down the hall, then knocked on the library door. Bade to enter, she opened the door in time to hear Lord Barclay's angry words. "How could you think so little of me?"

"May I interrupt?" Both gentlemen looked at her in surprise. "I feel dreadful that I am the cause of this disagreement."

Through stiff lips the young man said, "This was none of your doing, Miss Newman. Only my father's lack of trust in my judgment."

"You are wrong, son." The earl put a hand up over his mouth for a moment as he pondered what to say. At last his hand fell away and he said, "Your conduct has always made me proud. This mistake was about my own foolish conduct at your age. It has tainted many of the decisions I've made for most of my life. I fear I suspected you had exercised the same youthful lack of judgment that has haunted me and you are nothing like I was as a young man." He put a hand on his son's shoulder. "I made a mistake. Will you forgive me?"

Lord Barclay's eyes widened. "I—I do, sir. Grandmama told me a little about what happened with my mother, so I think I understand." He looked to Felicity, then back to his father. "But I think Miss Newman deserves an apology as well."

She shook her head, "Oh, your father and I made our peace just before you arrived. We have quite agreed we are to be friends for your sake."

The earl smiled at the lady, and she, in turn, smiled back. "So we have, but I think our young travelers must be famished. Shall we join the others and allow them to dine?"

The earl shot a questioning look at his son. Barclay smiled at the pair standing there in happy accord. It certainly wasn't what he had expected. His father's distrust still rankled, but there was no point in going on and on when his father had received the lady's forgiveness. Barclay nodded agreement to the plan. "Aaron and I shall join you after supper."

Barclay watched his father escort Miss Newman across the room. A strange thought settled into his mind when his father leaned down and whispered something to the lady, and she looked up and smiled at him. Odd that there was such an intimacy between them, as if they'd shared confidences. But how could that be? They'd only just met that day. Then Barclay's eyes widened as he took in the complete scene.

"Papa!" Barclay called just as the pair reached the library door.

Lord Fennerly stopped and looked back at his son. "Yes?"

"When the devil did you start dressing like a caper merchant?"

Miss Newman suppressed a laugh as Fennerly shook a finger at her and said, "A-ha! As you see, it's not just me. It's dreadfully foppish." He turned to his son, arms extended. "This amazing outfit"—he waggled his eyebrows at the lady—"is courtesy of our hostess. It should be a lesson to you, my boy, never to leave home without proper dinner wear even if you've taken leave of your senses."

After the door closed behind the couple, Barclay turned to stare into the fire. What was going on between his father and Miss Newman? He had rushed here thinking to find them at each other's throats, instead they were like a pair of old friends. What did it all mean? He settled into a wingback chair to ponder his father's conduct and await his dinner.

Outside the library door, the earl stopped and put his hand on Miss Newman's, which lay on his arm. "That was kind of you to try and take the blame on yourself, but you know I deserved a trimming from Clay. I behaved rashly."

Felicity didn't quite understand why she was so willing to forgive him, but somehow he was different from the other fathers who had confronted her. Perhaps it was that he'd trusted her enough to confide his own painful history. All she knew for certain was that she found she liked the father as well as the son. "You behaved like any worried parent. Don't fault yourself. We have agreed to start anew, so let us not linger over the past. Shall we join the others?"

The storm raged unabated for much of the night. Felicity arose early in an icy chamber and rang for a maid. Wrapping her heaviest woolen shawl over her night rail, she stirred the embers and a flame sprang to life. She moved to the window. A gray sky hung over the moors and a pristine covering of snow coated everything. The sharp angles of the terrain were softened into mounded curves by the undisturbed blanket of white. It was beautiful but treacherous for travelers. A smile curled her lips, Lord Fennerly would be forced to stay for as long as a week unless the thaw set in quickly. She suddenly realized the thought pleased her, for he was quite the most unaffected of her aunt's guests, not fancying himself an artist or writer.

A knock sounded at the door and Jilly, the housemaid who always acted as her personal servant at her aunt's, appeared with a can of hot water and a pail of coal. "Good morning, miss. Yer up right early on a frightfully cold mornin'."

Thirty minutes later Felicity arrived in the breakfast parlor, dressed in an emerald green and white plaid gown of soft wool. It wasn't the latest fashion, but it was warm. She was surprised to find a few of her aunt's guests dining early as well. She served herself and sat between Mr. Marlin Summers, an unassuming young man whose mother had been friends with Aunt Lily at school, and Mrs. Charles Houston, a rather grim woman whose husband wrote poetry about animals who acted like humans. After several attempts to engage the lady in conversation, Felicity gave up and turned to the young gentleman. He'd recently inherited his uncle's estate near Norfolk and had brought his mother up to the house party. Felicity was asking how he liked living on the coast when Lord Fennerly arrived.

Once again dressed in his own clothing, the earl looked every inch the country gentleman, from his neatly groomed dark hair, to his comfortably cut blue coat and well-worn buckskins. Those present greeted the gentleman, then returned to their breakfasts. Mr. Summers grew shy when the earl sat across from him, but Fennerly soon had the young man discussing crops and cattle. It was a new experience for Felicity to see a titled gentleman make the effort to converse with one considered so beneath his station, and she liked the earl the better for his effort.

Halfway through breakfast, an urgent knocking sounded on the front doors. Soon a chatter of young voices echoed in the great hall. Thinking her aunt, who rarely rose before ten, had visitors, Felicity excused herself and entered the long hallway. The sight that greeted her left her momentarily speechless. The front door stood wide open. She could see the drifts of snow had been shoveled from the doorway to the castle wall, and beyond that were an army of footprints in the snow. Puzzled as to who would have come on such a day, she hurried down the hall. As she entered the larger antechamber, she spied the butler, Hughston, arms on his hips, his face a study in bewilderment, surrounding him were a cluster of young boys who looked as cold as they were scruffy. Their ages ranged from five to twelve.

The butler's face brightened at the sight of her. "Oh, Miss Newman, can you help? Her ladyship isn't down yet and I cannot think what to do."

"What has happened?" Felicity hurried forward and was appalled to see the lads' faces were red and their eyes runny from the bitter wind. Most had large holes in their shoes and clothing as well as nothing seeming to fit properly. "Close the doors, Hughston." To the lads she said, "Come, move closer to the fire. "

The young visitors needed no second invitation, they pressed forward, crowding round the great room's huge fireplace, where flames licked the bottom of the chimney.

Hughston closed the doors and returned to whisper in her ear. "These boys are from Bodder Hall, miss. 'Tis a school some miles down the road. They say the roof's collapsed from all the snow and Mr. Hanks, the headmaster, didn't come home from the tavern last night. They've nowhere else to go. What are *we* to do with them, miss? The road to town is impassable."

"Then we must make room for them, but first we must warm them up. Have Cook prepare something warm and hardy for"—she quickly counted—"ten. We will worry about what to do with them when Aunt Lily comes down."

"Very good, miss." He disappeared down the hall, seemingly relieved that someone had taken the decision from his aged shoulders.

Felicity had just begun to question the boys when Lord Fennerly and Mr. Summers exited the breakfast parlor. They came to her side. The earl inspected their shabby dress. "Is there a problem, Miss Newman?"

Felicity quickly explained the situation. "I cannot think that my aunt's servants will have the time to oversee them what with so many guests in the castle. Still, we cannot turn them away."

To her surprise, it was the shy Mr. Summers who said, "Oh, Miss Newman, the key to taking care of lads this age is to keep them much occupied." Seeing the look of surprise on the faces of the lady and the earl, the young man smiled sheepishly. "I was a tutor before I inherited Summerley."

Felicity stared at the boys in bemusement as two more of Lady Walham's guests came down for breakfast and seemed to cut a wide swath around the shabbily dressed lads. Keeping them busy was only part of the problem in her opinion, not that she knew much about children. They would require someone to take charge since they would need dry clothes and baths as well as regular meals. Even more important, someone must make certain they didn't get into mischief until they could be returned where they belonged. As she took a closer look at the sorry state of their clothes as well as the abundant dirt and grim or their faces, she wondered if they should go back.

Lord Fennerly saw the bewilderment on Miss Newman's face. "What would you suggest, Mr. Summers?"

The young man put his hand on the nearest boy's shoulder and smiled reassuringly at the lad, whose eyes were round with fear. "Surely the nursery here at the castle must be full of toys and books. After they are fed and"—his gaze dropped to the boy's filthy coat—"cleaned as best we can, we should settle them there so her ladyship's guests won't be disturbed. I'll gladly help arrange some projects to keep them busy."

Felicity smiled at Mr. Summers with gratitude. "An excellent plan, sir. If you will oversee the boys while they eat, I shall go up and scour the attics for old clothes, although I'm not much a judge of sizes for young boys."

Her brows shot up when Lord Fennerly said, "Allow me to assist in that, Miss Newman. I've a son and might be better able to determine what we need." He moved near the fireplace. "Lads, form a line like soldiers." The boys stared at the fine gentleman with awe, even while they scrambled to do as he asked. The earl walked down the line, measuring the boys height against his waistcoat.

While the earl was judging sizes, Hughston returned just then with a tray full of cups of steaming porridge and buttered bread, which the lads eagerly took. Mr. Summers ordered them to sit in front of the fire and eat. Felicity informed the butler of the plan. "The nursery, miss." He seemed to take offense that these scruffy, unwanted boys would touch anything that had belonged to the late baron's family.

Clearly the butler wasn't happy, but he ordered a footman to show Mr. Summers and the lads to the nursery when they'd finished their meal. He informed Felicity that the attics were unlocked. With an indignant sniff, he said, "I hope you remember the way, miss, for I've got to get back below stairs to oversee things for our *true* guests."

Felicity urged him to go, then led Lord Fennerly up several flights of stairs to a door that was smaller than the others along the narrow passage. They entered a dusty room stuffed with trunks and broken furniture. Fennerly proved quite competent at the task and soon had a stock of clothing that had once belonged to the baroness's sons.

Halfway through the search, Lady Walham arrived, puffing from the climb. "Oh, my dear Felicity, Hughston told me what has happened. How can I thank you for taking charge?"

Felicity held up a blue coat for inspection that looked about right. "Lord Fennerly and Mr. Summers are the ones who knew what to do, Aunt. I fear I have little experience with children, but I will do what I can to help."

The baroness patted the earl's arm. "Sir, I can see where young Lord Barclay comes by his kind nature, but you needn't worry over these matters. I shall send for Hope or Perry to help Felicity. You must come down and join the other guests. Mr. Hairston and Lord Galen are to read some of their poetry this morning. "

"A rare treat indeed, Lady Walham, but I cannot abandon Miss Newman at this juncture." His gray eyes held a look of entreaty as he turned to Felicity.

A smile touched her lips as she fully understood his message. Anything, including a morning with ragtag schoolboys, was preferable to her ladyship's pompous guests. "Aunt Lily, the earl has raised a son and his expertise is invaluable to me. Do go join your guests and we'll come down again at nuncheon or when everything is taken care of in the nursery."

Lady Walham hesitated, not wanting to be a bad hostess to her guests, but not thinking it proper for an earl to be involved in the care and maintenance of a group of unknown children. "If you think I should, but should you tire of your task at any time, do join us in the Queen's drawing room." She gave the earl one last worried look, then shrugged and departed.

The gentleman took the lady's hand and brought it playfully to his lips. "Miss Newman, I am forever in your debt for saving me from two hours of dreadful poetry."

The breath caught in her throat a moment, then she realized he was merely teasing her. "Are you not being rather premature in your judgment of the gentlemen's work?" Felicity asked.

"Any man who is foolish enough to pronounce Scott's *Lady of the Lake* drivel, as Hairston did at dinner last evening, cannot know the first thing about good writing."

Felicity had to agree. They returned to searching out clothing for the children, but her thoughts returned to the feel of his lips upon her hand. It had sent a strange tingle through her. What did it mean? Just then the gentleman held up a jacket to ask her opinion, and she was forced to bring her thoughts back to the task at hand.

Once they had a stack of stockings, breeches, shirts, and

jackets in varying sizes the gentlemen pronounced usable, they each took an armful and headed back down to the nursery.

In the large schoolroom, Mr. Summers sat beside a newly built fire, reading to the boys from a book of fairy tales. The children were fully engrossed by the tale, never taking their gazes from the former tutor's face, even as Felicity and Fennerly entered and lay the garments on a table.

Felicity rang for hot water, and the process of cleaning and dressing the boys began. She quickly determined the rooms were too cold for a bath, so she supervised the washing of hands and faces, while the earl and Mr. Summers let the boys rummage through the stacks of clothes and select suitable garments. Two at a time the boys retired to a small room just off the schoolroom and changed into the dry clothes.

When at last everyone was clean and dressed, they settled on the floor to listen to Miss Newman take her turn reading from the book. Mr. Summers began to search the shelves, looking for games and puzzles to occupy the boys during the long, cold afternoon. As he'd predicted the shelves were well stocked. Also, he found paper and a box of old crayons which would be a treat for the lads from Bodder Hall.

Lord Fennerly stood quietly by the nursery door and watched the lady's expressive face as she did different voices for the characters of the story. It was obvious that she was enjoying the moment, and he was struck by the thought that it was wrong that such a lady would never marry and have children. How could Society have been so cruel to such a young lady to force her to make such a choice?

His musings were interrupted when two footmen arrived with bowls of lamb stew and apple tarts. The boys waited until Mr. Summers called them to sit at the table to eat, then ate as if they'd been stranded on a desert isle for years. The hall boy arrived to say that her ladyship had sent him to see to the lads while they went down to dine. Mr. Summers instructed him to summons them if there was a problem, then hurried out into the hall.

"Come, Miss Newman, we shall join the others for nuncheon," Fennerly called from the doorway.

About to join the gentlemen, she hesitated, then said, "Well, lads, enjoy your meal then stack your bowls on the tray. You are welcome to play with the toys on the shelves and if you mind Jacob, I shall return and take you down to the ballroom to play games later."

She then joined the gentlemen, realizing she was peckish too. As they walked down the stairs, she said, "Gentlemen, I cannot thank you enough for sacrificing your morning to help. I do assure you I will speak with my aunt and we shall find servants to take your place this afternoon."

The earl looked at Summers and grinned. "I don't know about you, young man, but for me it was far more interesting listening to Freddie and young Joe tell how to catch a proper tadpole in the stream than to hear Mr. Hairston prose on about the anguish in a fox's soul."

Martin Summers laughed. "I hardly agree, sir. If you've no objection, Miss Newman, I shall join you after nuncheon to help with the games. Something like musical chairs or drop the kerchief would work well indoors."

His lordship pulled a linen handkerchief from his coat. "And I will provide the kerchief if I may come as well?"

Felicity smiled. "All comers are most welcome, sirs. Shall we dine first before the games begin?" She took Lord Fennerly's offered arm and the trio went to join the other guests.

Over the next three days, Felicity, Lord Fennerly, and Martin Summers helped when they were needed in the nursery. Not surprisingly, Hope, Aaron, Perry, and Lord Barclay, on learning of the unexpected visitors, all arrived with offers of help. They were immediately assigned several of the lads to entertain. Felicity suspected they were enjoying the games of jackstraws, bagatelle, and the dissected maps, not that they would have admitted such, all considering themselves beyond such childish entertainments.

The weather did little to improve, snowing a second time on the third day after the boys' arrival. Her ladyship had been unable to send a servant to town to inform the vicar about the boys or inquire about their headmaster, since travel was still unthinkable. Felicity was seated at the window of the nursery, darning one of the boys' freshly laundered shirts. It was one of the few she'd been able to salvage from the garments they'd arrived in. As she stopped a moment to look out at a ray of sunshine which peeked through the clouds, one of the children slipped into the window seat beside her.

She looked down into the innocent face of young Joe, an adorable nine-year-old with curling black hair and eyes the color of a morning sky. "What, have you tired of the games?"

"Me and Harry done finished putting that map of the world back together." He beamed with pride at the accomplishment. Then he looked down at the floor and nibbled at his lip.

"Is something wrong?" She sensed he had something more on his mind.

He shrugged, not looking up at her. "Miss, are we goin' to have to go back to Bodder Hall?"

She sat the sewing aside. "Joe, is there some reason you don't wish to return to your school?"

He still didn't look at her. "I didn't say that, miss. It's just me and the others were thinkin' we like it 'ere at the castle with you and the other nobs. We ain't been in no trouble, could we not stay?"

Felicity felt dreadful, knowing there was little she could do to change the way things were. Their families had sent them to Yorkshire, and there was little that anyone could do. Over the course of the days since the boys had been there she'd suspected they weren't all that well treated. Not a single one had uttered a word of complaint against their headmaster, but still their condition on arrival and their rail-thin appearance alarmed her. She'd questioned her aunt, but the lady had assured her that the local vicar visited all the surrounding schools to make certain the boys were properly treated. Unless there was some proof there was nothing she could do.

"None of us live at the castle, Joe, save my aunt. After the storm passes we will all return to our own homes in other parts of England." She looked up as Lord Fennerly came into the nursery and smiled at her. A sharp pang twisted in her heart. Over the last few days she'd come to like and admire the gentleman despite their misunderstanding on that first day. The thought that he would no longer be a part of their daily lives left her feeling decidedly disheartened.

Putting her personal considerations aside, she asked, "Do you have any family, Joe?"

"Just me uncle, but he's no time for a lad my age. That's why he sent me to the Hall."

Felicity suspected all the boys had similar stories. She promised herself she would make certain that the Hall was a proper place before she sent any of the lads back. "Well, there is no need to worry about such things at the moment since no one can come and go to the castle in all this snow." But as she spoke she could see that the sun was now shining beyond the window. Depending on the temperature, it could only be a matter of a day or so before they were no longer isolated.

The lad nodded his head but didn't say anything.

Thinking to distract him, she picked up the shirt she'd been darning. "Do you know whose shirt this might be?"

The lad lifted the repaired sleeve, then said, "It's Ollie's. It used to belong to his brother."

She looked over at the small blond-haired lad who was quietly drawing a picture alone. He'd said almost nothing since his arrival, unlike the other boys, who had warmed up to the adults rather quickly. "Where is his brother?"

"Sent off to work, miss. Their family would only pay for one, so Mr. Hanks sent Owen off to work."

Felicity could barely ask the next question, her throat was so tight. "Where was he sent?"

"Don't know, but a flash cull comes to the school every now and then. If yer fees ain't been paid, Mr. Hanks sends ye with him to Leeds." There was a hint of fear in the boy's voice. Before he could say what frightened him, Harry called to Joe as he poured out a box of blocks with letters carved into them, and Joe hurried to the table to join his friend, his woe forgotten for the moment.

Eyes welling with tears, Felicity couldn't speak. She'd heard tales that children were being used in the mills, but the very thought made her heart hurt as she watched the roomful of young boys enjoying just being children. Unable to speak, she rose and hurried out into the hall.

Moments later Lord Fennerly appeared at her side. "Miss Newman, what is wrong?"

She turned to look up at him, her eyes glistening with tears of anger. "I—I think their horrid headmaster has been selling boys to the mills or maybe even the mines." Hearing the words spoken aloud suddenly made it all seem so much worse, and she began to weep openly.

The earl drew her into his arms. Felicity yielded into his embrace, trying to tell herself that it was only for his comfort but aware of the strange new sensations which surged through her.

He stroked her hair as he put his head next to hers and spoke in a soft voice. "Summers and I have suspected things weren't right at the school from little things the boys have said. I promise that once the weather clears I shall look into matters at Bodder Hall."

A shiver of awareness ran through Felicity as his warm breath whispered past her ear. She was in the arms of a man, and she quite liked everything about the feel. Shock raced through her. This led to dangerous thoughts. She pushed her emotions aside and concentrated on the lads.

She drew back and gazed up at the earl. "You will make certain that they are well taken care of after they return to school? That this man will be dismissed if he's been mistreating the boys."

Fennerly looked down into her beautiful tear-stained face, and something seemed to clamp around his heart. She was the most desirable woman he'd ever known and it wasn't merely that beautiful face. It was that vulnerability he'd seen. Over the last few days he'd also seen a goodness deep inside that was rare in a woman of their class. She truly cared about others, but especially the less fortunate. In a husky voice, he said, "I promise."

Time seemed to freeze as she gazed up at him so trustingly. He suddenly realized he wanted to kiss Miss Newman. As they stood alone in the hall, the only light was that from the open nursery door and the gentleman threw caution to the wind. He lowered his head and tasted those lovely lips, which quivered as they moved against his with passion.

Inside the nursery, Lord Barclay was in the middle of a game of jackstraws when he looked up to see his father and Miss Newman in a passionate embrace in the hallway. Shock raced through him. He'd never before seen his father so much as look at another woman, much less embrace one. Then a slow smile tipped his mouth. Why had he not thought about the lady for his father? She was smart, kind, beautiful, and very much in need of a gentleman to rescue her from her father's disreputable life. Fortunately she was no simpering schoolroom miss but just the right age for a man of his father's years and temperament.

When the pair drew back from one another, there was an awkward moment. Miss Newman turned and fled down the stairs. His father stood a moment, his face a study in confusion, mixed with a hint of astonishment, but whether from his actions or his response to the kiss, Barclay didn't know.

His lips twisted upward from a mixture of delight and amusement. His father was falling in love and didn't seem to realize the fact.

The earl came out of his reverie and strode back into the nursery. He looked about at the various lads engaged in some task. Instead of joining one, he went to the window and stared out, clearly lost in deep thought. His face was in profile to his son, yet the young man knew that face well. His father was deeply unsettled.

Tommy tugged at Lord Barclay's sleeve. "It's yer turn, sir."

Uncertain whether to approach his father, or let nature take its course, Barclay remained where he was. He played at the game halfheartedly, his gaze returning to his father often. Soon all the straws had been picked up, so Barclay excused himself from the lads, who were ready to start a new game. He joined his father at the window.

The earl mustered a smile and gestured out to the landscape. "It looks as if a thaw has begun. We should be able to leave tomorrow or the next day at the latest."

"Are you in such a hurry to depart, Father?" Barclay asked, surprised. "I thought perhaps"—he suddenly felt shy about speaking with his sire about such a personal matter—"that is . . . well, there is Miss Newman."

The only sign that the lady's name meant anything to the earl was a slight twitch of a muscle in his jaw. "The lady has her hands full since her aunt saddled her with the responsibility of these lads. We would be more help by moving to an inn in Bowes. I want to take a closer look at this Bodder Hall before the boys are allowed to return."

At that moment two servants arrived with the lads' evening meal, and all the games were abandoned. Fennerly arched a brow. "I suppose we must go change for supper."

Barclay saw Aaron helping Hope put the toys away. "Go ahead, sir. I shall help clear the tables so the boys can eat."

The earl nodded, then left. Barclay went and encouraged Hope to go; he would help her brother finish up. She blushed and dimpled up at him, but he was so distracted he paid little heed to her girlish crush.

The two young men quickly put everything back on the shelves and left the boys under the watchful eyes of the footmen. As Barclay walked down the stairs he halted at the first landing and said, "I think my father's taken with your sister."

"With Hope!" Shock filled Aaron's face.

"Not with Hope, you nodcock. Did that villain rattle your brains? With Felicity."

Aaron shrugged. "Well, she's a beauty. Many a man's lost his heart to that lovely face." He started down the stairs, unimpressed that another gentleman was smitten with his sister. It was old hat to him.

Barclay hurried after him. "But you don't understand. I think my father would marry her. We would be family." He was assuming a great deal on that single kiss, but his father was not a man who took such things lightly.

Aaron stopped and looked at his friend, then shook his head. "Lord Barclay—"

"Call me Clay, my family does."

Aaron smiled but there were shadows of sadness in his eyes. "Clay, I should like nothing better, but I thought you knew. Felicity's vowed for years she'll never marry. Just think, would you want my father and his debts in your family?"

Barclay stood frozen on the stairs as Aaron walked on down. The question had given him pause. After several minutes of pondering the question, a determined set came to his jaw. If his father wanted to marry Miss Newman, he should. He would match the earl's strength against the viscount's weakness any day of the week. With that thought Barclay hurried to dress for dinner.

In their respective rooms Lord Fennerly and Miss Newman's thoughts weren't so assured. The kiss had left them each wondering what it had meant.

His lordship decided he'd taken leave of his senses. What was he doing kissing this young lady in such a manner. Why, he'd only met her days earlier. In truth she was little more than a stranger, but that word didn't feel right when he thought about her. They'd been in each other's company more than in all the weeks he'd spent with his first wife before he'd married her.

As thoughts of his late wife returned, he was surprised that the usual bitterness didn't well up at her memory. Perhaps it was that Felicity Newman had shown him that not all gently bred ladies thought only of themselves. Thoughts of her again brought the kiss to mind. He couldn't deny that he'd felt a deep abiding desire to possess her and to protect her from any more of Society's hurts.

Then he shook his head. This was madness to be thinking about such a woman this way. He was settled in his life. He had his heir and his work on the estate. That should be enough. He didn't need some female disrupting what it had taken him a lifetime to attain. Besides had she not told him she had no intention of marrying? He must take her at her word. Once he fulfilled his promise to her to make certain Bodder Hall was a proper school for the boys, he would return to Fennerly Hall. His decision set in his own mind, the earl rang for the footman to help him don another hellish outfit of the late baron's for the evening ordeal.

As for Felicity, she had returned to her room and sat staring into her looking glass for some quarter of an hour. For ten years she'd promised herself she wouldn't marry and inflict her father's reputation and debts on another man. In all that time it had been easy because not a single man had touched her heart. But Lord Fennerly was different. For the first time she found herself thinking about a man whose very presence made her happy. A man who made her heart quicken and her knees grow weak. What would her life be like if she were loved by such a man?

A tremor of longing raged through her. Tears welled up in her eyes as she realized that nothing about her life had changed except that she had fallen in love. She grabbed a brush and began to drag it through her blond curls, pulling out the pins. Her father was still the same man who was deeply in debt, and she shouldn't allow her feelings for the earl to sway her resolve. She would simply keep her distance from the gentleman until he departed, which would likely be quite soon. Suddenly she threw the brush onto the dresser and slumped over to put her head down on her arms and gave in to despair.

That was exactly the way the maid, Jilly, found her some ten minutes later when she came to dress the lady for dinner. The girl noted that Miss Newman was dry-eyed, but there was a lack of her usual sparkle of wit and kindness that evening, as if her thoughts had taken her to some dark place. The servant could only wonder at what had put the lady in the doldrums, but she suspected it had something to do with Lord Fennerly. Like most of Lady Walham's servants she had a fondness for Miss Newman, and she hoped for the best.

That evening Barclay noticed that his father and Miss Newman were taking pains to avoid being in one another's company. He was worried. It seemed that their pride would keep them from experiencing the joy of love. His father might be planning to leave as soon as the roads cleared, but Barclay had something else in mind. He pondered the matter throughout most of the evening, and by the time he went to bed he'd come up with a plan. Surely given enough time in each other's company, they could resolve their differences, for there was one thing Barclay was certain of, his father and Miss Newman would made a splendid pair.

Chapter Four

Despite a restless night, Felicity rose early the next morning. She dressed herself and was about to depart when she discovered a note had been slipped under her door. It simply said, *"Meet me in the library at eight."*

Who would send such a mysterious missive? She had avoided Lord Fennerly at every turn the night before, but she had caught him gazing at her on several occasions. Something in his eyes had sent a pleasant tingle up her spine. Did he wish to put an end to the awkwardness after their kiss? She sighed and folded the missive. It would be even more awkward if she refused this request. She would have to steel herself against his charms and remind herself he would soon be gone. Then she could regain her conviction that her life was meant to be endured as a spinster.

Felicity made her way downstairs, her mood unusually dark. The butler stood in the great hall as she made the final turn on the landing. He looked up, a near smile on his usually stoic face.

"The roads are open, Miss Felicity." He lifted his hand to exhibit a stack of letters. "Muddy but passable. Howard was able to retrieve the post from Bowes."

A strange pang filled her, for she was certain that the earl and his son would depart later that day. She laid a hand over her blue velvet bodice as if she could ease the stab of longing for things to be different. But it would not go away and she allowed her hand to fall to her side, knowing she changed nothing. With a deep breath, she tamped down the feelings of despair. She had the lads to take care of, and she put her mind to that.

"Hughston, if the roads are open, I should send word to Bowes that the lads from Bodder Hall are here and safe. No doubt the headmaster has been looking for them if he was able to make it back and see that the roof had collapsed."

"Very good, miss. After you write a message, I'll send one of the grooms immediately."

Felicity went into the library and dashed off a quick missive to the local vicar. She sealed it and brought it out to the butler, who disappeared below stairs to summon someone to take it to town.

The long clock beside the library door chimed the hour of seven. She had another hour before she must put on her mask of indifference and face the earl in the library. She hurried to the breakfast parlor, opened the door, and halted at the sight of the room's lone occupant. Lord Fennerly sat slouched at the end of the table, a cup of steaming coffee in front of him. His mien brightened at the sight of her. He rose and bowed. "Good morning, Miss Newman."

She knew a sudden urge to turn and run. A mixture of hope and dismay churned in her stomach. She struggled with wanting to throw herself in his arms and the despair that she mustn't or she would be lost. After a moment she stiffened her resolve to be strong for his sake and said, "Good morning, sir. I didn't expect to see you up so early."

A half smile tipped his mouth as his gaze riveted on her face. "I have business this morning." He arched one brow as if she would know what that meant, but Felicity couldn't seem to gather two coherent thoughts as she stared into those entrancing gray eyes. Not only was she dumbstruck, but it was difficult to catch her breath. In an effort to regain her senses, her gaze dropped to the table, where she saw a crayon beside his cup. Had he found it in his pocket from the day before in the nursery? The gentleman's promise to see about matters at the boys' school came to mind. Was that the business he wished to discuss with her? Had there been nothing personal he'd wished to say? A feeling of disappointment raced through her as she gathered her wits.

"Ah, yes, do you intend to visit Bodder Hall today? Hughston tells me the roads are passable." She moved to the buffet, hoping to appear unaffected by his presence.

The gentleman remained standing until she returned to the table, but before she could take her seat, he stepped into her path. "Miss Newman, about yesterday . . . I wanted to apologize for taking advantage of you in the hall."

Felicity's gaze remained locked on her plate of eggs and bacon, which lay so unappetizingly before her. "There is no need, sir. You were only trying to give comfort and I do not fault you. I realized it was a gesture of the moment and did not mean anything."

He remained in front of her in silence not allowing her to pass. At last she looked up into his gray eyes, and her heart raced at the pained expression she saw. His voice was husky. "Felicity, do not say it meant nothing—"

Before he finished what he was saying, an urgent hammering sounded on the castle doors. It startled them both, and Felicity wondered who would be at the castle so early. Whatever he had been going to say was lost. When she looked back at the earl, his face was once again an unreadable mask.

Before she could question him, a quarrelsome voice could be heard. Some kind of altercation began to take place, and Felicity felt obliged to intervene on her aunt's behalf. "I must see to the visitor." She sat the plate on the table and hurried from the room.

In the hall she beheld a very tall, burly man in a fashionable drab brown coat of some cheap material which seemed to collect lint. She would have mistaken him for a dandy except for his coarse features and heavy brogues, which no self-respecting dandy would be caught wearing even in the country. The visitor had her aunt's first footman by the lapels of his livery, shaking him like a rag doll. "I'll not be denied entry, my boy. I'll see her ladyship at once, or I'll have the magistrate out here. It ain't right that you're keeping what's mine."

"What is the meaning of this, sir?" Despite his attire, Felicity instinctively knew that the stranger must be the missing headmaster. Who else would be demanding to see her aunt with just such a tone and so early in the morning. His face was flushed red, his bulbous nose almost crimson, either from the cold or years of too much drink. The set of his mouth beneath a drooping moustache was menacing. He had the look of a brute, despite his attempt to dress like a gentleman. Still she demanded, "Who are you, sir?"

The man released the footman and shoved him aside as he stepped toward Felicity. He ogled her with a glimmer of smug intimidation since she appeared such a slip of a girl beside his girth. "I'm Claudius Hanks, miss. And who might you be?"

"I'm Miss Newman, Lady Walham's niece."

"A niece, eh! Well, I've come for the lads what run off from Bodder Hall the other night while I was away. Ye've no right to keep 'em since they was entrusted to my care." His voice was loud and carried though the great hall.

Every moment in his company made Felicity certain he wasn't a man who should care for children. "The boys are well and safe in the nursery. Have you repaired the school roof, sir?"

His face twisted into a threatening grimace. "That ain't none of yer concern. There'll be a roof over their heads by nightfall, I'll guarantee."

"Until you have repaired the house, Lady Walham will never allow them to leave—" Before Felicity could finish, the man shoved her aside in a mad dash for the stairs, which caused her to fall to the floor.

"I'll not be kept from them lads. They're my livelihood." He moved across the floor then looked up the stairs at several frightened faces of her ladyship's guests who'd been disturbed by the ruckus. It seemed to occur to him that he didn't know the lay of the huge building. He turned to her and demanded, "Where's the nursery? If I have to I'll get the magistrate. You cannot keep me—"

Felicity sat on the rug, jarred by the rough treatment, the footman hovering at her side. She had never before been so roughly treated, and she was trying to gather her wits when she saw Lord Fennerly stride from the breakfast parlor straight toward Mr. Hanks. Her heart leapt into her throat, for while the earl was tall, he was smaller than the headmaster. On seeing the gentleman approach, Hanks balled his hands into two beefy fists. Without so much as a word of rebuke to the brute, Lord Fennerly planted the man a direct facer on his nose. To her utter amazement, the single blow made the giant of a man sink to his knees, then weave back and forth a moment before he fell face-first onto the oriental rug on the floor.

Standing over the unconscious man, Fennerly said, "If you ever put a hand on Miss Newman again, I shall have you arrested."

In a daze at the events, Felicity said, "I don't think he can hear you."

The earl came straight to Felicity and motioned the footman aside. The gentleman's face was full of concern. "Did he hurt you? I'll have him sent straight to the gaol in Yorkshire if he did."

She shook her head, her face only inches from his. It took all her resolve not to throw her arms round his neck and hug him. "N—no, he only startled me. I am well."

Fennerly helped her to her feet, then took her in his arms,

not caring that the footman stood gawking at them as well as the few guests who had been brave enough to come see what was happening. "When he shoved you, I thought my blood would boil." His hand caressed her chin. "I cannot continue to deny to myself that I love you, Miss Newman. You may think this is rather impetuous, having only met a few days ago, but I know my own mind. The moment I received your note to meet you, I—"

"My note? But 'twas I who received a note to meet you."

His brows grew together for a moment, then a slow smile tipped his mouth. "It would seem someone has been playing matchmaker and to good purpose." His voice grew soft. "I adore you, my dear Felicity."

She closed her eyes and seemed to savor the words for a moment. Then she shrugged free of his arms. She looked at the footman and then at the gawking guests. She took his arm and drew him across the great hall to the library. After closing the door she moved to the desk, where she stood with her back to him, her head bowed, not wanting to see the hurt her words would inflict.

"We cannot be together."

In an instant he was at her side. He turned her to face him but didn't take her back in his arms. "Do you feel nothing for me? Did I behave too much the fool when we first met for you ever to forgive me?"

Felicity looked up at him, her eyes full of pain. "Would that I didn't love you, sir. It would make life simpler." She ran her hand along the edge of his strong jaw. "I could never ask you—"

He captured her hand and brought it to his lips, where he pressed a kiss on her palm, which sent a shiver through her. "You are not asking anything I do not wish. 'Tis I who would ask you to marry me. Remember, my love, I am not some green lad who knows nothing of life's hardships. As I stood watching you try to protect those boys from Hanks I saw your courage and determination. I want you to be my wife and I understand all that entails. I know what your father is. I will deal with his problems as I must. You are worth it."

Felicity's eyes widened. "Are you certain? You cannot know what trouble he is in at the moment and I would—"

"But I do know why you are here. Clay explained the night he arrived . We will deal with your father and his debts together. I am quite positive that I cannot live without you. Marry me and make me the happiest of men."

She stared into that beloved face, then melted into his arms."Oh, dear Fennerly, I love you and I will marry you."

The earl's mouth closed over Felicity's only seconds after she uttered those words. This kiss made the first pale in comparison, for neither held back their passion. At last they drew apart and stared into each other's eyes with joy.

Suddenly the library door burst open. Hope and Lord Barclay appeared. It was clear they had been disturbed from their sleep by Hanks's shouting, for they were still in their bedclothes. Their reactions to seeing the couple were the exact opposite. At the same moment they both spoke.

Barclay said, "Jolly good."

But Hope demanded, "Unhand my sister."

Fennerly grinned, "Never dear, child. She has just agreed to be mine forever."

Barclay ran a hand through his still-tousled hair and nodded his approval. "I knew how it would be when I sent those notes."

The girl's eyes widened as she stared at the earl. "But . . . but only days ago you were accusing her of eloping with Lord Barclay. How can this be?"

The earl looked down at his future wife, a twinkle of mischief in his eyes. "Why, she is the Notorious Miss Newman, what else can one expect?"

Felicity laughed, then moved to her sister, who still eyed

the gentleman warily. "Has he not been everything that is wonderful to the boys from Bodder Hall?"

Hope nodded, "Yes, but . . . are you sure?" She leaned closer to Felicity and lowered her voice. "We have only just met him and . . . and he is quite old."

Felicity struggled not to laugh at the expression on Fennerly's face. "No, my dear, for a spinster like me he is perfect."

Hugh and Felicity gazed at one another with such intensity that even young Hope saw the truth. After hugs and kisses were exchanged, the earl suggested that Barclay and Hope go up and dress for breakfast and join them for a hardy meal. As they exited the library, Felicity noted that Mr. Hanks was no longer on the floor, the ever-efficient Hughston had already had the headmaster removed, but to where Felicity hadn't the least clue. Still she was worried.

"What are we going to do about the lads?" she asked Hugh as their respective relatives hurried up to change.

The earl slipped an arm round his fiancée. "I shall discuss the matter with Summers. That young gentleman has a good head on his shoulders and a thorough knowledge of schools. He might have some suggestions."

They went into the breakfast parlor to await the return of Hope and Barclay. Ten minutes later the pair arrived. The foursome had all just sat down to breakfast when another knock sounded at the front door.

Hugh frowned, "Who could that be? 'Tis worse than a posting inn this morning."

Felicity put a hand over his. "I warned you how it would be. We are the Notorious Newmans, after all."

She rose and he did also. He slid his arm through hers. "I shall join you this time just in case you need me to plant another facer." Seeing the look on his son's face, he said, "I'll explain later."

They hurried into the great hall, leaving Hope and Barclay

to finish their meal. As they entered the castle's antechamber, Felicity gasped. "Papa, what are you doing here?"

Lord Newley looked exhausted as the footman removed his driving cape, which dripped mud and water on the floor. "Oh, Felicity, child, you cannot know how good it is to see you safe and well." Relief at the sight of her unharmed caused him to slump into a nearby chair.

She moved quickly to her father, thinking that he looked rather ill, as if he hadn't slept in days. "Why would I not, Papa? You knew that Perry was accompanying us and Aaron arrived safely the same night."

The viscount reached up to touch his daughter's cheek. His voice was emotional. "That man I borrowed money from, he—he sent me this." The gentleman pulled Felicity's ravaged black velvet bonnet from his portmanteau, which sat beside him on the floor. The flowers were crushed and there were stains on the yellow ribbon which looked like blood.

"Oh, Papa, no. I have not worn that hat in ages. They must have stolen it from Newley Manor to frighten you."

"Well, they did." He leaned back and closed his eyes a moment before he said, "I have made arrangements to pay my debts."

Felicity looked at Hugh, who stood back and quietly watched his future father-in-law. "But how, Papa? I thought there weren't sufficient funds."

Newley opened his eyes. "I've made arrangements for my man of business to sell the town house. That came to me from your mother and is mine to sell. That should cover my debts. I've been such a fool, child."

Tears came into Felicity's eyes. She knew what a sacrifice that was for one who loved the excitement of Town as much as her father. "Oh, Papa, I'm sorry. But perhaps it's for the best."

The viscount's gaze shifted to Hugh. Newley sat up. "Who are you, sir?"

"Fennerly, sir, at your service." The earl politely bowed.

"Lord Barclay's father? What the devil are you doing at Walham?" Newley's eyes narrowed.

Hugh stepped forward and took Felicity's hand. He kissed it, then brought it round his arm and presented a united front to the old gentleman. "I came to stop your daughter from marrying my son."

Felicity dimpled up at the earl. "You know what a jade I am, Papa."

"What nonsense is this?" Newley looked from one to the other. "You marry that young pup? I cannot even make you consider a proper marriage." Then he looked from the earl to his daughter, and his gaze dropped to their entwined hands. The viscount's eyes widened.

Hugh kissed her cheek. "My dear, I would speak with your father alone."

Felicity hesitated. She glanced from her father's speculative gaze to the man who had changed her world. There was a determined set to his mouth. "Very well, my love."

The lady made her way back to the breakfast parlor, glancing back at the two men, a worried expression on her face. As the door closed behind Felicity, a grin settled on the viscount's face. "Why, if that don't beat all. Just when I've given up on the chit, she goes and falls for one of the richest men in England." The gentleman bounded to his feet. "Why, if I send an express letter I can stop the sale—"

The earl stepped into his path and placed a firm hand against his chest "No."

Newley's eyes grew stormy. "What do you mean no? As part of the settlement you could clear all my debts. There is no need for me to give up my town house. I—"

"There is every need that you give up your town house."

When the viscount opened his mouth to speak, Hugh held up his hand for silence. "You endangered your children's lives with your reckless gaming. I give you clear warning. If that happens again, I shall inform everyone in London that I won't be responsible for your debts nor will any of your children, who will be welcome at my home permanently. Do you truly wish to lose your entire family? I'm not saying you cannot game, for likely that is like asking you to not breathe, but not in London. The town house must go, or I won't pay your future debts." The earl arched one brow as the older man's face grew red, but from embarrassment or anger he could not determine. "And you know as well as I that there will be future debts. You are the type of man who could find a wager in a church."

Newley hung his head and stared at his muddy boots a moment. His gaze shifted to the crushed bonnet of his daughter that Whiner's man had shown him, and he was filled with remorse. It had been a hoax this time, but cent-percenters were ruthless. Newley couldn't deny his own weakness any longer.

"Very well, Fennerly."

The earl put out his hand and after a moment's hesitation the viscount shook it. "I shall have my solicitor draw up the exact terms of our understanding, as well as the settlements for Felicity. You will sign them before the wedding. Shall we join the others?" Hugh gestured in the direction of the breakfast parlor.

Newley sighed. "After you."

When the two gentlemen arrived in the breakfast parlor, Felicity rose and went to them. The viscount kissed her. "I wish you happy, child."

Felicity hugged him. "Thank you, Papa." Then she took the earl's hand and her world seemed complete.

By noon that day Lady Walham had broken out the champagne to celebrate her niece's engagement, Mr. Hairston and Lord Galen had vowed to write an ode to their love, and the boys from Bodder Hall were informed they would no longer have Mr. Hanks as headmaster since Lord Fennerly was going to buy out the school. Mr. Summers had agreed to be one of the trustees, along with Lady Walham and the earl. They would see that it was run properly.

It was nearly three in the afternoon before Felicity and Hugh found a moment alone together in one of the rear parlors. He took her in his arms and hugged her to him. "I do not think I can wait to marry you, my love. Marry me at once."

She drew back and looked at him. "If you are speaking of a runaway marriage to the border, I would not wish such even though I should like to be your wife at once." She sighed, "Everyone would say that the Notorious Miss Newman beguiled you into such rash conduct. I see how it will be."

Hugh kissed her forehead, then wound a golden curl near her ear round his finger. "So everything must be prim and proper. Well, what say you to a marriage in the chapel at Fennerly Hall with a special license, dear one."

Felicity grinned. "I say that would suit me fine, but what of your family? What will they think?"

"Have no fear, once my mother sees you she will know that the Notorious Miss Newman is perfect for me."

Felicity chuckled a moment before his mouth closed over hers. She didn't know there could be such happiness. Her arms slid round the earl's neck and all worries about schoolboys, families, and weddings disappeared in a haze of tender yet passionate emotion.

Lord Hawksmoor
Takes Flight

Laura Paquet

Chapter One

"That one, Mama! The one with the spot in the middle of his head!"

Caroline Farris tried to follow her son's pointing finger. It was rather difficult, since Edward was jumping up and down.

"The one on the left?" she asked.

He looked up, confusion in his blue eyes. "Which one is left?"

Caroline grinned. Sometimes she forgot Edward was only five.

"This one," she replied, lifting the puppy in question from the wriggling mass in the basket at Mr. Porter's feet.

"Yes! That's him!"

Caroline reminded herself that this puppy was likely not Edward's final choice. In the last half hour, he had made several "final choices," only to be distracted by another puppy that seemed friendlier or livelier.

"That's a good 'un," the gray-haired dog seller said, his mouth quirked in a knowing smile. "He'll be a good hunter. Smart and quick."

Edward shook his head. "I'm not allowed to hunt yet, sir. My mother says I must be as tall as she is before I can get up on a big horse."

Mr. Porter laughed. "Your mother is wise."

"How long do you think it will be before I'm as tall as Mama, sir?"

The dog seller pretended to consider the question seriously. "At least a few years, I would say."

Edward's face fell.

"That's a long time, sir."

"It's not so bad," Caroline said, kneeling down beside her son and replacing the squirming puppy in the basket. "If you were as tall as I am, you'd be much hotter in the summer."

"Really?"

"Of course! My head is much closer to the sun."

Edward laughed. "You're making that up."

"Maybe. Come on up and see." She picked up the little boy, and he flung his pudgy arms around her neck. Edward was getting heavy. It wouldn't be long before she could no longer carry him.

"You *were* making that up! It's just as cool here as down below."

"You caught me," Caroline said with a laugh. "Shall I put you down now?"

But from this higher vantage point, Edward had spied something of interest. "Look! That man is buying a puppy, too."

Caroline looked. She had been dimly aware of the gentleman kneeling a few feet away, examining the teeth of another spaniel from the dog seller's basket, but she had paid him little heed.

Most of the other customers at the dog seller's stall had weighed in with their thoughts as Edward had considered the various pups. Several had joked with him; all had seemed amused by his obvious excitement. All except the soberly clothed young man she studied now.

His brown coat and buff breeches were fashionable but plain. Perhaps he had chosen the coat to match his curly chestnut hair.

He clearly knew a lot about dogs. The pup was calm, barely struggling in his large hands as he examined it.

As Caroline and Edward watched, the man stood, the puppy in his arms. He was much taller than she had originally thought; his long legs brought him up to a height of nearly six feet, Caroline guessed.

"How much for this one?" he asked the dog seller. His voice was low, the words short and measured.

"Three quid, ten shillings, my lord. An excellent bargain, at that price."

"Not really." The gentleman frowned. "I spoke with one of your . . . your competitors not an hour ago, just down the street, and he was selling fine young spaniels for two pounds."

"I reckon you were talkin' to Archie Jones. He's got good dogs, he does, but they're not the hunters mine are. Are you a hunting man?"

"Occasionally." The man put the puppy down, but the animal showed no inclination to return to its basket. Instead, it flopped down on the gentleman's polished Hessian boots. "But I'm looking for a pet today."

"So are we!" Edward struggled down from Caroline's grasp and scampered over to the quiet young lord. "My mama says I am finally old enough to have a dog. Did you have a dog when you were my age?"

"Edward—" Caroline began to admonish her son for speaking to strangers. But to her amazement, the man knelt down until he was at Edward's eye level.

"Yes, I did. He was a cocker spaniel, just like these puppies."

"So you know about spaniels? Are they nice dogs?" The little boy's words tumbled over each other.

"The very best. Mine was my dearest friend, when I was just about your age."

Edward nodded. "That's why I want a dog. I don't have any brothers and sisters, so I want someone to play with in the park."

Caroline's heart contracted. Often, she regretted the fact

that Edward was an only child. There was little she could do to rectify the situation, however, since her husband had died four years earlier and no one else had appeared willing—or able—to replace him.

The man smiled, the expression lighting his large brown eyes. "A dog will be a very good companion."

"Do you have brothers and sisters, sir?"

He shook his head.

"Did you ever wish you did?"

"Sometimes," he said, ruffling the boy's hair. "I would have liked a little brother just like you."

Edward puffed out his chest with pride. But soon he was on to the next question. "Maybe you could have a son like me. Are you somebody's papa?"

Edward's inquisitiveness had gone on long enough. "My apologies, my lord," Caroline interrupted. "My son's curiosity sometimes gets the better of his manners."

The chestnut-haired gentleman looked up. "It is no matter," he said slowly, rising to his feet. "It is good to be . . . to be . . . curious."

All traces of the humor that had illuminated his expression when he was chatting with Edward had fled. His face was shuttered. What on earth could make him wary of her? Caroline wondered. She was the least threatening person on earth.

"Mrs. Farris, have you met Lord Hawksmoor?" The dog seller's voice cut into her thoughts.

Caroline shook her head. "I have not had the pleasure," she said simply, as her mind raced ahead.

She had certainly *heard* of the Earl of Hawksmoor, although she knew very little about him. Hardly anyone in her circle had ever clapped eyes on the man. *Ton* gossip made him out to be notoriously high in the instep, as he declined almost every party invitation he received. For years, he had been on many hostesses' minds, as any young man with a title such as his would be. Gossip had it that he had a fair fortune, and that made him even more attractive in the eyes of the *ton*. But as time went on and he remained aloof, ambitious mamas set their sights on more sociable swains than Hawksmoor the Hermit.

Mr. Porter introduced Caroline and Edward to the gentleman, and Lord Hawksmoor bowed as Caroline bobbed a curtsy. He did all that was proper, but he still wore a hunted expression. Perhaps he felt hobnobbing with the unwashed masses was beneath his dignity.

His next statement did nothing to erase this impression. "I must be going, Porter," he said brusquely to the dog seller. "I shall take this one, if you will let me have him for two pounds eight."

"I'd be losin' money at that, pardon my frankness. Three quid six would be the best I could do."

Lord Hawksmoor raised an eyebrow and said nothing.

"Well, for you, my lord, I suppose I could go down to three quid even."

Caroline watched in grudging admiration as the gentleman put his hands in his pockets. He could gain more leverage with a silent stare than most men managed with a torrent of words.

"All right, then, two quid twelve," Mr. Porter said with an exaggerated sigh. "But that's me limit."

"That will be fine," said Lord Hawksmoor, reaching into his pocket.

"Oh, no, my lord, you need not pay me now," the dog seller said, his eyes wide. "I know you are good for it."

His response wasn't surprising, Caroline thought. The aristocracy rarely paid cash for anything; the word-of-mouth their custom brought was considered more than ample reward for the risk of extending them credit.

"I insist." Lord Hawksmoor extended a handful of coins.

"Well, then, if you insist, I thank you." The money quickly disappeared into the pocket of Mr. Porter's ample waistcoat.

"Good luck with your own purchase, Master Edward," Lord Hawksmoor said, ruffling the boy's hair once more. "And good day . . . Mrs. Farris." He scooped up the puppy and would have walked away had Edward not tugged on the hem of his coat.

"Wait!" the little boy cried.

"Edward!" Caroline cried. Really, what must the young lord think of her son? She must work harder on instilling respect and decorum in the boy. This was what came, she reflected, of raising him in her father's harum-scarum household. He was afraid of no one and said whatever pleased him.

With relief, she noted that Edward's forwardness had apparently not offended Lord Hawksmoor. He turned and looked down with a small smile.

"We're going to buy a puppy, too. Right, Mama?" the child piped up.

Caroline nodded. "It is your choice, Edward. But don't delay Lord Hawksmoor. I'm sure he is a very busy man."

"Not really." His enigmatic smile remained.

Edward scuttled back to Mr. Porter. "We will have that one, please, sir," he said gravely, pointing to the puppy that had attracted his eye earlier. At least, Caroline thought it was the same one.

As Mr. Porter lifted it from the basket, Edward returned his gaze to Lord Hawksmoor. "All these puppies are brothers and sisters," he informed the gentleman. "They might be lonely when they come home with us. Maybe yours could play with ours someday?"

"Perhaps." His voice was noncommittal.

"Do you live nearby?"

"I live in Grosvenor Square," Lord Hawksmoor replied.

Caroline had been about to interrupt her son's incessant questioning, but her surprise at the gentleman's reply caused her to say instead, "How remarkable! We live not two blocks from Grosvenor Square. It is strange that we have never met." Even a recluse, she reasoned, had to venture out of his house occasionally.

The young lord turned his chocolate brown gaze on her, and she found herself slightly unnerved at its intensity. "It is not so odd. I am rarely in London, unless my resp— . . . unless my duties require it. I will return to the country once Parliament has risen."

Edward was not to be distracted from his goal by a discussion of neighborhoods and politics. He tugged again on the gentleman's hem. "Mama says we can walk the puppy in Hyde Park in the mornings. Early, when it's still nice and foggy. You could bring your puppy too!"

No matter how understanding Lord Hawksmoor was of her son's brashness, the time had come to draw the line. The child would likely be disappointed when the earl refused his request. "Edward is just excited about his new pet," Caroline said. "Please forgive his forwardness."

"There is nothing to forgive. The boy is right to think of his dog's welfare," Lord Hawksmoor said in his odd, measured voice. "Perhaps I shall see you in the . . . park someday, Master Edward. Thank you for the invitation."

With that, he turned on his heel and left, the puppy still in his arms. Bemused, Caroline watched him go. What an odd man, she thought. Even if he did cut a fine figure in his carefully tailored suit.

She turned her attention back to the dog seller. "How much for the puppy, sir?"

Mr. Porter grinned. "I can hardly charge you anything but two quid twelve now, can I?"

Caroline smiled in return. "So I am to benefit from Lord Hawksmoor's superior bargaining skills?"

"It appears so, missus."

She purchased a small leather collar and a lead from the

dog seller as well, and soon she and Edward were on their way back to their home in Hart Street, the puppy in tow. Their progress was slow, as their new friend alternately snuffled into every doorway and sat on its small haunches, refusing to move. She left Edward to the task of negotiating with the puppy as she reflected on the curious encounter with Lord Hawksmoor.

He seemed as toplofty as *ton* gossip made him out to be. At least, when he had been speaking to her, his manner had been distinctly chilly. While chatting with Edward, however, he had seemed almost a different person. She remembered the smile in his eyes when he remembered his childhood dog, and his patience with Edward's questions. He even seemed to speak more quickly.

With a mental shrug, she put the odd young earl from her mind. She had more pressing issues to consider, not the least of which was her column, which the editor of the *Weekly Monitor* was expecting on his desk tomorrow afternoon. It was almost done; she just needed to come up with a more persuasive argument to open the piece.

Edward's voice broke into her thoughts. "Are we going to have another rehearsal tonight, Mama?"

There was another thing on her plate, Caroline thought: the annual family theatrical. She'd been organizing it for years, and even though most of her siblings were grown—some even married, with children of their own—there would be a near riot among the Larch clan if she discontinued the tradition. Truth to tell, she loved the foolish make-believe and outlandish costumes as much as the youngest of her relations did.

"Yes, Edward, I think we shall. Your Uncle Lucas still needs help remembering his lines."

"Me, too," Edward said. "Can Scamp be in it?"

"Scamp?"

Edward nodded toward the puppy, which had managed to twist its lead around the base of a fence post.

Caroline knelt to untangle the leather string. "I think we can find a part for Scamp. Would he make a good lion in the Coliseum scene, do you think?"

"Oh yes! I can train him to look very fierce. Although we don't want him to *be* fierce, do we, Mama?" He frowned. "If he is, perhaps Lord Hawker won't let him play with his puppy brother."

"Lord Hawksmoor," Caroline corrected. Lud, she hoped the child wasn't putting too much stock in meeting the earl in the future. If so, he was likely as doomed to disappointment as every eager debutante in London. "We may not see Lord Hawksmoor at the park, Edward. He is an important man with many responsibilities."

"But he loves dogs," Edward argued. "He won't want his puppy to be lonely."

Caroline devoutly hoped the earl would make an appearance at least once—for Edward's sake—but she doubted that they would see the quiet young man again.

Chapter Two

"Thank you, Crawford," Gerald Kendall, Earl of Hawksmoor, said as he relinquished his hat and gloves to his butler. The puppy shot between his feet and scurried through the foyer and down the polished marble corridor, his tail wagging.

It was a shame there was nowhere else for the puppy to expend his energy than a cold hallway, Hawk thought as he shrugged out of his brown coat and handed that to Crawford as well. Perhaps it had been wrong to acquire a dog when he knew he'd be trapped here in London for at least another month. But the basket of puppies had been irresistible, their wheeking noises reminding him of childhood pets he had kept at his home in Nottinghamshire. On a rare nostalgic impulse, he'd bought one.

This austere town house was no place for a pup, though. Glancing up at the heavy chandelier and elegant moldings, Hawk thought yet again how much he loathed the place. For all its glamour, it had no paddocks, no pond, no rolling hills. None of the things he loved. He couldn't wait to get back to Nottinghamshire, where he could leave off what little town bronze he managed to acquire each Season.

"Lord Tavister is waiting for you in the library, my lord," Crawford informed him as he stowed the hat in an ornate armoire.

Hawk smiled as he thanked the servant and strolled down the

corridor to the library at the back of the house. He had not been expecting a visit from his old school friend, but the surprise was not unwelcome. If nothing else, it would take his mind off that unsettling encounter with young Mrs. Farris and her son.

It wasn't that they were unpleasant people, Hawk reflected as he twisted the knob on the library door. Quite the contrary. They were just so . . . boisterous. Boisterous people had always made him nervous.

The puppy slid through the opening in the door and scampered across the parquet floor of the library, yipping excitedly. Tavister, who had been sitting in a chair by the fire reading a newspaper, got to his feet.

"Hello, old boy." He bent down and offered the dog his hand to sniff. "And who are you? Another addition to your menagerie, Hawk?"

"Er, yes," Hawk admitted. He should have expected Tavister to tease him. "As for who he is, I haven't decided yet. I was thinking Rogue would be a good name. He has a certain gleam in his eye."

"An excellent name. He's the very picture of roguishness." Tavister settled into a large, comfortable chair by the fire.

"Port?" Hawk asked, moving to the sideboard and lifting a crystal decanter.

"Wouldn't say no."

Once they were both seated with filled glasses, Tavister took a deep breath. "Debate on the child miners' bill has been scheduled. It will start by the end of the month," he said in what Hawk knew was a falsely casual tone.

"Indeed." He sipped his port.

"I have my speech partially prepared, and I'm rather pleased with it, if I do say so myself."

"That's excellent. You've a gift for rhetoric, and this bill could do with some support. There are more than a few peers with mining interests who would be all too happy to see it fail." Too late, Hawk realized he'd left his friend an opening.

It was probably too much to hope that Tavister would let it go by.

It was. "That's why we need your help," Tavister said, leaning forward in his chair. "I don't like to beg, but I will if I have to. This bill is important. What is happening to those children is a national scandal."

"On that point we are agreed."

"We need everyone to speak out against child labor in the mines. But we especially need you."

"I would be no help to the cause." Hawk realized he sounded curt, but he had to leave his friend in no doubt about his feelings on this issue. He had to use short words if he wanted to sound authoritative.

"You believe that child labor must be eradicated."

"Of course I do. You know that."

"And your estate sits right in the middle of some of the largest coal seams in the Midlands. Your voice would hold more weight than those of ten lords from the home counties." Tavister thumped the arm of his chair with the flat of his hand.

"Tav, we've been over this and over this. You know I will not speak in P-P-Parliament, and you know why."

His friend set his glass on a rosewood Sheraton table with a clatter. "I know that you are being stubborn and obstinate. Can you not put your fears behind you, for the good of the cause?"

"My *fears*, as you call them, are well founded. I can't see how I can be the least use to you with my mouth flapping uselessly like a landed fish, and everyone from the back benches to the ladies' gallery laughing. No one will listen to a word I say. They'll just be gig-gig-giggling." He spat out the last word disgustedly. "S-s-see what I m-m-mean?"

He was sorely annoyed, and when he was annoyed, his stammer got worse. He cursed his stupid tongue.

"Just because some oafish boys years ago made sport of

your speaking voice doesn't mean that a roomful of adults will be as cruel." Tavister's words were harsh, but his voice was kind.

"They may not be cruel, but they still won't listen. I shall work behind the scenes," Hawk said, running a finger beneath his neck cloth, which suddenly seemed tight. "I can rally support by pulling in a few favors. That's where I'll be the most use to you."

The blond man shook his head. "That will help, and I appreciate it. But if you were to give a speech—"

"Save your breath," Hawk replied, not caring if he sounded rude. "There is as much chance of me sp-sp-speaking in the House as there is of me p-p-performing on stage at Drury Lane. That is the end of it."

Tavister cocked his head to one side. "An intriguing idea, Hawk. I could see you as Hamlet. You certainly have the hangdog face for it."

Hawk let out a bark of laughter, breaking the tension that had suspended itself between him and his old friend. They moved on to less contentious topics. But, Hawk feared, this would not be the last he would hear on this issue.

He wished Tav would let the matter drop. It wasn't as though he had so many friends that he could afford to alienate even one.

Chapter Three

"Lovely day for a walk, Caroline. Thank you for coaxing me to come." Sir William Larch, Caroline's father, eyed the dewy lawns around him appreciatively.

"I suspect these walks will be a regular event, if Edward has his way," Caroline replied as she watched her son running across the grass toward the Serpentine, dragged by an enthusiastic Scamp.

"Be careful not to go too close to the water, Edward!" she called after him. A half-audible assent floated back to her.

"The puppy was a good idea, m'dear. The boy is positively glowing."

Caroline could say the same about her father. His canary yellow waistcoat, bright blue superfine jacket, and cherry red pantaloons combined to give him the appearance of a round, cheery parakeet. But she had long grown accustomed to his eccentric attire. Any comment on it would simply encourage him to greater sartorial excess.

"It is boring to wear sober colors," he'd told her once. "Why should you ladies have all the fun?"

And since it amused him and harmed no one else—save some of London's more conservative tailors—Caroline had long ago resolved to hold her tongue where her father's clothing was concerned.

"Edward is certainly taken with Scamp," she agreed, bringing her mind back to Sir William's comment. "It was all I could do to convince him that the puppy shouldn't sleep under the coverlet with him last night."

Sir William laughed, and they walked on in companionable silence for several minutes, keeping one eye on the child as he scuttled across the landscape, which was still shrouded in early morning mist. It would be several hours before the park was thronged with Londoners longing for a bit of greenery or a chance encounter with friends.

Just as they caught up with the child and puppy, a muffled shout drew their attention to a small hill a short distance away.

"What the devil could that be?" Sir William wondered, just before another puppy crested the top of the rise and came hurtling toward them, a rope leash dragging behind it. Another shout echoed across the park, and then a figure came into view behind the pup. His brisk stride was surprisingly smooth, considering his tall, angular form and the fact that he likely had few occasions to run.

"Lord Hawker!" cried Edward, spying the pair. "You brought Scamp's brother for a visit!" The escaped puppy tumbled over Scamp, and the two rolled away in one scrabbling mass.

"Well, I don't know if 'brought' is the right word," Lord Hawksmoor replied with a low chuckle. He did not seem the slightest bit winded by his dash across Hyde Park. "If anything, Rogue brought me."

Caroline schooled her face into what she hoped was a bland smile. With luck, it would mask her astonishment that such a high-flown lord as the Earl of Hawksmoor was walking his own pet. Usually the peerage   particularly the ones who felt themselves above the rabble—delegated such tasks to servants.

"Rogue! What a wonderful name for a dog," she exclaimed, bobbing a small curtsy. "Lord Hawksmoor, may I introduce you to my father, Sir William Larch?"

The two men exchanged pleasantries. Then her father said,

in a teasing tone, "I've heard you are a rather rare bird to spot in these parts, my lord."

Caroline felt a dull ache in the pit of her stomach. *Please, dear Lord, don't let Papa make one of his usual faux pas. It would be nice to retain Lord Hawksmoor's good favor, for Edward's sake.*

Lord Hawksmoor frowned. "Indeed? And who says that?"

Please don't tell him I remarked to you yesterday that he was a bit of a hermit, Caroline silently willed her father.

"No one in particular," Sir William replied to Caroline's relief. "Just the usual *on-dits* one hears about Town."

"Ah, I pay little heed to such . . . gossip," the earl replied. "Perhaps that is why I am the last to know of my reputation as a . . . rare bird."

Thankfully, Edward burst into this awkward exchange. "Lord Hawker!" he cried. "Scamp knows his name already! See?" Edward turned to the writhing bundle of puppies and whistled. "Here, Scamp! Scamp!"

Scamp stopped trying to chew off Rogue's paw and bounded over to Edward, almost knocking the little boy over as he slammed into his leg.

"And I'm teaching him to walk on his lead, and to sit when I tell him to. He's not very good at that yet," Edward confided.

"Well, you have only been training him for a few days. Even boys take longer to mold than that." What looked suspiciously like a grin tugged at the corner of the young lord's mouth.

"That's what Mama said. She said I must be payment."

"Patient," Caroline corrected.

"I have to learn to wait," Edward explained for Lord Hawksmoor's benefit. "Does your dog like lettuce? Cook says it is the strangest thing she ever saw. Scamp adores vegetables, especially lettuce. Cook saves all the tough bits for him, and he eats them so fast you hardly even see them touch the floor. Mama says she wishes I liked vegetables half so much."

"Rogue has not shown any interest in veg . . . etables, but I will be sure to ask Cook to save him some tonight," Lord Hawksmoor replied, winding the rope lead around his hand.

"Scamp likes meat, too, of course. And bread. And cheese! He is very fond of cheese."

"Edward, do not talk Lord Hawksmoor's ear off." She smiled apologetically at the earl, who appeared a bit taken aback by Edward's flood of information.

Scamp, who had been busily gnawing on the toe of Edward's boot, suddenly spied a duck and her brood of ducklings on the edge of the Serpentine, and ran toward the shoreline, barking madly. Edward ran off in pursuit, and Caroline lifted her skirts an inch or two, preparing to give chase and ensure that her son didn't come to any mishap at the water's edge.

"I'll watch him, Caroline," her father said before she could move. "You stay here with Lord Hawksmoor." Sir William left them at a brisk stroll, the fastest pace his girth allowed.

Caroline, reassured that Edward would come to no harm, turned her attention back to the earl.

"Don't worry about your son's chatter. I find his stories charming," Lord Hawksmoor said. Once again, as she had remarked on their initial meeting, she noticed that his voice was significantly cooler and more formal when he spoke to her than when he conversed with Edward. She was at a loss to understand what she might have done to offend him, but she resolved not to let it bother her. Life was too short to hold grudges against anyone.

"Well, Scamp has charm to spare himself," Caroline replied. "He needed every last bit of it to soothe me when I found him in my dressing room this morning, with a corner of my favorite mobcap in his teeth. One soulful look from those big puppy eyes, though, and I didn't have the heart to do more than give him a gentle scold."

Lord Hawksmoor smiled. "A mobcap? Forgive me for saying so, Mrs. Farris, but you hardly seem the type to wear a mobcap."

"Why ever not? They are very handy when one needs to keep one's hair out of one's eyes." She wore one mainly when she was bent over her writing desk, working on one of her columns, but Lord Hawksmoor need not know that. Few people in London knew the identity of the author who had taken over John's newspaper duties.

"I don't know. I think of elderly widows and . . . spinsters wearing them, not someone as young and . . . lively as you."

Caroline had to clamp her jaw closed to keep it from dropping open with surprise. Could the reclusive earl be *flirting* with her?

What a preposterous notion. What makes you think that you, alone in all London, could bring Hawksmoor the Hermit out of his shell?

She countered his comment with a flippant reply. "I am not elderly, but I *am* a widow. Mobcaps are commonly worn by bereaved women; I'm surprised the parish does not send a selection to the house after the funeral. So I feel it is only seemly to don mine once in a while."

His grin faded. "My—my apologies, Mrs. Farris. I did not realize you were a widow, and I did not wish to offend."

"No offense taken, truly. My husband died four years ago, and while I miss John greatly, my grief is neither fresh nor painful." This conversation was becoming much too personal. "Do you come to the park often?"

"Hmm?" Lord Hawksmoor seemed startled by her question. "Oh yes, the park. I come here as often as I can. It is a pleasant . . . respite from the streets and noise. Sometimes, I am even lucky enough to spot a bird I have not seen before."

"Birds? Are you a bird watcher, then?"

"I am a bit of an amateur. Mostly, I enjoy collecting nests."

Again, Caroline tried to conceal her surprise. "Forgive me, my lord, but I cannot exactly picture you halfway up a tree."

Lord Hawksmoor laughed. The severe set to his jaw disappeared, and he suddenly looked younger and far less formidable. "I was a dab hand at tree climbing when I was a lad, and I do scramble up the odd oak at home in Nottinghamshire. These days, however, I buy most of my nests at the fair on Dulwich Common, or from street sellers."

Caroline's fascination with this unusual hobby had been stayed by something else the earl had said. "Nottinghamshire? Is that not near several of the major coal mines?"

Lord Hawksmoor frowned. "Yes."

"Then you must be involved in the upcoming debate about child labor in the industry." Her voice rose with excitement. This was the topic of her current series of columns, but she had not realized that Lord Hawksmoor's estate lay in such proximity to the mines. Perhaps he was also trying to limit the use of children underground.

"I am working with some . . . colleagues to shape the bill, yes." His voice was even colder and more remote than before. He couldn't possibly be thinking of watering down the bill's provisions. Could he?

"To strengthen it, surely?"

"Of course. Life in a mine is no life for a child. It is immoral to put anyone so young in such danger. And it can even be argued that doing so takes a job from a grown man who needs it more, although there are . . . people who dispute that." He shook his head, and Caroline was suddenly aware of the faint scent of sandalwood. "With the . . . scientific . . . advances we have made in the last few decades, surely there is some inventor who could devise a machine that could do the work now . . . assigned to children."

Caroline blinked. This was the longest string of words she had ever heard Lord Hawksmoor utter.

"So you will speak in the debate, then?" She found herself most curious as to how this reserved young lord would comport himself in Parliament. His manner of speaking might have been halting, but she suspected that he could hold a room in thrall with the force of his ideas if he so chose. The man had *authority*.

"No." His voice was flat.

"No? But as a landowner from Nottinghamshire, your voice would—"

"I know. But I will not speak." He slipped the dog's lead into his pocket and smoothed his hand over the resulting wrinkle in the fabric.

Lord Hawksmoor's adamant refusal to support his own cause baffled Caroline, and she groped for possible reasons. "I know you must be one of the younger peers, but everyone's point of view should be heard."

"I agree."

"Then why not—"

"I would . . . prefer not to talk of this, if you don't mind." He looked toward the Serpentine, and the frown that had creased his face cleared somewhat. "Here come the troops. Your father looks as though he could stand to be relieved of his post."

As Edward and the puppies barreled toward them, with Sir William in slow pursuit, Lord Hawksmoor turned his back on Caroline to await their approach.

What a selfish popinjay, she thought. What sort of man would not fight for a cause he believed in? Did he think it below his dignity?

Probably, she decided, as she knelt down and held out her arms to Edward.

And he probably didn't realize that if you didn't fight your battles when they first came up, you might never get another chance.

Hawk grimaced as he watched Mrs. Farris hug her son. What a fool he had made of himself, again. Her interest in his stance in Parliament had been both understandable and genuine, and he had treated her as though she were an insolent child. It was one thing to tell Tavister curtly to leave him alone. Tav was an old friend, first of all, and he knew Hawk's history and understood his reasons for silence. Probably the last thing that would occur to this ebullient, articulate woman was that Hawk would die of mortification if he so much as opened his mouth to speak to the child labor bill.

"Lord Hawker!" He felt Edward tapping him on the shin.

"Lord Hawksmoor," Mrs. Farris corrected.

Hawk looked down. "Why don't you just call me Hawk, Master Edward? All my friends do, and it is much easier to . . . pronounce."

"I hardly think it fitting for a child to call a peer of the realm by a nickname," Mrs. Farris protested.

Hawk paused. As an earl, he was used to others' deference, but it never ceased to amuse him. If they only knew. "Would Lord Hawk do?"

The dark-haired young woman's brows knitted together as she considered this suggestion. She could hardly know it, but the look of concentration on her face was most appealing. "Well, I suppose it would, if it does not offend you."

"It does not offend me in the . . . slightest." He knelt down and gravely shook the little boy's hand. "You must call me Lord Hawk from now on."

"And you must call me Edward," the child replied, equally grave. "I am not Lord anything, and Master sounds so old, so Edward will be suff . . . suffish . . . good."

Hawk suppressed a grin at the boy's attempt to use grown-up words. "Very good, Edward. I am pleased you consider me a close enough friend to be on familiar terms."

"Our puppies are brothers, after all," Edward replied happily. "We are practically related!" As he said that, a thought seemed to strike him. "Since we are almost relatives, you should come to our theatrical tonight!"

"Your theatrical?" What on earth could the child mean?

"Oh, Edward, Lord Hawksmoor would not be interested in our silly playacting." Mrs. Farris chuckled. "It is a family tradition," she explained. "We perform a play each year in my father's drawing room, for relations and friends."

"What sort of play? Sheridan and so forth?"

Her chuckle became a real laugh. "Heavens, no, nothing so polished. We write the lines ourselves, and it is usually a satire of some sort. This year we are acting out scenes from ancient Rome, but many of the characters are actually veiled parodies of prominent people and various relatives. It is all done in good fun, but it would probably seem rather childish to you."

It seemed rather mystifying, in fact. Why would anyone go to the trouble?

"You would like it. Scamp is going to play a lion!" Edward's face was pleading.

He hated to disappoint the boy. But Mrs. Farris obviously thought him a lackwit without the gumption to speak his piece in Parliament, so she could hardly be eager for him to visit her home. And even the thought of mixing with a large room of strangers made his neck stiffen with tension.

Some men feared war. Gerald Kendall feared small talk.

"Will you be performing?" he asked Mrs. Farris.

What he could have sworn was a blush tinted her pale cheeks. "I shall."

"Mama is Calpuna and Hessian and Dinah and many other people," Edward informed him.

"That would be Calpurnia and Hestia, I presume?" Hawk hazarded.

Mrs. Farris nodded.

"And Diana?"

Another nod.

A sudden picture popped into his mind of the ebony-haired Mrs. Farris dressed in some sort of flowing robe to play the beautiful goddess of the hunt. She would be most suited to the part. Perhaps he could attend without needing to talk to so very many people.

And perhaps, by doing so, he might redeem himself in her eyes somewhat.

He didn't know why that was important. He didn't even know the woman, and she certainly wasn't the type he would choose to know better if he did. She—and her whole family, in fact—were far too lively and outspoken for his liking.

"Please, Lord Hawk," Edward said again. For whatever reason, the child had become fixed on his attendance.

It wasn't as though he had an avalanche of invitations on his mantelpiece to compete with the theatrical. Those had stopped arriving years ago.

"I do believe I shall accept, with thanks," he informed Edward. "Just let me know the time and the place."

"Nine o'clock, Three Hart Street," Sir William piped up. "We would be most pleased to have your company, Lord Hawksmoor."

Hawk did not miss the sharp look Mrs. Farris gave her father at this remark. Yes, he suspected it was going to be the most interesting evening he had spent in many months. Even if it did involve a roomful of strangers.

Chapter Four

"What on earth possessed you to encourage Lord Hawksmoor to attend?" Caroline asked her father as she struggled to draw a clean line of kohl along her eyebrow.

Sir William smiled. "I thought he might make good company for you."

She rolled her eyes. "With one child, four siblings, and several in-laws to coax through this production, I am hardly lacking for people to talk to." As if on cue, her sister Harriet appeared at the door.

"Caro, what am I to do with this foolish thing?" Harriet held up a wreath of laurel leaves made from green paper and wire. "I cannot get it to stay fixed, and Molly is no help." Molly, their long-suffering ladies' maid, lived in dread of the annual theatrical, as it taxed her minimal hairdressing skills to the limit.

Caroline looked at her father. "See what I mean? The last thing I need is *company*." She motioned her youngest sister into the room and attached the rather wilted-looking wreath to Harriet's blond curls with a series of hairpins. "There you are. You are a vision of loveliness. Off you go—we need to be ready soon. Have you run Lucas through his lines one more time?"

"I did, and he is still having trouble with that scene from *Caesar*," Harriet said as she hurried out the door.

Caroline leaned back in her chair and sighed. How hard could it be to crumple into a heap and cry "*Et tu*, Brute"? Yet

Lucas managed every time to find some new and hilarious variation on the line. Yesterday it had been "I think not, Brutus."

She giggled. Despite herself, she couldn't be angry with her fifteen-year-old brother. He tried so hard, and it was only playacting after all, as she had explained to Lord Hawksmoor.

Lord Hawksmoor. At the thought of seeing his serious, sober face in the audience, Caroline's stomach contracted. What *would* he think of them all?

What did it matter? she asked herself as she picked up her kohl pencil again and focused on her other eyebrow. Lord Hawksmoor was a stuffed shirt, and the last thing she needed was his good opinion.

"He's not a bad-looking fellow," Sir William said. Caroline started, and the kohl traced a jerky line down the side of her face.

"Who?" She feigned innocence as she picked up a rag soaked in witch hazel and began carefully wiping the black streak from her cheek. Thank goodness women—well, most women—no longer wore cosmetics. Applying them was difficult work.

"Lord Hawksmoor, and don't pretend you don't know who I mean, gel."

"He is all right, I suppose." She remembered how he had looked when he had knelt to shake Edward's hand, his normally serious face lit up with a smile. She also remembered how the soft wool of his coat had stretched tight across a pair of rather broad shoulders, but she quickly suppressed that memory.

What good were broad shoulders when the man in question would not take the weight of the world on them—or even the weight of one cause?

"He is also lord of one of England's oldest estates. And, if the scuttlebutt about Town is to be believed, he has finally succeeded in redeeming that estate from the financial entanglements his father left behind."

Despite her intentions to pay the stuffy lord as little heed as possible, Caroline's ears perked up. "Oh? I had not heard about the father. What little I know of the family has revolved around the son's snobbishness."

"I knew the sixth earl slightly. A loud, showy man he was—you could not imagine a more opposite father and son. Fond of his drink, and fond of deep play when he was in his cups. Lost an entire unentailed property in Kent one night at faro."

Caroline gasped. "Deep play indeed."

"That was not the half of it, child. When he died ten years ago, the estate was rumored to be in debt for more than fifty thousand pounds."

Caroline shook her head. "No matter how much I've dabbled in cards, I cannot imagine losing such a sum."

Sir William shook his head. "You've always played for fun. The old earl played for spite, or vengeance, or some other such emotion. It was a compulsion for him, and it was not pleasant to observe." He glanced at the small carriage clock on the mantel of the breakfast parlor. The room was serving tonight as a dressing room for the amateur players. "I see that it is almost time for the show to begin, my dear, so I shall take my leave. I am looking forward to finally seeing what you have prepared this year."

By long family custom, Sir William never performed in the theatricals and was kept in ignorance of most of the content. The tradition dated back to the days when he was their only audience member.

He kissed his eldest daughter on the cheek and took his leave. As the door closed behind him, Caroline leaned back in her chair and closed her eyes.

Her father couldn't be trying to throw her together with the Earl of Hawksmoor, could he? Good heavens, what a dilemma that would be if Papa truly put his mind to it. He could be a most determined parent.

She opened her eyes and shook her head. The idea was ridiculous. No one could be less suitable to Caroline's temperament than the selfish young lord. For one thing, she could not imagine anyone more unlike John.

John had been outspoken, enthusiastic, eager to grasp life by the tail, and fearless about fighting for his many causes. Lord Hawksmoor, by comparison, seemed as dull as a sparrow compared with a peacock.

Although he was a pink of the *ton*, she had to grant him that. No wonder London's ladies had taken years to give up on him.

She drew a pot of rouge toward her, dabbed some on her fingertips, and began applying it to her cheeks in broad, light strokes. To her surprise, she noticed that her fingers were trembling.

How odd. She was never struck with nerves during one of their performances. On the contrary, she found acting thrilling. More than once she had caught herself regretting the fact that a life on the stage was considered beyond the pale for a gently reared young woman. In another time and another place, she suspected she would have rather enjoyed becoming a minor Mrs. Siddons.

As it was, she had to make do with the annual Larch theatricals, which she had always enjoyed. But tonight, her stomach was clenched, and a thin sheen of perspiration coated her forehead.

She couldn't possibly be nervous because some stiff-rumped earl would be in the audience. Expunging that thought from her mind, she reached for a feather puff and powdered her shiny forehead.

The hubbub in the drawing room was almost overwhelming. On all sides, Hawk was surrounded by laughing, excited people, from tiny children to aged dowagers, all of whom seemed to know each other and to enjoy exchanging information at the top of their lungs.

"Good heavens, Lottie, when did you chop off your curls?

You look most fetching!" exclaimed an elderly woman in a fussy gown, as she tugged a much younger woman toward her.

"Not a farthing would I have given for that horse—not one pence! Yet Morris bought it. Better his blunt than mine," said a young man whose high shirt points and purple breeches almost put his host's sartorial splendor to shame.

Almost. Tonight, Sir William had outdone himself. Hawk suppressed a grin as he observed his host's yellow trousers, embroidered waistcoat, and bright blue jacket, adorned with vaguely military epaulettes. His neckcloth, thankfully, was plain and snowy white. It was the only thing remotely reserved about his attire.

One couldn't help but like the older gentleman, despite his outrageous fashions. In fact, his colorful clothes were part of his charm. Hawk was fascinated by Sir William's utter lack of concern for what others thought of him. Surely, Hawk reasoned, the wags at the gentlemen's clubs must have had their share of amusement at the old dandy's expense. He'd bet that Sir William was the subject of more than one caustic wager in the betting book at White's. As far as he could tell, Sir William could not care less.

Hawk settled back on his gilded chair, and glanced once again at the makeshift curtain drawn across one end of the room. The play would likely begin soon. He had no idea what to expect, but he found himself strangely anxious for the performance to start. For one thing, it would absolve him of the necessity of engaging the other members of the audience in conversation.

As though she had overheard his thoughts, a middle-aged woman in a conservative green gown settled down beside him. To his surprise, he recognized her.

"Lord Hawksmoor. What a pleasure to see you here! I did not realize that you knew my brother's family."

"Mrs. Norton. Good evening." He had not known that Emma Norton was related to the Larches. The Nortons had been friends of his late father, and although his acquaintance with them was slight, it was cheering to see a familiar face in the throng.

"I am a relatively new member of the Larch circle," he continued. "Mrs. Farris purchased a puppy for her son from the same litter as my new pup, and we met through the dog seller."

"How remarkable!" Mrs. Norton was one of those lucky people who found even the most mundane aspects of life exciting. "Well, it is lovely to see you again. I don't believe I have seen you since your dear father passed away."

"Dear" was not an adjective Hawk would have applied to his parent, unless it was meant in the sense of "costly," but he had no desire to debate his late father's merits or lack thereof with Emma Norton. "It has been a long time," he acknowledged.

"You are in for a rare treat tonight. These children are *so* talented! Of course, it is Caro—I'm sorry, Mrs. Farris—who marshals them all into line. She writes the plays, as well. We were all afraid she would stop after Mr. Farris passed away, but when her period of mourning had elapsed she came back to it. She knew the younger ones would be disappointed if she let it go."

"What happened to Mr. Farris?" Hawk asked, knowing he might sound too inquisitive but unwilling to let the opportunity pass.

"It was the saddest, strangest thing. He simply fell down dead one afternoon, walking home from the *Monitor* office. A young man like that, just one-and-thirty, with a new son and in excellent health! The doctor later said it was likely that something in his brain had just collapsed, or exploded. It was most unfortunate."

Before Hawk could ask more, Sir William's booming voice sounded above the room's chatter. "Ladies and gentlemen! If you could please take your seats and direct your attention to the front of the room, our performance is about to begin."

The older man strolled through the opening in the curtain. "Most of you have been witness to these performances for many years, but for those who have not, a word of explanation. What you are about to see is a series of vignettes, rather than a complete play. Think of it as a series of afterpieces, rather than the main event. There may be pantomime, or farce, or even some semblance of comic opera." He grinned. "As usual, I have been kept in the dark about the content, but I can guarantee you an evening of unmatched entertainment. I may be biased, but I do think my children put on rather a good show."

A round of enthusiastic applause swept the drawing room as Sir William took his seat.

What must it be like to have such unequívocal approval from a parent? Hawk wondered. It must affect one's outlook substantially. No wonder the Larches—the three he had met, anyway—seemed so eager to meet life head-on.

At the front of the room, the makeshift curtain was drawn back jerkily. He caught a muttered epithet as the bed sheet snagged on a knot in the rope from which it hung. Then, with one last tug, the "stage" was revealed in its entirety.

In one corner, a row of three wooden columns of mysterious provenance—Corinthian? Ionian?—teetered, marking what Hawk supposed was a make-believe Roman Forum or Coliseum. In the opposite corner was a raised platform adorned with a spindly potted plant. Just left of center stood a miniature chariot. Hawk wondered whether Scamp would be pressed into service as its equally diminutive horse.

The stage was oddly devoid of one thing, however. People.

A rustling and a muffled thud issued from the doorway on the back wall, which had been draped with what appeared to be a torn cape. Then, in a rustle of fabric, a tousle-haired youth in an improvised toga emerged, his garland of leaves askew. He strolled toward the columns, looking both proud and slightly panicked.

From beyond the curtain came Mrs. Farris's clear voice. "What mean you, Caesar? Think you to walk forth? You shall not stir out of your house today."

"Caesar shall forth: the things that threatened me never looked but on my back," the young man muttered nervously. Then, perhaps realizing that half the audience could not hear him, he shouted the line once more, tossing it over his shoulder.

"Caesar, I never stood on ceremonies, yet now they frighten me," Mrs. Farris replied as she strode through the curtain. What she said next, however, Hawk could not have remembered if he had been under examination by a magistrate.

She continued to speak, but he was sorely distracted by her costume. It was similar to Caesar's, but the effect was as different as silk and burlap.

Another white bedsheet, apparently, had been pressed into service. And while the toga was in most ways less revealing than the scanty dresses currently in vogue among the young women of the *ton*, its effect was far more shocking, in Hawk's mind at least.

For Mrs. Farris's left arm was completely bare, and the swath of fabric below it was tucked in all-too revealing ways.

She looked nothing at all like the boisterous young mother who had conversed with him in Hyde Park. She looked more like a statue in Montague House—as classically composed, but far more compelling.

He realized he was staring, and hastily shifted his gaze to Caesar, who seemed to be having some trouble with his lines. The boy stumbled over a sentence, recovered, then plowed ahead for several more lines until he stopped dead.

"What can be avoided . . ." emerged an encouraging female voice from the shadows beyond the makeshift stage.

Caesar's eyes lit up. "What can be avoided whose end is purposed by the mighty gods?" the young man repeated. The audience, blessedly, had the good grace not to heckle him.

"Do not go forth today: call it my fear that keeps you from Almack's, and not your own," Mrs. Farris/Calpurnia urged, reaching out to Caesar and laying a hand on his arm. Hawk sensed that this was the moment when the play would diverge from its classical origins.

Mrs. Farris continued, "I have consulted the astrologer—well, the society column of the *Monitor*—" She paused to let some chuckles ripple through the audience. "And the astrologer says it is a most inauspicious day for you to be seen in the august precincts. Men who want your ruin—nay, not only your ruin, but to steal this Season's merriest widow from under your very nose—are about and mean you harm."

"What need have I of a merry widow? I am already a married man, am I not?"

"That has rarely stopped a man from pursuing fair hand at Almack's in the past—providing that fair hand does not come attached to parson's mousetrap."

Another chuckle rippled through the audience. Hawk was astonished at the rather frank nature of the satire. There were women and children in the audience. Surely it could not be seemly to allude—however obliquely—to the young married women some men were wont to chase at the celebrated assembly rooms?

No one, not even Sir William, seemed the least offended by the dialogue, so Hawk decided he was being far too prudish for his own good and returned his attention to the scene. His thoughts soon wandered away from the play, however, and back to the intriguing Mrs. Farris.

Her normally animated face was alight with excitement as she delivered her lines. It was more like torchlight—fiery, intense—than the gentle glow of a lamp or a candle.

Where had that thought come from? Hawk was not predisposed to flights of poetic fancy. He twitched his shirt cuffs to straighten them under his blue superfine coat, and immediately felt more like himself.

Mrs. Farris strode across the stage, the folds of her toga swirling about her in a most distracting way. Was the ridiculous garment securely sewn or pinned together? He hoped so. Well, the better part of his nature certainly hoped so. Admittedly, the better part of his nature seemed exceedingly small tonight.

He reached a hand to the back of his neck to adjust the collar of his coat. What the devil possessed him this evening? The last thing he needed was to develop an infatuation with a flamboyant widow who came complete with an eccentric family.

He knew all too well where flamboyance could lead. People who flew too close to the sun and all that.

While he had been woolgathering, the play had continued. Several other actors had arrived, and Mrs. Farris had quit the stage. An argument of sorts was ensuing, a mixture of Shakespeare and modern cant that seemed to revolve around Lady Jersey. Then a young man brandishing a knife—well, what appeared to be a piece of wood painted yellow—moved behind the hapless Caesar, who crumpled to the ground with a histrionic scream.

"Choose your second, Brute," Caesar howled, to the audience's immense amusement as he expired with heaving sighs.

Hawk enjoyed the subsequent vignette, a related parody of Almack's which involved a young blond woman being thrown to the "lions" (a confused-looking Scamp) for the sin of waltzing with a young cavalry officer without the patronesses' permission. She, too, died a rather showy death. Mrs. Farris, it appeared, had a bloodthirsty dramatic streak.

He had become quite caught up in the next installment of the show, a pantomime involving several Roman deities debating in Parliament, when Mrs. Farris reappeared—in the guise of Diana, he assumed. Her costume was largely unchanged from her turn as Calpurnia, except that she carried a small bow.

"Mars you may be, but your stance is far from warlike,"

she admonished the young man who appeared to have recovered quickly from his death as Caesar. "If you believe in your cause, then you must fight."

Easy for Diana to say. Mars probably doesn't sound like a candidate for Bedlam every time he opens his mouth.

Hawk refused to dwell on that self-pitying thought. When he turned his attention back to the stage, he enjoyed the rest of the admittedly amateur performance. Finally, he sensed the evening was drawing to a close when all the players—including Edward and even Scamp—assembled on the dais.

"We'd like to thank you all for sharing this evening of foolishness with us," Mrs. Farris addressed the crowd. "For the final amusement of the night, though, we need your help. Harriet? Lucas?"

The young blond woman who had been thrown to the lions, along with the erstwhile Caesar, hopped down from the platform and knelt to retrieve two large baskets from beneath a side table. One basket, Hawk noticed, was heaped with wreaths of paper laurel leaves similar to the ones the players wore. The other contained a stack of papers.

What next? he wondered.

The siblings moved through the small audience distributing the items. He accepted his with alacrity, although his face must have betrayed his bafflement, for the young woman leaned toward him and whispered, "Truly, my lord, they won't bite."

He smiled, although his face felt tense. Whatever was about to happen next, he suspected it would involve him acting ridiculous. His father had done enough of that for several generations of earls.

He looked down at the sheet of paper. It appeared to be a parody of a popular drinking song.

Good Lord, were they expected to sing?

"Does everyone have a wreath and a sheaf of paper?" Mrs.

Farris's clear voice rang out across the little crowd. A murmur of assent went up.

"*Good*. Now this is how we're going to divide the parts—"

That was all Hawk needed to hear. When he had agreed to come to this evening—which, admittedly, had been most enjoyable—there had been no mention of performing. It pained him to seem rude and to leave the festivities before they were over, but enough was enough.

It was certainly not seemly for an earl to don a silly hat and sing some foolish song in mixed company.

He glanced around the room. Well, Lord Chemley was here, and he seemed to have no qualms about putting a piece of fake greenery on his head.

But then again, the Chemleys had had a pristine reputation going back to the Restoration and beyond. They could afford to unbend a little every now and then. Hawk couldn't. Although it did look as though everyone was expecting to be amused.

With a trace of reluctance, he rose from his seat and excused himself, walking past a group of excited young ladies who were already giggling over the mildly scandalous words to the song. The rising hilarity was his cue to leave.

He had to get out. Now. Quickly, he stopped by Sir William's chair to offer his thanks for the evening, and brushed aside the older man's surprise at his early exit.

Hawk was in the foyer, collecting his cape and hat, when he felt a hand on his arm. The jolt of awareness that shot from his elbow to his heart led him to suspect that it was not Sir William who had pursued him.

Slowly, he turned to face Mrs. Farris. Up close, her toga was even more intriguing. It was, he also realized, coming slightly loose on one side. Quickly, he raised his eyes.

"Lord Hawksmoor? Is everything all right? I saw you leaving so quickly, and I was afraid that you might be ill." Her eyes were filled with such genuine concern that he cursed himself for worrying her.

But how could he tell her the truth—that he thought her family's games undignified?

"Er, yes, I am somewhat fatigued," he said, surprised at how easily the fib came to him. He was unaccustomed to lying, and the effort left a sour taste in his mouth.

He evidently wasn't very good at it, either, judging by the frown line between Mrs. Farris's wide-set blue eyes. "I see," she said.

In the silence that followed, he could hear the pendulum of the case clock in the foyer swinging monotonously back and forth.

He felt like a scoundrel.

"And I must retire early. But I do thank you for your . . . hospitality."

"You are most welcome." Her smile did not reach her eyes.

Dash it! He couldn't leave like this without being honest. He would just attempt to be diplomatic about it.

"In truth, Mrs. Farris, I am not leaving due to exhaustion or to other . . . commitments," he began. "It is just that I am unaccustomed to . . . performing in public, and I thought I would leave before I made a . . . spectacle of myself."

There. That sounded suitably neutral.

Her eyes narrowed.

Well, perhaps it had not.

"Do you think that a group of people having a bit of innocent fun is unseemly?"

"Well . . . perhaps not unseemly for everyone—" Damn, he was making it worse! How could he explain that he didn't care how others comported themselves, but that he had to be most careful about what he himself did? And that any sort of utterance in public on his part was likely to lead to disaster?

"—just unseemly for an important lord like yourself," she finished for him.

"Yes! I mean, no!" How could she twist his words so easily? She stared at him, waiting for an explanation.

Suddenly, he was angry. He did not need to explain himself to her. He had thanked her for the entertainment, and surely that was all that was necessary. Her insistence on probing more deeply was simply rude.

He decided to stand on his dignity. It had never failed him before.

"You had best get back to your . . . guests," he said, infusing his voice with unmistakable hauteur. His father might not have taught him much that was useful, but he had shown him how to convey authority when the occasion demanded it. "Good evening, Mrs. Farris."

As the door closed behind him, he pretended not to hear his hostess's huff of annoyance.

It was her own fault, really. If she had just let him leave with his polite fiction intact, he would not have to have behaved so badly.

If it was her fault, then, why did he feel so low?

Chapter Five

Grimly, Hawk inserted a bootjack into one of his polished Hessians and pulled it up over his foot. When it stuck briefly, he muttered a mild oath.

"Displeased today, my lord?" asked Crawford. Most servants would not have dared even this slight familiarity, but Crawford had been with the family since before Hawk was born.

Hawk looked up from his seat on a bench near the front door. "Just talking to my boots. My annoyance will pass."

In short order, he was suitably garbed for a walk in the park. With Rogue twisting circles around his feet, Hawk left the town house and beat a hasty path through the early morning streets to Hyde Park.

He could almost enjoy London at this hour of the morning. Most of the beau monde was still abed, coddling aching heads from the late night before, so the thoroughfares were not as cacophonous as they would be in the afternoon. But that did not mean the streets of Mayfair were deserted. There were maids hurrying back from the market with choice fish and vegetables for aristocratic tables, and tradesmen directing their carts into the mews behind the great houses. A few nurses and even several ladies supervised children in the fenced squares. And on every street were knots of costermongers, flower sellers, and match girls, proffering their wares.

"Posy fer yer lady, milord?" asked a tiny girl at the corner of South Audley Street and Upper Grosvenor Street. Eight years old at the most, she craned her neck to look up at him, her blue eyes wide in her dirty face. "Nice vi'lets, sir. Lovely t'day, they are."

Of all London's street sellers, he found the children hardest to resist. Crawford often teased him when he returned from a walk, his pockets laden with walnuts or bits of lace, which immediately found their way below stairs.

Hawk rarely bought flowers, as he had little interest in them himself, and his servants had more use for practical items. But perhaps . . .

"What price for a bunch?" he asked.

"A penny, sir." Her voice was hopeful.

"I shall take two," he said. He felt it only right that he should offer two bundles of flowers to Mrs. Farris, since he had been rude to her on two occasions.

The child's face broke into a gap-toothed smile. "Cert'nly, milord." With a flourish, she selected two of the plumpest bouquets from her tray and thrust them into his hands. In return, he gave her a shilling.

"I'll have yer change in a moment," said the girl, digging into a grimy sack hanging from her belt.

Hawk shook his head. "The change is for you," he said as he strode away with his violets.

"Thank you, milord!" The child's voice echoed behind him. "Bless you!"

The pleasure Hawk felt in the little girl's happiness was immediately dampened by self-recrimination. *So you may be able to help one flower seller. But you shy away from helping hundreds of children trapped in far more deplorable conditions. You cannot congratulate yourself.*

Pushing such pointless thoughts from his mind, he turned into Upper Grosvenor Street. As they neared the stone gates, Rogue began straining at the rope leash. Hawk found himself equally anxious to reach the park. If he were fortunate, he would find Mrs. Farris and her son, make his apologies for his past rudeness, and put the eccentric family from his mind for good.

He had spent entirely too much of the previous night thinking about Mrs. Farris and her commanding presence on the makeshift stage. He was at a loss to understand his fascination with the outspoken young widow. He certainly was not interested in her in a romantic way.

When he married—as he knew he must one day, to perpetuate the earldom—he would choose a meek and proper young miss who would bring no scandal on himself or the title. And, coincidentally, one who wouldn't remind him of his own shortcomings.

That philosophy had stood him in good stead so far. Rather than the showy actresses and singers Tavister pursued, Hawk was fond of the young women who worked behind the scenes in the theater. He had been the protector of several, until they had attracted husbands who did not mind their somewhat shady pasts.

He crossed Park Lane and entered Hyde Park. As always at this time of day, it was largely deserted. He suspected that if he were to encounter Mrs. Farris at all, he would find her by the Serpentine. Rogue, apparently, knew that, too, as he was already dragging Hawk in that direction.

As he reached the edge of a clump of trees, Hawk spotted the little family group not twenty feet away. Sir William, of course, was easy to see. Even amid the spring blooms, he stood out like a flowering tree in a country garden. Beside him, Mrs. Farris was leaning down to unfasten Scamp's collar. Edward was dancing from one foot to the other with seeming impatience.

Hawk slipped the hand with the bouquets behind his back.

Rogue let out a series of sharp, excited barks as they approached, and Mrs. Farris jumped.

"Sorry we . . . startled you," Hawk said, willing himself to speak smoothly.

Mrs. Farris turned. "It is no matter. It is good to see you again, Lord Hawksmoor," she said. Her words were all that was polite, but Hawk noticed that her face was blank. None of that torchlight glow that had struck him last night. It was no wonder, really. He had acted like a greenhead.

"I wish to . . . apologize for my hasty exit last evening," he began. Why wasn't there a simpler word in the English language for expressing regret than *apologize*? Perhaps there was one, and he just couldn't think of it right now.

"Edward, why don't you and I take the puppies for a run up that hill?" Sir William boomed. "Well, you and they shall run, and I shall supervise."

A grimace shifted briefly across Mrs. Farris's features before she appeared to school her face once more into an impassive mask.

Edward agreed that a run was an excellent idea, and within moments Mrs. Farris and Hawk were alone.

"No apology is necessary, my lord," she began, but he cut her off.

"Please do not let me off so easily. I had my own reasons for . . . departing, which had nothing to do with you, but they are no excuse for my rudeness. In fact, I have been rude to you twice in as many days, so I really feel I must make amends." He presented the flowers. "Please accept this small . . . gift."

Her smile this time was genuine. "You did not need to do this, although it is very sweet. Thank you."

Abashed by her pleasure in such a simple token, he plunged on. "I more deeply regret my sharpness yesterday when you raised the . . . matter of the child labor . . . bill." *Slowly, man, slowly, and you'll get through this.* "It was quite normal that you would assume I would speak to the issue in P-P-Parl—"

No. Not now.

"—in P-P-Parl . . . Parl . . ."

Demmed voice box.

"—in the House . . . House of . . . House of Lords."

There. It is out. Finally.

Mrs. Farris's eyes were wide. He braced himself for the cutting comment. But instead, she said, "You're not a snob at all, are you?"

Whatever he had expected her to say, that was not it. "I beg your pardon?" he asked, with all the aloofness he could muster.

"I thought you were simply high in the instep, that you thought yourself too good for tawdry debates in Parliament and silly amateur theatricals. But you're shy!"

That was going too far. "I am not *shy!*" *Shy* was a word for young girls in the schoolroom, not for a grown man. "Really, Mrs. Farris, this conversation is inappropriate." He couldn't simply turn from her—that would be base rudeness. But how was he to shift this demmed discussion into less troubled waters?

He glanced behind him, as if he would find the answer to his dilemma writ in the trees.

"Thinking of running away again?" Caroline couldn't believe it when she heard her own words. She had to stop saying the first thing that popped into her head. That unfortunate habit had landed her in a great deal of trouble in the past. And if the thunderous look on the earl's face was any indication, it was about to do so again.

"I am not r-r-run . . . r-r-run . . . Damn!" the earl bellowed.

Caroline knew her eyes must be like saucers, but she couldn't help herself. She would not have believed the subdued earl could be so emotional.

"And now I must ap . . . say sorry again, for my uncouth . . . language." Lord Hawksmoor looked away and inhaled deeply. "I do not know what has come over me."

"I provoked you. I should not have called you shy, and I should not have said you were running away." Caroline paused, unsure how to make her next statement, and then decided to plunge right in. How much angrier could he get with her?

"How long have you stammered?"

The earl crossed his arms across his chest and glared at her. "Since you were a child?"

His scowl, unbelievably, became deeper. Caroline quailed, but soldiered on.

"That is why you often stay quiet, or speak slowly."

He hesitated, then seemed to deflate somewhat. He was still more than formidable, however, as he nodded.

That was a breakthrough, she supposed. "And that's why you avoid strangers, correct?"

Another nod. His eyes were hooded. It appeared he would never speak to her again.

"Have you ever sought treatment?"

That broke his silence. "Treatment?" His laugh was bitter. "Aside from a few slaps on the hand with my father's crop, no."

Caroline tried to mask her shock. "So you were punished for stammering?"

"Of course. It is a foolish habit."

"It is more than a habit, my lord, begging your pardon. There are causes both in the body and the mind for it, and they can be addressed."

"How have you become such an expert on the topic?"

She felt a blush staining her cheeks. "I am no expert. But I remember reading something about it. One of my brothers is studying to become a physician, and he occasionally brings home scientific papers for me to read. I found the topic interesting, particularly from a theatrical point of view."

When he said nothing, she plunged ahead. "All of my siblings and I, to some degree, have suffered nerves when we perform our little plays."

"Forgive me, Mrs. Farris, for saying that I can't imagine you suffering nerves on any occasion."

She ignored that comment. "While none of us has stammered, some have lost our place in the script, while others have forgotten lines altogether. My brother Lucas panics and makes up new lines, as I'm certain you noticed last evening."

"You mean Caesar didn't challenge Brutus to pistols at dawn?" For the first time in their conversation, Caroline noticed a gleam of mirth in the earl's eyes. It was progress, she supposed.

"Correct. Nor did we intend for Mars to shout 'My kingdom for a horse!'"

"I suspected as much."

They lapsed into an uncomfortable silence. Caroline had never been able to abide silence.

"Perhaps I might be able to help you," she heard herself say. She almost lost her nerve when the earl raised one eyebrow imperiously.

That was an elegant trick, she thought. She must learn how to do it—it would be most useful on the stage.

She brought her attention back to the matter at hand.

"If you like, we could at least discuss the matter."

The eyebrow flew higher.

"I have much experience in developing an authoritative speaking voice," she plowed ahead, feeling as though she were running a great distance. She smoothed her damp hands down the front of her sprigged muslin day dress.

"First, I had to learn in order to assert my authority over my brothers and sisters. Our mother died young, and I helped my father in their raising and education."

Lord Hawksmoor nodded but said nothing. That was all the encouragement she could expect, she supposed.

"Later, when we began to put on theatricals, I had to learn to conquer my nervousness. I learned quite a few tricks that I would be happy to share with you, my lord."

"I hardly think that speaking to children and p-p-playacting in fancy dress are equiv . . . the same thing as speaking in . . . Parliament," he said, his voice icy.

"Well, no, but there are certain techniques—"

"Thank you for your interest in my im—impediment, but I must decline your help." Now the iciness was laced with sarcasm. "Unless you are a sor-sor-sorceress, it would be fruitless."

Caroline felt her hands clenching in frustration. All she had done was offer to help the man! She didn't need to have made the effort. And here he was throwing it back in her face, and belittling her besides. She'd be hanged if she'd stand here and take such treatment.

Pompous boor.

"Very well then, Lord Hawksmoor," she gritted out. "My apologies for having dared to offer my assistance." She looked into the distance, where Edward and the dogs were gamboling near a tree, under her father's watchful eye. "I must collect my son, now. I'll make sure my father brings Rogue back to you."

"Wait. I will come to collect Rogue." Did she hear an actual trace of shame in the earl's tone? Impossible.

"Do not bother yourself. I'm used to dealing with children and other unimportant matters. It should not tax my meager abilities to get your dog back to you." She had to leave now, before she did or said something she would really regret.

She turned and left him without looking back.

Chapter Six

Idly, Hawk turned a silver letter opener over and over in his hand, then tapped it against the glossy surface of his mahogany desk. When he realized that the sharp instrument might scratch the furniture, he put the opener down.

Next he reached for a stack of correspondence from his estate agent. There was nothing terribly urgent in it, but all of it needed to be dealt with at some point. Today seemed as good a day as any.

He unfolded the top letter and stared at it unseeingly. Soon, his gaze had drifted from the paper to an indeterminate spot on the opposite wall.

What the devil is that noise? He was about to ring a footman and send him off to investigate when he looked down and realized he was knocking the glass inkwell against the edge of an extended desk drawer.

He sighed and replaced the inkwell on the blotter. Really, he needed to go for a ride and expend some of this excess energy, or his desk would be a pile of kindling before the week was out.

A ride would mean braving Hyde Park. He had avoided the park entirely since his last encounter with Mrs. Farris, but he doubted she would be there at this time of day. *He* was rarely there this time of day. It was five o'clock, the hour when all the fashionable people would be parading about in their carriages. Usually he avoided the park at such times, but if he didn't get out of this demmed house and see at least a few trees and some green grass, he would go slowly mad.

He was about to head to his rooms to change into his riding habit when he stopped. The clots of people jamming the park would mean he'd be forced to walk his horse—at best, he'd be able to try a brisk trot. And a brisk trot would do little to chase away the restlessness that had dogged him since his unpleasant meeting with Caroline Farris in the park last week.

Hell, he hadn't even been able to expunge it by taking Rogue for a good run. Since their dispute, he had had one of the footmen take the pup for his morning walk. Cowardly, yes, but no one had ever accused the seventh Earl of Hawksmoor of being a hero.

He stood up and strode toward the door of the library. Perhaps a long stroll through the streets of Mayfair would help. Not many trees or birds, but at least it would quench his restlessness. Perhaps he would go all the way to White's.

An hour later, still restless even after his long walk, he sat in a quiet corner of the club, nursing a small glass of port. So lost in his thoughts was he that he was completely unaware of Tavister's presence until his friend slid into the vacant seat opposite him.

"Don't often see you here, Hawk," Tav greeted him, signaling the waiter for another glass.

"I was heartily sick of my house and decided on a change of scenery."

Tavister smiled. "Have you ever thought about remodeling the mausoleum?"

"I'd *sell* the demmed thing if I could, but it's entailed. Lucky thing, too, or my father would have wagered it years ago at Ascot. It may not be beautiful, but at least it is a roof over my head."

Tavister laughed. "That's what I like about you. You are an optimist."

Hawk grinned. Tav had always been able to help him laugh at himself.

"In a bit of a bad humor today, Hawk? Chemley over there warned me that you had a face like a thundercloud, and he was right."

"A bit," Hawk said with a faint smile. He realized how juvenile he was being, brooding over his dispute with Mrs. Farris. Perhaps his friend would suggest some sort of diversion to lift him out of his doldrums.

"Well, my news will not help your mood one bit," Tav said as he settled into his chair and accepted a glass from the waiter.

"Yes?" Hawk said, his voice steely.

"I'm glad I found you, and I shan't beat around the bush. Support for the child mining bill is faltering—despite your excellent efforts behind the scenes," Tav began. "So yet again I'm going to—"

"No."

"Be reasonable. We need everyone we can find to support this. And not only do you live in a mining district, but your maiden speech would attract attention all on its own."

"But—"

"As it stands now, the bill will be defeated. We will lose, Hawk. Countless children will die underground if we do." Tav set his glass on the table with a clatter. "Good heavens, man, don't you *care*?"

"Of course I *care*!" The sound of his voice ricocheting off the walls almost startled him. "That's pre-pre-precisely why I don't want to speak in P-P-Parliament. I'll just undermine the c-c-cause."

Several men had turned to stare. Hawk took a deep breath and willed himself to lower his voice.

"Stop kidding yourself." Tav's voice was cold. "You don't want to speak in Parliament because you're *afraid*."

Hawk stood. "Next you'll tell me I'm r-r-running away."

"If the shoe fits."

Hawk stared at his friend, putting all the hauteur and disdain he'd so carefully cultivated into his glare. Tav, damn him, stared back unblinkingly.

Damnation, what good was it being an earl if you couldn't even make people flinch? Granted, Tav was a viscount, and had never been much of a shrinking violet, but still—

Tavister's last accusation hung in the air between them. Finally, Hawk was tired of fighting, tired of being browbeaten on all sides. He'd give the demmed speech, it would be a disaster, but Tav would finally stop plaguing him.

And, more to the point, he might be able to expunge that look of disappointment he'd seen in Mrs. Farris's eyes the other day. If he were truly honest with himself—and Hawk prided himself on honesty above all else—he would admit that it was her lack of faith in him that would make him capitulate more than anything Tav had said. Tavister was a gifted orator, but he wasn't irresistibly persuasive.

The sadness in Mrs. Farris's blue eyes had spoken more loudly than Tavister's bluster ever could.

His decision to speak would mean he would need to redouble his lobbying efforts. And he would be wise to anticipate the damage that would surely be done by his wretched speech, and plan to repair it in advance.

On one point he and Tav were agreed. This bill was important, and he would do everything he could to make it pass.

"All right," he spat, continuing to glare at his friend. "I'll do it. And when I make a complete hash of it, don't say I didn't warn you."

"When you get through it without the world coming to an end—as you will—I shall be proud to celebrate with you."

"Save your toasts until you've heard me open my m-m-mouth."

Tavister would not be dissuaded from his glee at Hawk's decision, however, and stayed a few more minutes to chortle and gloat. Once he had departed—likely to convey the glad tidings to a select group of their fellow peers—Hawk slumped back against the leather seat.

The die was cast, and there was no going back. But he was going to need help, if there was to be any chance of him not making a complete fool of himself—and, by extension, their cause. And the only person he knew who had even claimed to be able to help him was Mrs. Farris.

Going to her now, after the disgraceful way he'd spurned her offer of assistance, was sure to be a humbling experience. Very well. Two people had already called him a coward, and he had allowed himself to be drawn into doing the one thing he had sworn not to do. Matters could not get much worse.

The chords of some rousing piano piece were echoing through the Larch home on Hart Street when the family's butler ushered Hawk through the foyer and into a small parlor. The music stopped briefly when the servant had left to announce him, but had restarted shortly thereafter.

As soon as Hawk entered the spacious room, he saw the source of the music. Mrs. Farris was seated at the instrument, seemingly lost in concentration as her hands flew over the keys. He watched, entranced, as the piece built to a shattering crescendo. Then Mrs. Farris thumped her hands down into a satisfying chord and sighed.

The butler cleared his throat. "Lord Hawksmoor, ma'am."

Caroline turned around on the small piano stool and smiled coolly. "My apologies for not stopping immediately, my lord. Until I've played a piece through to its end, I am haunted by the feeling of something unfinished."

She was wearing a deep blue day dress cut in what he assumed was the latest fashion. He paid little heed to such matters, but he was struck by the fact that the garment was a bit more revealing than he remembered dresses being even last Season. Not that he minded.

"No . . . apologies are necessary, Mrs. Farris. You play . . . mag-magnif . . . very well, and it was a delight to hear you."

The lady's eyes narrowed slightly at this comment. "Thank you, but I happen to know that my talents are nothing more than adequate."

Hawk searched for words to explain how her music had touched him, even if, as she claimed, her technical skills were not perfect. "Perhaps that is the case—I am no judge of music. But spirit and passion are just as important as technique, I believe. And on those scores, you seemed to be giving as much to your music as any . . . professional I have seen on the stage."

Her smile warmed slightly. "Thank you. I am glad you enjoyed it. I have always loved Bach. There is something very primal about him, do you not think?"

Watching the play of the sunlight over her ebony hair, Hawk was struck by a primal, physical response that had nothing to do with music. Clearing his throat, he said shortly, "Yes. Yes, indeed. Bach."

What the devil was the matter with him? Every time he found himself anywhere near Mrs. Farris, he found his thoughts wandering in all sorts of unsuitable directions. Granted, the woman was lovely, but she was so far from the type who normally appealed to him that he was astonished he was giving her a second thought.

That dress, for instance. It occurred to him that he had never seen her wear the same garment twice in the few weeks that he had known her. Refusing to dwell on the fact that he had actually noticed what she was wearing every time they had met, he fastened on the idea that she must be something of a spendthrift. A different dress for every occasion, and all in the latest stare of fashion? For a widow, such expenditures seemed rather excessive.

"Lord Hawksmoor?" From the tone of her voice, he realized that she had been addressing him for some moments.

"Sorry," he replied. "Woolgathering." He cleared his throat.

"I was just asking what brought you to my doorstep today." She nodded toward a settee upholstered in vibrant yellow silk and adorned with emerald and scarlet pillows. Apparently, the Larches' fondness for flamboyance extended to their household furnishings as well. "Please, be seated."

He sank into the well-padded settee and took a deep breath. He was not used to eating humble pie, and he suspected that he would not much care for the taste.

"Mrs. Farris, I have come to ask a favor."

Her eyes widened, and her right eyebrow twitched in a peculiar manner. "Yes?"

She was not going to make this easy for him, and he could not say that he blamed her. But he had faced more daunting foes than she.

"I have decided to speak to the child miners bill," he began, hoping that his words made it sound as though he had made the decision easily and had not been hounded into it.

Mrs. Farris clapped her hands and grinned. This time, the smile was genuine. "That is excellent news! But what of your nervousness about public discourse?"

He picked at a stray thread on his otherwise immaculate coat. "That is the reason I am here. You . . . mentioned that you might be able to help me."

"Even though my experience consists only of playacting and child-rearing?" she asked, her voice sly but not unkind.

Good heavens, the minx was enjoying this! Then again, he couldn't say he wouldn't have the same reaction if the tables were reversed. He nodded.

"However acquired, your knowledge of speaking . . . clearly and with authority far outweighs mine. I was wrong to mock it, and to mock your offer of help."

He prayed that his sincere words would turn her opinion of

him. How unpleasant it was to be in the position of a suppli-
cant.

A heavy silence filled the room as she considered his suggestion. Finally, she spoke.

"I would be happy to help, if I can," she said. "After all, the
bill needs as many supporters as it can get."

A tiny rivulet of disappointment seeped through him as
he realized she was doing this for the cause rather than for
him. Then he laughed at himself for his vanity. It did not matter *why* she had agreed to help him. The important thing was
that she *had* agreed.

"Thank you," he said. "I truly . . . appreciate it."

"Shall we start right now?"

He liked her forthrightness. "If you are not otherwise engaged, that would be excellent."

"There is no time like the present." Her voice was brisk.
"The debate is due to begin in a week, is it not?"

He nodded.

"Right, then. Let me think." She stared out the window for
a moment, twisting the string of pearls around her neck and
nibbling her bottom lip in concentration. "Are there particular
times when the stammering is worse? I've noticed, for instance,
that you rarely hesitate when you are speaking to Edward."

"That's true. I am very comfortable when speaking to children." He paused. How could he say this without sounding
like a green girl? There was nothing for it but to say it. "Adult
strangers, however, m-m-make me nervous."

She eyed him speculatively. "So, apparently, does saying
something you're uncomfortable sharing."

He drew himself up in his seat and straightened his shoulders. The woman was far too perceptive. "Yes."

"Don't worry, my lord. Your secret is safe with me."

"I am not ashamed," he lied.

"Good. Because we will get nowhere if you suffer from
self-loathing."

He blinked at this bald statement. "I am an earl. Peers of the realm are not prone to . . . doubt themselves," he said crisply.

To his frustration, she burst out laughing. "*Everyone* doubts their abilities, my lord, if you will pardon me for saying so."

He fixed her with his best quelling glare, but a few giggles continued to erupt from her.

"Perhaps this idea that you must somehow be more perfect than we mere mortals is partly to blame for your fear of public speaking."

"I am *not* afraid!" he thundered.

She held up both hands in a gesture of surrender. "Forgive me. What I meant to say was that your image of yourself might be responsible for your discomfort."

"Perhaps," he conceded, although the idea seemed rather featherbrained.

"So what we need to do first is to instill the notion that you will never speak flawlessly."

"Are you mocking me, Mrs. Farris?" he asked. "The whole point of this exercise is for me to learn to do exactly that."

She shook her head. The action loosened one dark curl, which came to rest along the curve of her heart-shaped face. "No one speaks flawlessly. Great actors like Mr. Kean and Mrs. Siddons sometimes forget their lines. Even the Prime Minister and the Prince Regent occasionally stumble in their orations. It is not a crime, or a sin."

Grudgingly, he nodded. "Granted."

"You must allow yourself to make mistakes."

This was not the practical sort of instruction he had hoped for. But what other choice had he? He didn't have time to find another teacher, and anyone he did find might spread the word among the *ton* that the Earl of Hawksmoor had descended to the point of taking *elocution* lessons. At least he trusted Mrs. Farris to be discreet.

"Secondly, you need to learn to breathe."

He chuckled. "I have been practicing that particular skill for the past thirty years or so."

He was gratified to see an answering smile. "Why, I do believe you do have a sense of humor under that starchy stiffness after all."

"I've become a master at hiding things well."

She stood up and paced toward the window, twisting her necklace again as she walked. "What I meant was that you need to breathe properly before saying something that makes you nervous. I don't understand precisely why, but a deep draft of air seems to calm the nerves." She turned to face him once again. "I always take a few long breaths before beginning our theatricals. My brother Lucas spends ten minutes in an empty room before every performance, with his eyes closed, doing nothing but breathing."

Hawk knew his astonishment showed on his face. "If he is that agitated about performing, why does he do it?"

"He enjoys it once he treads the boards. And he hates to feel left out."

Hawk nodded. He remembered that feeling as a boy, when the masters at Eton would call upon students to respond in class. While others had stood and recited their answers with varying degrees of surety, Hawk had lingered at the back of the room, praying not to be called upon and yet wishing that he could respond as his classmates did.

He took a shallow breath and released it noisily. "Is that the way I should breathe?"

Mrs. Farris shook her head, setting that enticing loose curl dancing once more. "Deeper, and from below the chest, not the throat. Like this." She stood in front of him and placed her hands across her flat stomach. He watched, fascinated, as her midriff expanded. She continued to inhale, and her bosom rose in a most distracting manner.

He felt lecherous for staring. But she had asked him to

watch. She held the breath for several seconds, then exhaled slowly. She looked at him and smiled. "See? It's easy."

"I've never seen anyone breathe quite that way."

She blushed slightly. "I learned about it in a book my cousin David sent us from India. Apparently, the holy men there are quite skilled at it. Some spend years just learning how to breathe."

"What else did you learn in this book?" He was honestly curious. He had heard a little about Hindu philosophy and customs from the men of the East India Company, who entertained the crowd at White's with tales of their exploits. But most of these were derogatory, emphasizing that the Indians were unschooled heathens. Given the engravings Hawk had seen of the elegant temples and palaces of India, he had never been able to convince himself that this was true. This breathing exercise was further proof.

Mrs. Farris's blush deepened. "Much of the book focused on poses that these Indian wise men assume in an effort to calm the mind and achieve what they call enlightenment. I have not tried any of those," she hastened to add. "Yet."

Hawk grinned. "I don't doubt that you plan to." A sudden vision of Mrs. Farris reclining in the exotic garb of the East startled him. What sort of book, exactly, was she reading? Was it suitable for a gently reared young woman? Even a widow?

She smiled back. "Eventually. But this talk is distracting us from the task at hand. Breathing properly is just one of the techniques I've used to quell my nerves. Opera singers and professional actors do these exercises as well—"

"As I've mentioned, Mrs. Farris, it is not a matter of nerves." He paused, then forced himself to be honest. "Well, not merely a matter of nerves."

She smiled. "Nerves are what I understand best. Let us address that subject first, and we shall concern ourselves with the physical aspects of your stammer later."

He nodded. "So what other suggestions do you have?"

"Focus."

"Pardon me?"

"Do you find you have more trouble when you speak to a particular person or group?"

Hawk's laugh was without humor. "If you ever visit the House of Lords and observe the yawning noblemen who are thinking more of the roast joint they hope to devour for dinner than of the next oration, you would know my answer to that question."

She returned to her chair, sat down and smoothed her skirts before continuing. "I sympathize entirely." When I realized you were in the audience for our theatrical the other night, I could barely concentrate on my lines." No sooner had Mrs. Farris made this statement than her hand flew to her mouth. "You see, we seldom invite anyone but longtime family friends. That is not to say you are not a friend. It's just—"

"I understand," Hawk cut in, eager to save her from her embarrassment even though it intrigued and thrilled him. So *he* had had the ability to make this confident female nervous? How very interesting.

"Anyway," she added in a more distant voice, "when I am distracted by other people, I look just beyond them. So although I appear to be paying attention to the audience, I am actually almost oblivious to their presence."

"Where do you look?"

"Long before the performance, I select something on the back wall of the drawing room—usually the large portrait of my mother that hangs over the fireplace. I am then reminded of her very good advice—that I could do anything I chose, if I just put my mind to it."

"I suspect your mother was right." Again, he found himself wondering how different his life might have been if he had grown up in a family like hers, rather than with a widowed father who expended all his bitterness on his only son.

Caroline chuckled. "My mother may or may not have been correct. But the important thing is that picking an object or spot gives my mind a place to rest, as it were, when I am tempted to panic. So for you, the next time you are in the House of Lords, examine the wall opposite your accustomed seat. Surely there will be something—a painting, a window, a crack in the woodwork—that can serve to focus your attention.

"Then, you need to practice speaking calmly and slowly while looking at that spot. Soon, you'll associate confidence with that view."

It sounded so simple. "And this will cure my stammer?"

Mrs. Farris shook her head. "I doubt it."

With great effort, he avoided slapping the arms of his chair with frustration, not wanting to look like a temperamental child. "Then why do it?"

She sighed. "I don't have the training or the medical knowledge to completely cure you of your affliction. In fact, I'm not certain anyone does. But I can help you control it."

She leaned forward to emphasize her point. "I warned you that you were going to have to learn to live with imperfection. In only a week, I cannot turn you into Charles Fox. So you must not be disappointed if you do stammer when you give your speech. I think these techniques will lessen the degree of stammering. But I doubt I can eradicate it. Are you still willing to proceed?"

"Of course," Hawk said gruffly, even as his mind raced ahead to the ridicule he would surely face in the House. "I have promised Lord Tavister, and I am a man of my word."

"I am glad to hear it," murmured Mrs. Farris. "So let us move ahead to memorization."

"You certainly have an array of tricks at your disposal," Hawk said.

"We've only just begun," Mrs. Farris replied enigmatically.

Chapter Seven

Caroline tried a few deep-breathing exercises as she waited for Lord Hawksmoor to arrive. As she was inhaling and exhaling in a steady rhythm, she also tried to banish her nervousness with rational thought.

There is no reason to fear Lord Hawksmoor, she told herself silently as she took a deep draft of air. *He is simply a gentleman in need of assistance, and I am helping him.* She counted to five, then released the breath slowly from her lungs.

She inhaled again. *And even if he does have the most appealing laugh, he indulges in it infrequently. The man is entirely too serious.* After a count of five, she exhaled.

Even as she thought it, she wondered. He certainly seemed to affect a grave mien. But was that all part of his efforts to control his voice, or to ensure that people thought him worthy of respect?

If he truly were a serious man, what would he think of her? For years, Caroline had refused to be serious about anything, save her newspaper columns and Edward's upbringing.

For four years, in fact. Ever since John died.

She inhaled. *What was wrong with taking life lightly?* she asked herself. It certainly made it easier to sleep at night. Although, she had to admit, her nights had not been peaceful for several weeks now. At odd hours she would awaken and be struck by memories of Lord Hawksmoor's face as he had patiently answered Edward's questions at the dog seller's corner.

More disturbingly, she often recalled his intense gaze on the night of the theatrical, when she had felt terribly exposed in her makeshift Roman toga. The portrait of her mother had come in most handy that night. She exhaled.

Sometimes it was his voice she would hear in her head, a voice that was low and pleasingly modulated, probably due to years of effort on his part to tame it. Whatever the reason, it was a soothing voice. Even when he stammered, the comforting undertone remained.

If Lord Hawksmoor radiated one quality, it was steadfastness. And steadfastness was the one quality Caroline had never found appealing. She inhaled.

Anything or anyone that smacked of stability usually drew her instant scorn. Stability meant stodginess and boredom. Caroline preferred a far livelier life, full of musicales and grand balls and theater and gossipy expeditions to explore the shops of Oxford Street. And in the evenings, a few rounds of cards for moderate wagers were always diverting.

She suspected Lord Hawksmoor found little pleasure in any of those things. So why could she not get him out of her mind?

Caroline exhaled in a rush. Her breathing exercises, normally so helpful, were doing her no good whatsoever. The moment she found herself wondering whether her guest, who was due to arrive any minute, would be wearing the buff breeches and blue coat that suited him so well, she realized that more drastic measures were needed.

Beethoven.

Bach was all well and good for calming one's emotions. But there was no composer like Beethoven for helping her release them.

She had just finished working her way through the first few difficult bars of a sonata when she heard a knock at the front door. Glancing at the silver clock on the mantelpiece, she saw that it was exactly two o'clock.

Lord Hawksmoor was always punctual for their meetings.

It was fortunate that he came to visit her, rather than the other way around. Not only would it be unseemly for her to visit him, but their lessons would also never start on time.

Caroline stood up from the stool as her guest entered the room. "Good afternoon, my lord," she welcomed him, curtsying. She knew it was shallow and unseemly, but she was delighted that he had chosen the buff breeches and blue coat today. The coat brought out the blue of his eyes, and the breeches . . . well, the breeches brought out thoughts that were better left unexamined.

The earl must spend a lot of time on horseback, as he cut a very fine figure in his closely tailored clothes.

"Good afternoon, Mrs. Farris. Please do not interrupt your playing on my account. I heard a bit of it through the open window while I was waiting on the front step. It is not Bach today, is it?"

She shook her head. "Beethoven."

"Beethoven." He repeated the name, just as he had done with Bach on his earlier visit.

"You are not a devotee of music, are you?" she asked.

He shook his head, with a wry smile that crinkled the corners of his eyes. "I wouldn't know Beethoven from a baker's oven. But that doesn't mean I can't appreciate music when I hear it. And I very much enjoyed your playing."

"Thank you," she replied, ringing a small bell on the side table. When a maid appeared at the doorway, Caroline asked for tea and cakes to be brought in.

As Lord Hawksmoor folded his lanky length onto the small settee, she asked, "Have you completed your assignments? If not, I shall have to think up a suitably governess-like punishment," she added.

He didn't rise to the bait. Her brothers, or her father, or John, would have had a teasing riposte. Lord Hawksmoor merely said, "Yes. I have tried the breathing and all those other techniques, and I have also looked about the House for a suitable object of focus."

"What did you find?"

"There is a small crack in the wall just behind Lord Camberton's seat." He leaned against the settee and stretched his arm along its curved back.

Caroline was struck by the grace of the gesture. Lord Hawksmoor might be a nervous speaker, but he was perfectly at ease with himself otherwise. "That will be ideal. Have you found the breathing useful?"

"Moderately—if I am careful not to breathe too deeply. Then I feel as though my head is about to detach itself from my neck."

She laughed. "Yes, I forgot to warn you about that."

"So what is on our agenda today?"

She tapped a finger on the edge of a small table as she thought. "I believe I would like to focus on some of the words that are giving you particular trouble. Hard consonants seem to be one obstacle. Words such as 'bill' and 'Parliament.' "

His smile was self-mocking. "Yes. Unfortunately, those words tend to come up a great deal in the House."

She rubbed her hands together. "So we are going to treat them like lines in a play. You shall repeat them over and over, in a quiet room like this, so that they will no longer loom so large when you must say them in public."

They practiced a number of words over the next few minutes, breaking only to pour cups of tea from the tray the maid had brought in. They had moved on to long words, such as "apologize" and "inappropriate," when Caroline suddenly became aware of the fast clicking of puppy nails on parquet. She turned to see Scamp skid into the room, followed closely by Edward and a slightly out-of-breath Harriet.

"Mama! Lord Hawk! Can we go to the park this afternoon?" Her son's face was alight with anticipation.

She shook her head. "I'm sorry, sweeting. Lord Hawksmoor and I need to practice his speech a bit more."

Edward perked up at that. "Can I help? I know about speaking on stage. Remember? I had two whole lines to say in the theatrical."

She ruffled his hair. "You did, and you delivered them very well."

The little boy looked pleased.

"But Lord Hawksmoor and I must do some work by ourselves before you can help."

"I have to make myself worthy of your expertise," the earl chimed in with a knowing look at Caroline.

Edward nodded sagely. "Will you go to the park with me, Aunt Harriet?"

"With pleasure." Harriet smiled at her young nephew, whom she adored. "Sorry to disturb you, Caro, but since I am here—are you going to Miss Shelton's soirée tomorrow night?"

"I believe I shall, for an hour or so at least after the theater. I don't want to stay too late, however, since I promised Lady Dawe that I would attend her niece's ball as well."

"Three events in one evening?" Lord Hawksmoor said, his tone intimating that Caroline had just announced her intention to become an opera singer.

She turned to him, amused. "The Season is short, and I must gather my rosebuds while I may."

"Speaking of rosebuds—I'll need your advice on my nosegay for this evening, Caro. I just don't have your taste, and I want to make sure it's not too overblown." Harriet paused for breath. "After you and Lord Hawksmoor are finished, of course."

"Certainly. I'd be happy to." Caroline smiled at her youngest sister.

"Excuse us, then," Harriet said, ushering Edward out of the room. Scamp paused to snuffle once at Lord Hawksmoor's boots before departing.

"You certainly have enough responsibilities to keep you busy," the earl remarked, a glimmer of amusement in his brown eyes.

"I don't lack for diversion, that is true," Caroline replied.

"Do you never wish for peace and quiet?"

"Quiet? I can't abide it. It makes me restless. I'm much happier surrounded by tumult. Speaking of which—I think we will soon need to test your speaking skills in a more intimidating setting than our drawing room."

"What did you have in mind?" His voice was neutral.

"An evening at Vauxhall." She held her breath.

As she suspected, Lord Hawksmoor was not pleased with the idea. "V-V-Vauxhall!" he sputtered.

She nodded.

"I can't think of anywhere in London I'd be less inclined to visit."

"Precisely, my lord. That's why we should go."

"We?"

"You don't think I'd set a lamb like you among the wolves all on your own, do you?"

"I'm not a lamb." His tone was mutinous.

"Excellent. Shall we meet here this evening before proceeding to Vauxhall?"

"T-t-tonight? Do I not need more p-p-practice first?" He plucked at his shirt cuffs in a manner that Caroline had quickly come to realize masked extreme agitation.

"The debate is scheduled for Thursday, so there's no time to waste." She attempted to raise her right eyebrow to emphasize her concern.

"Aha—I am not the only one who needs practice," he said with a slight smile. "You need to exercise that eyebrow. I assume you mean to express some emotion with it?"

She nodded.

"Unfortunately, your lack of skill in the . . . maneuver makes it look as though you have something in your eye. Concentrate more on holding the rest of your face still than on raising your eyebrow, and you'll be . . . much more successful."

She tried his advice, and felt much less awkward. "Sharing the secrets of lordliness with me? That's very kind."

"More the secrets of the Kendall family. It was one of the few useful things I ever learned from my father."

She had no idea how to respond to this bald statement, so she brought the conversation back to Vauxhall. "It is decided, then. We shall go to Vauxhall tonight."

"I don't recall deciding anything, or even agreeing to anything. Really, Mrs. Farris, do you always get your way?" Lord Hawksmoor asked, a chuckle taking the sting from his words.

"Generally," she admitted.

"Well, who am I to stand in your way? To Vauxhall tonight—I shall be here with my carriage at eight."

His carriage? Well, of course he would bring his carriage, you gudgeon. Did you expect him to accept a ride in yours, or to propose that we walk all the way to Vauxhall?

It made eminent sense for the earl to collect her. Why, then, did Caroline feel so intimidated about the prospect of riding alone with him? As was her wont, she blithely dismissed any feelings of trepidation and agreed that she would be ready at the appointed hour.

What would she wear? And why on earth did she care? She was certain that the stiff-rumped earl wouldn't notice if she came in sackcloth and ashes. And she certainly didn't give a fig what he thought about her attire, in any case.

With alacrity, she turned their attention back to the vexing problem of clashing consonants.

Chapter Eight

Hawk surveyed the ebullient crowds surging by their supper box at Vauxhall and tried valiantly not to scowl. He might have felt as though he'd been thrust into the seventh circle of hell, but he would die rather than let Mrs. Farris know of his discomfort.

At the minute, thank heavens, she was distracted by a long conversation about bonnets. At least, Hawk thought it was still about bonnets. One of Mrs. Farris's acquaintances, a Miss Wilks, had spied her in the supper box a few minutes ago and descended upon her for advice about some sort of millinery crisis.

It was not the first time since they had arrived at the gardens that Mrs. Farris had been drawn into conversation with one of the other pleasure seekers. Indeed, she appeared to be on more or less intimate terms with half of London. It was no wonder she had seemed surprised on first meeting him that they had never encountered one another before.

He glanced across the table to observe Mrs. Farris's increasingly pointed efforts to extract herself from the conversation. She had tried several times to involve him in it—they were here to increase his skill in speaking with strangers, after all—but it soon became apparent to them both that he had little knowledge to contribute on the subjects of ribbons and lace. Not that Miss Wilks noticed his absence one whit.

He caught Mrs. Farris's eye and smiled, to let her know that he did not blame her for her friend's rudeness.

In truth, he was just as happy to sit back and observe the passing scene as to participate. He hadn't been to Vauxhall since shortly after he had come down from Oxford.

Now, as then, he marveled at the carnival atmosphere of the place. The gardens had degenerated somewhat since his last visit a decade ago, but there was still a wide range of diversions on offer. On their way to the supper box, they had briefly watched a mannish-looking woman crossing a tightrope.

His gaze swung to the octagonal bandstand across the walk, from which he could hear the faint strains of what sounded like a country dance melody. Perhaps Mrs. Farris would enjoy a dance? He suspected that someone with her musical ear would.

Lost in thought, he was startled to hear a voice at his elbow.

"Hawksmoor! Didn't peg you for a Vauxhall type."

He turned to see Lord Chemley smiling at him, and he nodded in response. He didn't know Chemley well, but he had always thought him a decent enough sort.

"Not as a matter of course, but Mrs. Farris wanted to come."

"I had no idea you were a friend of hers. Almost dropped my hat when I saw you in the audience for the theatrical the other night. Said to m'wife that I hadn't seen you at any *ton* function in years."

"I have to break with tra-tra-tradition once in a while, just to keep people guessing." He began to mentally chastise himself for his stammer, then heard Mrs. Farris's words in his head as clearly as if she had just spoken them aloud.

Allow yourself to make mistakes.

He took a deep breath.

Chemley appeared not to have noticed his blunder. "Good for you. You're too young a man to stay at home reading a book." He rubbed his hands together. "Tavister tells me you are working with him on the child miners bill?"

"Yes, I will be speaking in P-P-Parliament next week." He took another deep breath.

Chemley gave him a knowing glance. "Nervous about your speech?"

If you only knew. "Not really." He braced himself for a barb.

To his surprise, the older man merely clapped him on the back. "No need for nerves, Hawksmoor. The lords are a group of somnolent old men. Keep it short, make them laugh once or twice, and you'll be fine."

The one thing he didn't want to do was make them laugh. However, he didn't want to discuss that with Chemley. "I'll try to . . . remember that."

While they'd been speaking, Miss Wilks had apparently exhausted Mrs. Farris's stores of knowledge on the subject of headgear and disappeared. Hawk suddenly became aware of the young widow's steady gaze at him across the table.

She had probably heard him tripping on that demmed word *Parliament.*

"Good evening, Lord Chemley," she said, nodding at the empty seat beside Hawk. "Would you join us?"

"Love to, Caro, but m'wife is here, somewhere, and she'll likely be wondering where I've capered off to. I'll leave you two to enjoy your evening." It was a cloudy evening and the lighting in the park was dim, but Hawk could have sworn the marquis flashed him a quick wink as he departed.

Good Lord. Chemley thought he was *courting* Mrs. Farris. Well, he supposed he could hardly fault the older man for making such an assumption. After all, wasn't that one of the chief attractions of Vauxhall for debutantes and their young swains? Hadn't more than one reputation been torn to tatters after a tryst in the Lovers' Walk?

"Would you care to dance, Mrs. Farris?" he blurted out, desperate to turn that tide of thought.

Her eyes widened. "I would love to, my lord."

"Good." He rose and extended his hand to her. Together, they made their way to the edge of the small dance area, where a set was just coming to its end.

As the winded-looking dancers applauded, the musicians nodded in acknowledgement. Then a young man who appeared to be the leader of the little orchestra turned to the crowd and announced that the next dance, in a moment or two, would be a waltz.

Mrs. Farris glanced at Hawk, her face fractured with an odd, small smile. "Do you mind?"

"Not at all." Well, truth to tell, it was a bit more intimate a dance than he had had in mind. But it wasn't as though he didn't know *how* to do it. He might spend most of the year rusticating in the country, but even he found himself at the local assembly rooms a few times a year.

And, although he would admit it to no one but himself, he was curious to see whether Mrs. Farris was as accomplished in dancing as she appeared to be in everything else.

Bother, Caroline thought as they took their places on the dance floor. Country dancing she could manage, barely, but the trick of waltzing had always eluded her. She was certain to make a complete cake of herself.

Lord Hawksmoor raised his left hand and his eyebrow simultaneously. "It's easier to waltz if we're holding hands." He grinned.

She couldn't help but smile back. "As always, you've quickly grasped the rudiments of the situation," she said as she stepped closer to him. His large, warm hand enveloped hers, and a twinge of . . . something . . . shot down her arm.

Nerves, probably.

A moment later, his other hand rested lightly at her waist. There was that twinge again, radiating to the tips of her toes and the top of her head.

She hadn't felt like this in years. No, if she were to be completely honest with herself, she had never felt *precisely* like this. It was as though every inch of her skin, every hair on her head, was sparking like a cat's fur on a dry winter day.

She took a deep breath. Immediately, a clean male scent of wool, sandalwood, and soap filled her lungs.

That wasn't helping matters at all.

Surely she couldn't be attracted to the cross, reserved, *stuffy* Lord Hawksmoor. Could she?

"Mrs. Farris? Are you all right?" She heard his voice dimly, as though he were calling to her from a room at the other end of a large house.

She nodded. "Call me Caroline, or Caro if you prefer," she said absently. All of a sudden, it seemed ridiculous that someone who could evoke such long-dormant feelings in her should be standing on ceremony.

He raised both eyebrows this time. "Certainly. And you must call me Hawk."

"You don't seem like a hawk," she said, as the opening bars of the waltz drifted over the crowd. Any further comment, however, fled her mind as he gripped her firmly about the waist and spun her into the crowd of dancers.

His speaking voice might trip him up, but his feet never stumbled.

Caroline instantly realized that all she needed to do was relax and let him lead. He certainly knew what he was doing—and where they were going—better than she did.

She closed her eyes as they swung easily around the small floor. It was like playing music, in a way. Lord Hawksmoor held her so securely, yet gently, that she didn't need to worry about the steps—

"Ow! Er, I mean—" came a startled male voice.

Her eyes flew open. She realized, to her chagrin, that she was standing on Lord Hawksmoor's toe.

"Oh, my lord, I'm so sorry! I should have warned you that dancing isn't my forte."

The corners of his eyes crinkled deeply as he laughed.

"Don't worry. I found out on my own." He extracted his boot from under her foot and propelled them both out of the path of an energetic couple. "Shall we continue?"

"Are you certain it's safe?"

He tilted his head and gave her an assessing look. "What is it you are always telling me—that you can't be afraid of making mistakes?"

She nodded. "Hoist with my own petard. Onward, then!" She held tightly to his hand as they made their way back into the crowd.

As they twirled away once more, Caroline felt safe and supported in the circle of the earl's arms. Why, then, did she still feel as sparky as a cat?

Far too quickly, the tune was over.

"Care for another dance?" Lord Hawksmoor asked, a knowing glint in his eye.

"I must say, I've rarely enjoyed a waltz that much," she told him, "but I suspect your feet have never enjoyed one less."

"My feet, perhaps. As for the rest of me, I was charmed." He held out his hand, encouraging her to try again.

Caroline blinked. "I'm flattered. But much as I would enjoy another round, dancing is not the best way for you to practice your speaking."

"I've been speaking to you."

"Yes, but you're comfortable with me."

This time, it was Lord Hawksmoor's turn to blink. "I suppose I am."

"Unless I'm treading on your toes, of course." She turned from the dance area. "Let's return to our seats. Perhaps another of our acquaintances will appear."

As they strolled back toward their supper box, the earl stopped suddenly and turned to face her. "Just before we began dancing, you said I didn't seem like a hawk. What did you mean by that?"

Caroline felt a slight blush warming her cheeks. Really,

one of these days she was going to have to learn to keep her lips shut once in a while. But she had said it, so she had no choice but to be honest. "It's just that I've always thought of hawks as devious, rather cruel birds," she mumbled. "Swooping down on innocent creatures and devouring them just doesn't seem to be your approach."

"Oh, I don't know," he said, with an odd look. "I can think of a few innocent creatures I might quite enjoy swooping down on."

"My lord?" This time, there was no mistaking it. He was most definitely flirting with her. And, to her utter astonishment, she was enjoying it.

But her face must have registered her surprise, because his grin changed immediately to a rather abashed grimace.

"My ap-ap-apologies, C-C-Caroline," he said. "I did not mean to be forward."

Before she could reassure him that she was neither innocent nor offended, a red-faced man of middle years crossed their path.

"Hawksmoor!" he bellowed. He was clearly well in his cups.

"Do we know each other?" Lord Hawksmoor's voice was cool and polite.

"Not directly, I s'pose. But seen you in the House. Never heard you, course. You're a quiet one. I'm Penfield." He puffed out his chest, looking absurdly pleased at his success in pronouncing his own name.

"Pleased to meet you, Lord Penfield." Hawk nodded and made as though to carry on, but the older man put a restraining hand on the earl's chest.

"Wait! Want to talk to you 'bout the mining bill."

Hawk sighed. "Of course you do. Everyone does."

"You're backing the thing, are you not?"

"Yes."

"Backing a bill that will cost mine owners—some of them peers like me—hundreds of pounds in lost labor costs?"

Hawk nodded. "On the other hand, it will save . . . many children from a . . . desperate life below ground."

Lord Penfield waved his hand as though brushing aside Hawk's argument. Caroline had never even heard of him before, but he certainly comported himself as though he were lord of all creation.

"Poor children will work somewhere. If not in a mine, then selling fish on the streets of London or climbing the chimneys of some provincial town." As he spat out these last words, he poked his finger into Hawk's broad chest. The sour fumes of wine on his breath enveloped the little group.

"Is it so much worse to work in a mine than to slave in a stable or an overheated mill?" Penfield continued, his voice rising. "And who cares, really, anyway? They're just letterless brats. One drops in harness, there are ten more where they came from, with a litter of siblings to feed at home."

Even in the dim lantern light, Caroline could see the implacable glint in Hawk's eyes. "Is a poor ch-ch-child less important than a rich man's son? D-d-don't they all d-d-deserve—" He drew in a sharp breath, but it was too late.

Penfield snickered. "I can see we have little to fear from your arguments in the House, Hawksmoor. Few of the lords will have the patience to sit still while you spit out a complete sentence."

The older peer must have been even more inebriated than he let on. Otherwise, he would have run as fast as he could to the furthest point in the gardens once he saw the look of bitter hatred in Hawk's eyes.

Chapter Nine

"Lord Penfield—" Caroline began, but Hawk laid a gentle hand on her arm and cut her off.

"If that's the b-b-best defense you can muster for your cause, we have won half the b-b-battle already," Hawk said, his eyes like granite chips. "I may not have the smoothest tongue in England, but I do r-r-remember my . . . rhetoric instructor telling us that ad hominem arguments were foul . . . play."

"No one ever said politics was a fair sport." Penfield sniggered again. "G-g-good evening, L-L-Lord Hawksmoor."

His mirthless chuckle echoed back to them as he ambled away.

"Pay him no heed," Caroline piped up, eager to fill the silence with something other than Penfield's mocking words.

Beside her, Hawk stared at the peer's retreating back. "I don't. He's just an old drunkard," he said slowly. She sensed he was trying to make himself believe the words even as he spoke them.

He seemed to have forgotten she was there. She suspected he was remembering other cruel people in other places, and reliving the torments they had visited on him. If he did that, he was going to undo all her careful work.

"Shall we go for a stroll?" she heard herself ask. She'd go anywhere, do anything, to wipe that bleak look from his face. She'd simply suggested the first activity that came to mind.

He turned to her and slowly seemed to realize where he was. "A stroll?"

"Yes. Perhaps the Dark Walk?" She had suggested it because it was as far away from Penfield as they could get and remain in the gardens. "I could use a bit of exercise."

"If you like." His voice was toneless. Nevertheless, he offered her the crook of his arm, and gratefully she slipped her hand through it.

Desperate to banish whatever ghosts were pursuing him, she kept up a stream of chatter as they walked toward the shady confines of the Dark Walk. As they entered the tree-lined path, Caroline was dimly aware of half-visible forms drifting off the gravel into the moonlit shrubs beyond. She suddenly remembered that the Dark Walk was also known as the Lovers' Walk.

Perhaps this hadn't been the wisest idea after all.

"Have you seen Kean's latest turn at Drury Lane? I thought it was quite astonishing, myself," she asked in a false, bright voice.

"No."

Of course he hadn't. He wasn't much of a public man. What had she been thinking?

"What about novels? I've heard that *Rob Roy*—"

He raised a hand to stop her flow of words. "Thank you, Caroline, for your attempts to distract me from my black mood. But really, there isn't much you can do to pretend you did not witness that."

"Witness what? Lord Penfield's shocking display of bad manners?"

He shook his head and gave a weary sigh. "Don't p-p-pretend. I made a fool of m-m-myself."

"You did nothing of the sort. Penfield came off the weaker man."

"That's not what they will think in the House."

She kicked a pebble out of her way and watched it skitter

into the grass. "Then the lords are bigger fools than I took them for."

The earl stopped, so suddenly that she stumbled. He reached out his free arm to steady her, then moved both hands to her shoulders and turned her to face him.

"Why do you believe in me?" he whispered. "Why do you even care?"

She didn't even stop to think before answering. "Because you're trying so hard to do what is right. And because you're ten times the man a drunken lout like Lord Penfield is."

And because my arms feel like they're on fire beneath your hands right now, she added silently.

Some of the bleakness left his face at her words. He stared at her with an intensity that would have frightened her, had she not known him to be an honorable gentleman.

Why did she suddenly wish he wasn't honorable? Why did he suddenly seem far less stuffy?

He lifted one hand to her chin and tilted it up. "You're . . . beautiful."

She could feel her cheeks flushing. "Not really. Harriet's the pretty one in our family. Of course, my mother was a great beauty—"

He moved one finger to her lips. "Shhh. Can you not let me get the last word, just once?"

"Oh." She paused. "All right."

He removed his finger from her lips, but continued to gaze at her as though he'd never seen her before.

The silence grew, until Caroline couldn't stand the tension one moment longer.

"What do you mean by the last word?" she blurted. "Are we going back to our supper box?"

He shook his head and smiled. "I suppose there's only one way to silence you," he said, as he lowered his face to hers.

If Caroline had felt like a sparky cat when they were dancing, she now felt like an entire electrical storm. Invisible, delicate bolts of lighting darted through her as Hawk ran one hand through her curls, and drew her closer to him with the other.

What was he thinking? What had possessed him? And, more to the point, where on earth had Hawksmoor the Hermit learned to kiss like *this*?

That was the last conscious thought Caroline had before she stopped thinking altogether.

Reluctantly, Hawk released his viselike grip on Caroline. Dropping his hands, he stepped back a few paces. He had to stop now, before the situation spun completely out of his control.

She looked up at him with heavy-lidded eyes full of unspoken questions, and it was all he could do not to reach for her again.

It had been a long time, if ever, since he had been swept up by such deep waves of emotion and need. He had spent his life avoiding them, after all. In his experience, people who let their passions run away with them usually ended up in debt, in disgrace, or in jail.

He cleared his throat. Caroline blinked, but for once said not a word. He adjusted his neckcloth. She remained silent.

Why, of all times, did her gift for conversation appear to have deserted her now? There was nothing left for it but to step into the breach himself.

"Umm."

As usual, he was the soul of eloquence. He tried again.

"Mrs. Farris—"

She grinned. "Isn't that a trifle formal for a moment like this?"

"Caroline." He sighed. "I shouldn't have done that, and I apologize."

Her grin faded. "Why shouldn't you have done that?"

"Because . . ." Well, why? It was a good question, and he didn't have an answer that he thought she'd want to hear.

She waited, one eyebrow quirked at an odd angle.

"You still haven't got it," he told her.

"Oh, the eyebrow? I'll keep working on it. Don't evade the question."

She's the one who should be debating policy in the House of Lords, not I. She's as tenacious as a terrier.

"It's just not what I do." He blew out an exasperated breath. "I don't make a habit of accosting young women on secluded p-p-pathways, I can assure you."

She tilted her head to one side. "You're nervous. Why?"

"B-b-because we're standing in the middle of V-V-Vauxhall Gardens, where anyone could c-c-come upon us! Think of your r-r-reputation."

"I'm a widow. I don't have to be as circumspect as a debutante." A slight breeze ruffled her hair, and she drew her shawl more tightly about her shoulders.

"Well then, think of my reputation." As soon as he'd spoken, he knew it was exactly the wrong thing to say.

Caroline crossed her arms in a most unladylike way. "What do you mean?"

He winced. "It's just that my family—you see—well, I have to be above reproach in all matters."

"And a simple kiss would bring the wrath of the *ton* down on your head?"

This was becoming deucedly difficult. He shook his head. How to extricate himself from this debacle?

"So it isn't the kissing that's the problem. Therefore, it must be me."

He tried to interrupt, but she was not to be stopped.

"Are you worried that being seen with me—a woman who dares to playact and sing silly songs in public—would diminish you? Or perhaps my whole family shames you. My father alone has committed enough crimes against fashion to stain your precious reputation." Her voice rose with every word.

"But heavens!" she cried with an odd laugh. "Just imagine what you'd think if you realized you'd been seen publicly embracing a *journalist!*"

All of a sudden, she stopped. And this time, it was she who looked as though she wished she could swallow her words.

"A journalist?"

Caroline paused, then uncrossed her arms and placed her hands firmly on her hips. "Yes. Not many people know, but not because I'm ashamed of it. It's just that people tend to take any sort of writing less seriously if they know a woman is behind it."

Hawk was still trying to wrap his mind around the fact that she wrote for the newspapers, without even beginning to think about why she'd concealed this fact from him. "What do you write?"

"A column. For the *Monitor.*"

Now it was his turn to cross his arms. "This wouldn't be the column that has been arguing strongly for the last few weeks in favor of the mining b-b-bill?"

She nodded. "The same."

"And your interest in helping me speak p-p-properly—" Damn! Why did his voice always fail him just when he needed it most?

He sighed. "You assisted me just to further the causes you champion." It wasn't a question.

She shook her head. "Perhaps that was part of my ambition, at first. But, truly, my main wish was to help you overcome your problem."

"Well, I can't say you've succeeded even in that. Look at my p-p-performance with P-P-Penfield."

"But at least you stood up to him! You didn't just walk away."

His smile felt stiff and forced. "I suppose that's something. Not much, but something."

They stood in silence, facing each other. The crowds continued to drift past them, and in the distance Hawk heard the faint playing of the orchestra they had danced to so carelessly.

It felt like a century ago.

"I think I would like to go home," Caroline said eventually, with a weary sigh.

"Certainly," he agreed, and turned back the way they had come.

This time, he didn't offer her his arm. It wouldn't have done him any good, anyway, as she strode several yards ahead of him in her haste to reach the carriage.

He was angry that she had manipulated him. And he was frustrated that she could not understand his need to preserve his family's unsullied reputation at all costs.

But although he had said he was sorry for kissing her, regret was the one emotion he wasn't feeling at the moment. He watched her stride down the path, and took a moment to appreciate the view. He remembered how wonderful it had felt to hold her warm, round body close to his. Oh no. He wasn't sorry one bit.

Chapter Ten

"They do go on, don't they, my dear?" Sir William remarked to his daughter as they sat in the Ladies' Gallery of the House of Lords.

"Mmm." Caroline wished she hadn't suggested her father accompany her this afternoon. She had forgotten how much politics bored him. As it was, she could barely follow the debate, due to his constant commentary.

She knew she should suggest they leave, but she couldn't. Not yet.

She shifted her gaze to the far, dim corner of the chamber. There, shuffling through a set of notes, sat Lord Hawksmoor.

He was dressed in the most self-effacing of costumes today, the shades of beige and brown making it seem as though he hoped to blend into the woodwork. Although some of the other peers were chatting among themselves, dozing, reading and generally paying little attention to the matters at hand, Hawk had said little to anyone in the hour since Caroline and her father had arrived. Indeed, he had barely taken his eyes from his notes, except to glance occasionally at a spot on the far wall. Caroline assumed it was the crack in the wall he had mentioned as his focal point.

Only once had his gaze swept the Ladies' Gallery. He'd stared at her for a moment or two, nodded almost imperceptibly, then turned back to his papers.

She couldn't blame him, really, for not making more of an

effort to recognize her. He probably found her presence more of a distraction than anything.

She lifted a hand to her mouth to cover a yawn. In the last few nights, she'd managed very little sleep.

Late into the night of their visit to Vauxhall, she had lain awake, seething and trying to figure out his continual insistence on being upstanding to the point of priggishness. But within a few minutes, her annoyance had evaporated. He had, after all, spent a lifetime trying to make up for his father's bad behavior. It was understandable that he would be more careful than other men.

Her irritation with him was displaced by something far more powerful—curiosity.

Because despite his oft-repeated assurances that he was a sober, refined gentleman not given to baser instincts, she suspected—no, she *knew*—that there was much more to the Earl of Hawksmoor than the quiet image he presented to the world.

No true prig would have been able to kiss like that.

She knew there were fires deep inside him just waiting to be stoked. But was she the woman for the task? And how, precisely, was she to manage it?

He did not look like a man on fire at the minute. He looked, more precisely, like a man on his way to the guillotine. His hands were rarely still, fidgeting with his cuffs and his neck cloth and the buttons on his coat.

Don't be afraid of making a mistake, she willed him. *You can do this.*

Preoccupied with her mental encouragement, she did not realize that the previous speaker had finished his address supporting the bill and had taken his seat. It was only when Lord Hawksmoor stood that she realized the moment was at hand.

A rare hush descended on the chamber. Even from this distance, she could see the gentle rise, then fall, of his chest. A count of five, then it rose again.

He was practicing the Indian breathing technique she had taught him. He may have dismissed her, but he'd held firm to her lessons. She closed her eyes and prayed that they would work.

"My fellow . . . peers," he began in his slow, measured voice.

In the back of the chamber, one of the elderly lords sneezed. Then, silence.

"I wish to address you today on a subject of grave . . . importance. One that touches the lives of thousands of ch-ch-children—"

A low, unpleasant chuckle emanated from the back benches on the other side of the House.

Caroline held her breath in a manner that she was certain the yogis of Calcutta would not countenance.

Keep going, she willed him.

Hawk glanced up at the wall and paused for what must have been just a second or two, though it seemed much longer.

"—all over England," he continued, as though he had never stopped.

She released her breath in such a rush that the elderly lady sitting in front of her twisted backward with an annoyed frown. Caroline smiled in what she hoped was an ingratiating manner, and turned her attention back to the floor of the House.

"As my estate is in the Midlands, I have a . . . p-p-particular interest in this issue," Hawk continued, this time not stopping at all when he stammered. "It is a crime against . . . childhood, and a black mark on England's good name."

Caroline smiled. He had managed the word "childhood," one of his stumbling blocks, with barely a pause. That must give him confidence.

And it seemed to, as he continued to speak with relative smoothness for the next five minutes. His arguments were strong and well reasoned, and his delivery—while unlikely to cause Edmund Kean to renounce the stage—was adequate to the task.

When he stumbled on the hard consonants, he simply kept going, seemingly oblivious to the muttered comments that passed between certain peers. But his forehead was shiny, and Caroline knew that, if she were close enough, she would see a thin sheen of sweat coating his features.

And still, he kept going, presenting reason after reason why the bill should pass.

She glanced sideways at her father, and saw that even he was captivated by the sheer force of will at work in the chamber below.

Hawk paused. His chest rose and fell. Rose and fell.

"And so, in c-c-con-conclusion," he said. Grimaced. Stopped.

"In con-con-con—"

He stopped again.

You're almost there. Keep going.

Into the silence came a mocking voice. "Spit it out, Hawksmoor! Just because you're talking about children doesn't mean you have to sound like an infant."

Penfield, of course.

Caroline suddenly realized what happened to Eton bullies when they grew up. They became drunken old peers.

Don't look at him. Look at the crack in the wall.

But Hawk looked neither at Penfield nor at the wall. Instead, his gaze shifted to the ladies' gallery and came to rest directly on Caroline.

He held her attention with the same intense gaze that had pinned her on the walkway at Vauxhall.

For a moment, it was as though an invisible wire connected them across the vast space of the House. Caroline drew on her meager theatrical talents to put all her belief, all her encouragement, all her faith, in her eyes.

You can do this, she tried to say silently. *Don't be afraid.*

He smiled, with a brilliance that seemed to light up even the dim corner where he stood. He turned back into the House and looked directly at Penfield, who had continued to chortle. From her vantage point, Caroline could just barely see the imperious quirk of his eyebrow. Penfield stopped snickering. She absolutely *had* to get Hawk to teach her that trick.

"To finish," Hawk intoned, "I would just like to remind the members of this House of the concept of *noblesse oblige*. As peers, we have received much, but we have a r-r-responsibility to give in return. That is all I ask you to do today."

That was what Hawk was all about, she realized. He would follow his conscience, no matter what. Even if it meant he had to face his worst fears.

That was why she had found him so compelling when they first met. Not because he was attractive—which he was. Not because he had charmed Edward—which he had. But because, from that very first moment, she had sensed that he was a man of substance. A man who believed that an honorable life was the only one worth living.

A man like that could help her overcome the fear she rarely voiced—that everything of value in her life could easily come to an end in an instant. Why hadn't she seen that before?

Lord Hawksmoor folded his lanky form back onto his bench, as a smattering of applause mixed with catcalls echoed through the chamber. He looked drawn and elated at the same time. Once more, he turned his gaze to the upper gallery. And this time, Caroline hoped that all the love she now realized she felt showed in her eyes. His smile was warm, but fleeting. Within moments, he looked away. He was still afraid of her, and all she represented. And she didn't know if she could— or even should—change his mind.

Chapter Eleven

Hawk strode across the still wet grass of Hyde Park, Rogue scampering about his heels. It felt good to breathe cool, fresh air again, after spending most of the previous day trapped in the airless confines of the Palace of Westminster.

The day had been a very mixed blessing. The knowledge that he had spoken in public without the world ceasing to spin had come as a revelation. It was as though heavy manacles had dropped from his arms and legs, leaving him free to move through the world as others did.

He doubted he would ever be a great orator. Indeed, he might never get through an entire address without stammering. But he would get through it. He would do his duty.

However, not all the news was good. The argument in the House had not gone their way. Debate had continued for several more hours, long after Caroline had shepherded her obviously bored father away. And when the bill had been put to a vote, it had been soundly defeated.

"We knew it was a long shot," Tavister had remarked as they reviewed the arguments very late that night at White's. "But it was one we had to try. I can't thank you enough for adding your voice to the fray. I know for a fact that your speech turned a few of the hesitant peers over to our side."

"You mean they were swept away by the thrilling tide of my voice?"

"It wasn't how you said it. It was what you said."

Hawk had nodded and sipped his port. Perhaps, just perhaps, that was enough. They could always attempt another bill next year. And the year after that. Every year, in fact, until the peers came to their senses and voted for it.

In the meantime, though, there were other things he could do. In the last few weeks, he had put the wheels in motion to fund a small school on his estate, so that any child who wanted to learn could attend at no cost. It was a very small step to keeping a few children out of the mines, but it was a start, something he could build on.

He scanned the lawns ahead of him, but saw no sign of an ebony-haired young woman accompanied by a small boy, an elderly dandy, or a rowdy spaniel.

Perhaps she wouldn't come today. He couldn't blame her if she didn't—he'd given her reason enough at their last meeting to avoid him for the rest of her life. He suspected few women would be willing to encourage the attentions of a man who seemed ashamed of them.

That's how it must have seemed to Caroline, he realized now. How could he have made such a mess of things? It wasn't she he was ashamed of. It was himself.

He was ashamed that he had been afraid to live life to the fullest for so many years. That he had spent so much time on the edges of the playing field, while others took all the risks, got all the glory . . . and had all the fun.

He slipped a hand into his pocket, to check that the item he'd fished out of his closet this morning was still there. It was. Good.

Perhaps it wasn't too late to change. He was ready, finally, to take a chance on life. The trick was he needed to prove to Caroline that he was ready. That would be difficult to do if she wasn't here.

A fierce tug on the rope lead in his other hand brought his attention to Rogue. The puppy was twisting himself around

Hawk's feet, so that he had to keep jumping to avoid getting his legs tied up in the lead.

"I knew you could waltz, but I had no idea your talents extended to the Highland fling." Caroline's voice, throaty and laced with merriment, came from what sounded like a few yards behind him.

Before he could turn, however, Scamp hurtled past him, dragging Edward in his wake. Hawk gave in to the inevitable and dropped the lead, letting Rogue scamper off to join his brother.

"Good day, Lord Hawk!" Edward cried breathlessly, as the puppies dove at each other. "Scamp started running as soon as he saw you!"

"Good day, Edward," Hawk replied, slightly distracted as he watched Caroline approach. She was looking lovely, as always, in a green dress he had not seen before.

"Hullo, Caroline," he said, his voice cracking slightly. He was fully prepared for what he planned to do. He just hoped it would work.

"Hawk." Her smile was wary as she moved toward him.

It occurred to him that they had not stood side by side since he'd stepped away from her in the Lovers' Walk.

Perhaps that was why he found breathing suddenly more difficult.

"No!" Edward's voice cracked the still morning air. "Scamp! Rogue!" Scamp had broken free of his lead and was playfully growling at his brother.

"Don't worry. They won't hurt each other," Hawk reassured the child. "But can I trust you to keep an eye on them while I have a few private words with your mother?"

Edward nodded solemnly. "I promise not to go far."

"Good," Hawk said as the boy followed the dogs across the clearing, then sat down to observe them. Hawk turned his attention back to Caroline.

"You wished to speak to me, my lord?"

He smiled. "Are we back on formal terms?"

To his surprise, she looked away. "I am uncertain. Are we?"

It was just the opening he needed. But now that the time had come, he wasn't sure he had the nerve.

Nonsense, he told himself. *If you could confront the entire House of Lords, you can certainly face one headstrong young woman.*

Looking at her, realizing how much he wanted her—how much he needed her—he knew that this would be a much more nerve-wracking endeavor than his speech of the previous day.

Yesterday, he had just been trying to curry short-term favor with a bunch of indifferent noblemen. What he was about to do was much more important and much more permanent.

"Are we back to being formal?" he fired her question back to her. "I devoutly hope not. Because that shall make what I'm about to do even more acutely embarrassing."

Glancing behind him, he spotted a statue of some unknown luminary. "C-c-come with me."

She glanced toward Edward.

"We'll still be able to see him from where we're going," he told her.

"All right."

He held out his hand and, to his relief, she took it. It felt good to touch her again, however briefly. But he wanted more, much more, than this brief contact. Everything would hinge on what happened next.

They reached the statue and she looked at him enquiringly. It was now or never. He dropped her hand, placed one foot on the plinth of the statue, and vaulted up beside the marble figure.

"Hawk? What are you doing?"

He grinned. Really, being foolish was a great deal of fun. He should have tried it years ago.

From his pocket, he withdrew a crumpled green mass,

which he unfolded and stuck on his head at what he hoped was a rakish angle.

"A laurel wreath from our theatrical!" Caroline exclaimed, laughing. "You kept it!"

He nodded, but could say no more or he'd be distracted from his purpose. Taking a deep breath, as she had taught him, he looked around the park. It had become more crowded since he'd arrived with Rogue a few minutes ago. A few dedicated horsemen were cantering on a nearby path, and several nurses were about with their young charges. He even spotted a knot of battered-looking Corinthians who looked as though they hadn't seen the insides of their lodgings all night.

Well, this wouldn't work without an audience. He cleared his throat.

"Friends, B-B-Britons, countrymen. Lend m-m-me your ears!" he began in the loudest voice he could muster.

To his immense delight, Caroline's eyes shone.

"What are you up to?" she gasped.

He simply grinned. His heart was banging against his chest like a wild bird trapped in a cage. When he noticed that several passers-by had stopped to observe the curious little scene, he took a very deep breath. No matter. He could do this. She had shown him he could.

"I have come to m-m-marry Caroline Farris, *and* to p-p-praise her," he continued, looking directly into her eyes.

Dimly, he heard a delighted laugh come from one of the nurses who had stopped to watch. Even more dimly, he was aware that Edward had started wandering back toward them.

But mainly, he was aware of Caroline's astonished face.

"Marry?" she echoed.

He nodded.

"But you said . . . at Vauxhall—"

"I said a great many things at Vauxhall, and most of them were wrong," he replied. "The most wrong of all was my assumption that one could not have fun *and* be dignified." He looked up at the crumpled paper wreath on his head. "Well, if not dignified, at least not scandalous."

She laughed. "I must admit, you don't look much like a haughty earl at the moment."

He extended his hand. After a moment's hesitation, she clasped it and let him pull her onto the plinth beside him.

"So, Caroline? Will you . . . marry me?"

"I have just one question first."

He grinned. "Of course."

"Why the public display? Did you think I would respond only to such an exhibition?"

"No." He shook his head as he gripped her hand more tightly. "I wanted to let you know how much I'd changed. How much *you* had helped me change. The Earl of Hawksmoor you met a few weeks ago would have died rather than make a public speech in Hyde Park."

She nodded. "I know."

"Because of you, I know that *living* is more important than merely *existing*. I know that I don't have to be a sort of m-m-monk to avoid being the rakehell my father was. And I know that s-s-sometimes, you have to take chances to get the things you really want."

"The things you really want?" Her voice was faint.

"Or the people." He reached for her other hand, steadying his back against the marble soldier so that they wouldn't both topple onto the grass. "I've answered your question. Now, will you answer mine?"

"Yes, missus, answer him!" came a young woman's voice from the crowd.

A torrent of emotions washed through Caroline as she stood on the pillar, looking up at Hawk in his ridiculous head-gear. Pride in him, joy at the moment, even a touch of embarrassment at their predicament.

But the main feeling that coursed through her, down to her very toes, was love. She loved this man with all her heart, she realized, as she struggled to keep her balance on the plinth. Not because he'd ventured this public display for her benefit, which she knew was costing him more of an emotional price than the most valuable wedding ring was worth in gold. Not because he'd worked so hard to present his speech in Parliament. But because she'd always loved him. Probably from the moment he'd knelt down at the dog seller's stand to answer Edward's questions.

He was a good man, and she'd sensed it even when she had wrongly suspected him of being too cowardly to stand up for his convictions. But was she ready to marry again?

"Of all the t-t-times for you to lose your ability to speak, Caroline—" Hawk murmured in mock frustration.

She did not—could not—answer.

"Caroline?" Hawk prompted.

"Yes, Gerald?" she said at last, feeling oddly dazed.

"Gerald?" He frowned. "How did you know my name?"

She laughed. "It wasn't difficult to deduce. I looked you up in *Debrett's*."

"But no one calls me Gerald."

"I shall. *Hawk* seems a rather dramatic name for a woman to call her husband, don't you think?"

He nodded, an expression of glee upon his face. "I am beginning to enjoy drama, m'dear. But if I may call you wife, you may call me whatever you like."

And then, right there, on a pillar in the middle of Hyde Park, he bent his head and kissed her.

An Imperfect Proposal

Hayley Ann Solomon

Chapter One

"Amaryllis, dear, do come and meet Captain Fredericks of the Third Hussars! Captain Fredericks, this is my daughter, Lady Amaryllis Hastings and do not feel afraid to ask her for a dance, for I declare she is an obliging child and would not disappoint you for the world."

Amaryllis, thus summoned, felt her heart sink into the very toes of her fashionable slippers. Oh, how mortifying to be paraded thus! Poor Captain Fredericks would be bullied into offering to dance with her, and though it would be very pleasant to take up the set, it was humiliating in such circumstances.

Why could her mama not leave her be? She was perfectly satisfied with her dance card which was a respectable half full. There was no need to be thrust forward like this.

But her mama seemed to think there was every need, for after Captain Fredericks it was the Earl of Cathbrook, then Mr. Fry, who was rumored to be a nabob, then Lord Patterson—the list went on and each time Amaryllis felt worse. She was a pretty wisp of a girl—far too thin, in her own opinion—but her shyness in company made her awkward, and the delicious lights of laughter that sprung from her inner depths never seemed to surface at functions such as these.

Small wonder when she was laced and corseted and had had dressers fussing over her all evening, shaking their heads over her pale coloring—wan, they called it—and her golden locks that refused to curl and were gentle in tone rather than the ravishing guinea gold that was all the rage.

Her redeeming features were her eyes, which were a magnetic midnight blue, framed in lashes that were dark and thick and wondrously long. But even these came in for criticism, for her dresser was certain that no one would believe that artifice had not been employed in the darkening of those brows and lashes. She was in a positive quake that one of the patronesses would accuse Amaryllis of using paint and unfortunately passed those qualms on to Amaryllis, who felt shier than ever.

Suffice it to say, then, that whilst Amaryllis never precisely lacked for a partner, she was also never as sought after as Miss Lila Trewellyn, her dearest friend, or Miss Martha Caddington, the lady she least liked of her acquaintance.

Both of these damsels were currently engaged in the waltz, Miss Caddington catching her eye with infuriating sympathy (or was it triumph?), and Miss Trewellyn winking merrily as she twirled past, feigning ecstasy, for she was in the arms of a particularly dashing partner, and she was certain Amaryllis would agree.

Amaryllis did agree, for it was hard to ignore Lord Redding's very fine physique, or the elegant cut of his dark, tailored frock coat, which sparkled, a little, with diamonds. Nor could one exactly miss the muscled thighs that defied even the clocked stockings to disguise their perfection of form. As for the velvet knee breeches, well, they were positively indecent, so fitted as they were! Amaryllis was glad, for once, she was not waltzing, for she was flushing like a schoolgirl and would have been rendered speechless had her hand been solicited by such a paragon.

She need not have worried, for it wasn't, though she did think, for a fraction of an instant, that she had caught a reassuring smile in those handsome hazel eyes. But how foolish! Lord Stephen Redding, the Earl of Devonport, was as likely to notice her as he was to offer for the local costermonger's daughter. She ignored the flush on her cheeks and dropped her eyes down to her fan, berating herself for such foolishness.

Lila was curtsying politely at the cessation of the waltz and edging her way round the potted palms to her side. Suddenly, for some unknown, urgent reason, Amaryllis wanted to fly. She wanted to escape the glittering, jeweled hall, festooned with bright silks and decorated in the Spanish style in memory of Salamanca.

She wanted to flee the sympathetic sighs of the dowagers who caught her eye and shook their heads; she wanted to creep past her mama, engaged in conversation with Lord Sedgebrooke (doubtless telling him how delightful a partner she would be) and find some fresh air somewhere. She was engaged, after the quadrille and the bourrée to Mr. Ratchins. It was to be the waltz, at last, which lifted her spirits, somewhat, for there was nothing so fabulously exhilarating as the waltz, especially when the gentleman encircling your waist was altogether too attractive for one's own good.

Not that Mr. Ratchins fitted that category precisely, but one could be generous when one was waltzing, and overlook such small matters as protruding teeth and a collar starched far too stiffly for comfort. If it had only been the Earl of Devonport— that would be another matter entirely. Amaryllis suddenly knew why she was avoiding Lila. She did not want to hear her animadversions on this paragon. It was enough, surely, that she'd had to watch from the sidelines?

Miss Trewellyn's progress was stopped by Miss Baskerville, so Amaryllis breathed a little sigh and took her opportunity to escape. She gathered up her skirts and disappeared into the anteroom just off the main ballroom, then frowned as she saw Miss Caddington's form silhouetted on the adjacent balcony. If Martha were to corner her here, she would delight in saying something catty and hurtful, and Amaryllis was in no mood for such sport. She therefore edged her way out of the antechamber and found herself in a dark suite of rooms that were obviously not intended for the use of the ball, for no tapers had been lit and only the firelight in the hearth lent a rosy glow to the vacant room.

She sank back thankfully, though a little guiltily, into one of the winged chairs and listened, for a moment, to the first strains of the quadrille as the orchestra tuned up. It was uncustomary for her to be so sunk in gloom, for normally—when she was not being paraded like a prize pig on the marriage mart—she was cheerfulness itself. Her sunny nature and kind heart did not permit of a fit of the dismals, so busy was she in decocting potions, writing snippets for her diary—a wonderfully eclectic notebook of all matters ranging from Miss Marsham's receipt for a head cold to the proper way of pressing flowers to the innermost yearnings of her heart. She also rode almost every day if it was fine, read feverishly from Hookham's and Hatchard's, and could often be found ascending the stacks at the Temple of the Muses, Finsbury Square, in search of bargains.

This, indeed, was how she had met Lila, for Lila, too, was an avid reader and delighted in spending a comfortable day in front of the fire armed with a pile of books ranging from the Gothic to the most up-to-the-minute serials like *The Athenaeum Weekly Review*.

Now, however, Amaryllis found it hard not to choke back her tears. Everyone was being perfectly kind, but she could hardly help being disheartened. Her family expected her to marry and had expended a fortune on two Seasons and a court appearance, and there was not the remotest prospect of anyone—not even stiff-necked Mr. Ratchins—obliging her with an offer.

The strain was enormous. Every time her mama went to so much trouble to secure her a partner and her papa refused to relocate to their country seat—where she knew he would be happier—she felt responsible. Though not a word of reproach had been leveled at her, sometimes she felt her mother's encouragement was a little hearty, and her dresser's attempts at ringlets a smidgen desperate. Even dear, kind Papa's face was a trifle too anxious as he asked whether she had met anyone interesting that day.

Amaryllis, when she dreamed of growing up and marriage, had never thought out what this might mean, how burdensome would be the task of finding a husband for herself. It had never occurred to her that she might not like the man she was to marry. She'd always imagined herself with someone who was ravishingly handsome and had a smile that lit up his countenance and a humor that exactly matched her own. She had stupidly not even dreamed that she would have difficulty finding this paragon, or that filling up a dance card would become a daily trial of nerves, or that, worse, someone hideous would offer for her and she would have no choice but to accept.

These thoughts oppressed her dreadfully. She reached into her beaded reticule, stitched handsomely with little rhinestones that glittered elegantly in the firelight, and hunted for a handkerchief. Of course, she had forgotten, in her agitation, to put one in, so she was forced to close the reticule with a sigh and brush her hands across her lashes as she did. She was just feeling more depressed than ever when a slight rustle from the brocade sofa on the left caught her attention.

There was probably a mouse, and it was probably terrified, poor thing, what with the noise and the unexpectedness of her entry into this darkened room . . . she stood up and peered over the edge of the sofa. Not a mouse, by George, but two children, wedged behind the chair and regarding her with horrified eyes.

"Hello!"

Amaryllis smiled in the friendliest way she could, her own

troubles set aside for the moment. There was a silence as the girls—for such they were—stared at her for a moment.

"I am Amaryllis. Are you also hiding from the ball?"

Her tone was so sweet and confiding that the children, after a speaking glance at one another, decided it was safe to emerge.

"Are you hiding?" they asked in surprise, for they had never encountered a grown-up who hid. Amaryllis, in her glittering gown of rose sarcenet embroidered with gold fichu trim looked very grown-up indeed.

She laughed. "Yes, I am, but don't tell anyone if you please. It is very bad of me."

The children promised solemnly, for there was nothing—as they told Amaryllis—that they liked less than a sneak.

"So what are you doing out of your nursery? Enjoying the music?"

"No, for we can't hear much over the buzz of conversation."

"Peeking at the dancers?"

"Yes, for they are all very elegant, only we have seen heaps of balls before so it was not so much that as . . ."

"Yes?" Amaryllis prompted.

The girls looked at each other. They must have decided Amaryllis was perfectly acceptable, for they both started simultaneously speaking. Amaryllis was forced to laugh and stop up her ears and tell them to talk one at a time.

"Well, you see, we are hungry!"

"What, is no supper sent up to your nursery?"

"Only bread and butter and jam and two glasses of cold tea."

"But that is outrageous!"

"No, it isn't, really, for it is a punishment. Usually we have all the tidbits Cook is preparing for the ball, and some of the sweetmeats, and the little pink sugar fairies . . ."

"But how inconvenient to be punished on such a day!"

"Yes, if we had thought about the matter we would have tipped ink into Mr. Petersham's hat tomorrow, after the ball, but we were so angry we really couldn't think properly."

Amaryllis's eyes danced. "No, indeed," she agreed gravely. "And who, if I might inquire, is Mr. Petersham? I feel certain he must be positively odious!"

"Oh, he is! He teaches us deportment, which is a trial enough without him having to report poor Evans, our governess, for improper conduct. Simply because she happened to doze off in one of his classes!"

"Sounds like he deserved ink in his hat."

"Oh, indeed, and it was splendid sport to see his face as it trickled down his ears! Unfortunately we giggled at the wrong moment which caused him to march us off to our uncle."

"Your uncle? "

"Yes, the Earl of Devonport—he is our guardian, you know, whilst our parents are excavating in Italy."

Amaryllis ignored the leap of her heart at the mention of this illustrious name. But curiosity overcame her. "What did he say, your uncle?"

"Oh, he threatened all manner of dire consequences which personally we don't believe, for he is a thundering good sport when he is not called upon to punish us and I cannot believe he would ever lay a hand upon us, never mind a birch rod, which is what he threatened."

"He threatened to birch you?"

"Yes, the next time we take to pouring ink into hats or even shoes, which he added as an afterthought and I must say I wish we'd had the idea ourselves! But he sent us off to bed without any dinner. It is really very vexing when we can smell all the smells from the kitchens and Cook has baked a simply sumptuous frosted cake and like as not everyone will eat it and there will not be a scrap of it left for us in the morning."

"How horribly unfair!" Amaryllis's lips twitched.

"Isn't it? But we do have one consolation!"

"Which is?"

"Uncle dismissed Mr. Petersham! He said he did not much care for talebearers and since Mr. Petersham obviously objected to the governess he had selected, it was wiser all round if he found employment elsewhere."

"Bravo! What did Mr. Petersham say?"

"He was as mad as tacks but there was not a thing he could do save deplore our deportment and lack of any redeeming qualities."

"What an odious, odious man!"

"Indeed, for we would not have taken such drastic measures were he not!"

"So you came downstairs because you are hungry?"

"Yes, we thought we might be able to dart in, undetected, and seize a plateful of macaroons, or even some of the game pie though I daresay there is none of that left . . ."

"No, for I saw a footman remove the salver."

Amaryllis was too polite to say that the chances of two small children, tousled and in their nightgowns, remaining undetected, was zero. Instead, she hesitantly suggested an alternative.

"What you need, my dears, is an accomplice."

"Yes, but who? We asked Darcy the second footman but he says the butler has his eye on him and Matilda is so useless we haven't even bothered asking . . ."

"What about me? May I procure you some refreshments? I doubt my reticule will stand anything like jelly or pigeon pie, but if I am careful I should be able to fit some slices of that strawberry frosted cake you mentioned. I saw it in the supper room and it looks delightful."

The children stared at her in blank amazement. "But you are one of the guests!"

"Indeed."

"But you are a grown-up!"

"Only just!"

The girls chuckled.

"You really are the nicest person we have met. I'm Vicky," said the eldest of the two sisters.

"I'm Clementine but my friends call me Clem."

"Good to meet you," Amaryllis replied gravely. "I am Amaryllis Hastings."

The girls exchanged glances. There was something about her name that seemed to intrigue them, but when Miss Hastings asked, they only grinned cheekily, so she thought she must have imagined this. They muttered something about a list, but the matter made no sense at all.

"Well, then, I shall go . . . gracious, is that the second set already? I am engaged for the next dance but after that I should be able to amble over to the refreshment table and purloin a morsel or two!"

"Look for us above the balcony. If we crouch down low we shan't be seen and it is less risky than here, where everyone comes to snatch a kiss . . ."

Amaryllis was shocked, "Gracious! You were not hiding when . . ."

"Yes! Mortifying, too, and I nearly sneezed which would have been perfectly frightful!" Vicky giggled.

"Please, please, please don't tell Uncle! We should very likely starve for a week."

This was one promise Amaryllis made easily. The thought of telling the Earl of Devonport that his nieces had been very improperly witnessing some equally improper behavior . . . it did not bear thinking upon.

"Off you go quickly, then. I trust there is a suitable escape route?"

"Yes, out that door which leads to the gallery and the private suites. It is usually locked but Molly is growing so careless . . ." The girls giggled and produced a huge key.

Amaryllis tried to frown, but the attempt made her chortle instead, a fact that endeared her still further to her new acquaintances.

"Go then! I shall not, I trust, fail you!"

With that, she swept up her skirts and returned to the crush of the ballroom.

Chapter Two

It was not one dance but two dances later that she was able to keep her promise. Her cousin, Mr. Stanley Bandox-Brow, had just remembered that he'd promised to do his duty by Amaryllis and this he gallantly did.

As a matter of fact, he would not take no for an answer, for he told Amaryllis flatly that her mama would harangue him to death if he did not take a turn with her across the floor.

This unflattering invitation was, not surprisingly, ill-received, but Amaryllis did her best to swallow her annoyance. She could not, however, feel grateful—as Mr. Bandox-Brow clearly expected her to be—especially as he did not seem to have mastered the finer steps of the dance.

The consequence was that her pretty slippers were sadly crushed and her feet positively ached. Be that as it may, she curtsied gracefully and thanked him politely before setting about her more interesting pilfering spree.

She would have been shocked to realize that for all her precautions she had not escaped unseen. The Earl of Devonport, happening to glance her way, found his eyes arrested at the sight of two slices of strawberry frosted gateau and—yes, he could swear it—a pair of sugar plums—disappearing into a certain beaded reticule. He had not, up to now, thought much about the shy little mouse who had been invited on the strength of her antecedents alone, but now he felt a tug of curiosity he had not previously foreseen.

As Amaryllis swept up the banisters, my lord's eyes followed the shimmer of her gown, though he made no movement to catch up with her. His puzzlement changed to laughter as he saw the recipients of her bounty—hidden behind a china silk screen, but not well enough for his curious glance. He turned his back on the proceedings. If he knew nothing of them he could hardly be forced to object—and invited a particularly dazzling beauty—a Miss Paterson-Vermont—to partake of the supper dance.

The evening was well advanced when the earl next caught sight of Miss Hastings. Her reticule sat innocently upon her lap as she tapped out the rhythms of Mr. Handel's water music. She was alone, for her mama was once more busy with cards, and her circle of friends all seemed to be engaged with partners. Of an instance, he felt sorry for her. She was too innocent for flirtation, and too insipid for his tastes, which ran to more buxom beauties, especially of the Spanish kind.

Still, she made a pretty picture in her shimmering gown, and her slippers were beguiling as they tapped away in tuneful harmony with the orchestra. They were a delicate pink and ribboned to her ankles, which he noted with satisfaction were more than satisfactory. (Amaryllis would have been mortified to realize she was revealing her ankles beneath the long, flowing fabric of her gown, but fortunately no one was at hand to tell her so.) As she looked up, she caught the eyes of the earl and could not help blushing, though why she had to behave like such a silly ninnyhammer she could not imagine.

The earl smiled. She half thought there must be some more eligible young lady behind her, but she realized her mistake at once, for his eyes held her own and there could be no mistaking their interest.

Of a sudden, Amaryllis felt shaky and tongue-tied. She hardly knew what to say, for he was advancing toward her . . . gracious! Had he seen her pilfering the sugar plums? But he did not look angry, he looked . . . he looked serene and amused.

"Miss Hastings?"

He was a hairbreadth away from her now, and looking down upon her with a gentle smile upon that handsome countenance.

Amaryllis nodded, hardly daring to breathe, for Stephen, Lord Redding, was beyond her touch and she hardly knew what to say. Fortunately, she remembered her curtsy and my lord's brows lifted infinitesimally at this unnecessary formality.

"Would you care to dance? I know it has been very remiss of me not to fill out your card and if you are engaged . . ."

"No, yes! I mean, no I am not engaged . . ."

"And yes you would like to dance?" The smile was more pronounced, now, but still gentle.

"Yes, please, your lordship."

Stephen nodded and took her arm. "We shall wait until the end of this set and then take up our places. Your gown is very fetching."

"Thank you!"

Amaryllis thought she must be dreaming. The ballroom suddenly seemed brighter, as though a thousand tapers had been lit. Jewels and rhinestones sparkled liked a million shimmering raindrops, my lord's gloved hand upon her arm was so warm it seemed to burn into her skin . . . but oh, that was just the start of these lively sensations. The next dance was the very waltz she had so yearned to put into practice.

Her nerves beat so wildly she was convinced she would miss the steps, forget the beat, or miss a count. She moistened her lips nervously and counted softly under her breath until my lord laughed down at her and whispered that she must relax and allow him to lead her. His hand tightened about her waist, which was hardly conducive to any kind of relaxing.

What is more, Amaryllis could not rid herself of the notion that he found her gauche, having to count her steps.

She tensed, then relaxed as if to appear nonchalant, then finally, because she felt so unutterably exhilarated and perhaps a little because Miss Martha Caddington was watching them with a disagreeable pout of envy on her lips, she began to forget her worries and give herself up to the excitement of the dance.

Her partner, sensing this sudden change, felt an unexpected wave of tenderness sweep through him. He wanted this little chit of a thing to have a splendid time, to have one memory at least that was not bittersweet.

Lord Redding was more observant than society gave him credit for. He was accustomed to seeing Miss Hastings obligingly take the baggage carriage so her friends could ride unfettered outside. He was used to her making up a fourth at piquet when there was no one more interesting to take up the challenge.

She always smiled sweetly and seemed grateful for any small attention, no matter how negligent or carelessly bestowed. He realized with a qualm that he himself was guilty of taking her for granted as her acquaintances seemed to do.

Why, he wondered, had he not immediately inscribed his name on her dance card as he had with most of the other ladies invited as his guests? It would have been the most common of civilities, yet he had been discourteous, or negligent. He wondered why, and realized with a qualm that there was not a whisper of reproach in her bright eyes as they met his, for the veriest fraction of an instant.

The dance was over sooner than Lord Redding expected, and he realized with annoyance that he could not linger, he had bespoken himself to Miss Ingles, and that lady was already regarding him anxiously from the sidelines. It would be ill-bred to leave her disappointed, so he made his bow to Amaryllis, hovered with her hand for a fraction of an instant upon his lips, then strode off in the direction of Miss Camilla Ingles.

Camilla was entirely different from Amaryllis. As my lord approached, she feigned surprise that it was his dance already, and made a great show of consulting her card as if she had forgotten that the earl had inscribed his name there. Normally his lordship was amused by such wiles, but this evening he found the behavior slightly distasteful. Fortunately for Miss Ingles, his good manners showed none of his sudden annoyance.

Indeed, when she flirted with him—Camilla was determined to fix the earl's interest this Season—he responded agreeably, so Camilla was able to catch the eye of her good friend Martha Caddington in a rather "I told you so" sort of fashion.

Martha, however, was not so elated as she might have been. The earl was definitely the pick of this Season's crop, and it was naturally *she* who would have been desirous of my lord's attentions. Still, she had had one waltz with him, so she supposed Camilla could enjoy her little quadrille. After all, a quadrille was not nearly so distinguishing as a waltz, not to mention exhilarating, for she had made certain that her glittering bodice pressed accidentally against my lord's own expansive chest, and that she edged a trifle closer to him than the requisite three inches.

She was just feeling pleased with herself when her eyes alighted on Amaryllis, engaged in animated conversation with Lila Trewellyn. Her face darkened, for she could not think how insipid little Amaryllis could have stolen her limelight. She moved closer to the pair and waited until their own delicate steps brought them into speaking distance.

"Oh, *dear* Amaryllis!" she trilled. "How . . . how perfectly provincial is your dress! Do you hope to start a trend?"

Amaryllis made the fatal mistake of looking flustered, but Lila Trewellyn was more up to snuff. She smiled sweetly. "It is a trend the Earl of Devonport obviously likes, Miss Caddington. Did you not notice how he asked Miss Hastings for the last waltz? Miss Caddington smiled, but the blaze in her eyes was spiteful rather than merry.

"But naturally I did! How fortunate you are, Miss Hastings, to have been chosen as his token wallflower this evening. His lordship is so punctilious about such things, you know. He always makes a point of distinguishing one partnerless lady at every function. So *civil*, I always say."

"You are a cat, Martha Caddington!" Lila's eyes flashed, but the damage was done. Amaryllis looked unsteady on her feet and so pale her friend thought she might faint. But she was more spirited than that, and a lady if nothing else. She smiled at Martha and murmured that yes, indeed, she had been fortunate.

Martha nodded spitefully and moved on to fresh targets.

"Pay her no heed, Amaryllis! She is just jealous and spiteful."

"I know that. She is, nevertheless, quite correct. His lordship was just being kind."

"Nonsense! When you forget your nerves, Amaryllis, you are positively beautiful!"

"You are a dear for saying so, Lila, and I love you for it, but I cannot think of myself in such terms! But come, let us not spoil the evening in this fashion. I daresay if we are quick enough we can coax a sherbet out of that footman. I am positively parched."

So, head held up high, Miss Amaryllis Hastings concluded her evening with both poise and dignity. She had never, however, felt so low, especially as Mr. Ratchins required her for a second dance and indicated, in that circuitous and pompous manner of his, that he would be calling on her the following day.

Amaryllis's heart sank. The thought of an offer from Mr. Ratchins was very lowering, for though she had been despairing of ever receiving a formal proposal of marriage, the thought that one might now be imminent was depressing to the spirits. She scolded herself for being such a flighty flibberty-gibbet. But no matter how many times her dresser told her, as she set aside her baubles and brushed through her hair, that she looked passing pretty, she could not overcome her feeling of gloom.

Chapter Three

As it happened, Mr. Ratchins must have had second thoughts, for there was no distinguishing visit from him all morning, despite Amaryllis forcing herself to wear her newest muslin, adorned with rosebuds and a sash of the softest flamingo pink.

Her mama, when she had seen her thus attired, had raised her brows and inquired whether Amaryllis was expecting any visitors that day.

"No, Mama."

"Well, I wish you were, for you are in excellent good looks, my dear, and I feel certain that if only Mr. Darrow or even, yes, I shall dare to look so high—the Earl of Devonport—should set eyes on you thus . . ."

"Oh, Mama! Let us not speak of such things! There is not the remotest chance that either of those gentleman will show the smallest interest in me . . ."

"No? I heard you waltzed with a certain earl last night. I could have kicked myself for missing the spectacle, but I was engaged in the most riveting game of piquet . . ."

"It was nothing, Mama."

"Nothing? When it was the talk of the ballroom? Now, my dear, do not look so coy, I am very pleased with you and if only we can put our heads together to think of a way . . . I know! We can invite a select circle to a picnic at your uncle's country seat. It will be unexceptional at this time of year, and

I feel sure I can include Lord Redding, for after all, his mama and I were once close acquaintances . . ."

"Mama!"

"What?"

"I forbid you to think of such a thing! Oh, it is embarrassing and so horribly transparent . . ."

"But, my dear, how do you expect his lordship to become better acquainted with you if you don't make the slightest push to meet him?"

"I don't expect it! Mama, fixing one's eye on Lord Redding is like expecting to make a match with Czar Alexander himself! It is . . . it is . . . romantic nonsense."

"Then you like him?" Lady Hastings regarded her daughter keenly.

"Yes. Yes. Of course I do." A delicate pink suffused Amaryllis's cheeks. "But what is that to the purpose?"

"The purpose is that his lordship distinguished you last night with a waltz."

"Yes, and Martha Caddington and Lila Trewellyn . . ."

"Only a quadrille and Martha is of no account. There is a reason she has had three Seasons already. She is the most spiteful widgeon alive and I cannot think his lordship will be cajoled by her forward manner."

"I cannot think he will be cajoled by my insipid one!"

"Amaryllis Hastings, I should wash your mouth out for such nonsense! You are not insipid, you are charming."

"Mama, I am a wallflower! I have not taken, and you know it! You cannot think how thankful I am when I manage to get my card half full . . ."

Lady Hastings blinked back a tear. Amaryllis spoke the truth, though she could not think why, for her daughter had character and a generosity of spirit that was rare for her age.

How stupid gentlemen are when they come to look for a bride! How tiresome not to recognize her daughter's sterling qualities! Oh, if only Amaryllis would consent to wearing the latest, low-cut necklines! With her slender figure and rounded curves . . . oh, it was a shame she was so modest, for she hid her greatest attributes—her face and her figure—behind potted plants. It was nothing but a matter of shyness, if she could develop a more flirtatious manner . . .

"Mama, I know what you are thinking! I am not going to bat my eyelashes for Mr. Darrow, I should look a quiz!"

"It is not Mr. Darrow I was thinking of, Amaryllis!"

But Amaryllis would not be baited. With a flush high upon her cheeks, she announced there was no point continuing on with such a tedious discussion. She had work in the herbarium, for Lady Atholl had advised her of a new way of propagating lemon grass and she was anxious to try it out.

The next few days Amaryllis threw herself into her work. She enjoyed gardening very much indeed and Lady Hasting's London residence benefited much from her expertise. She found it impossible to stitch, or do needlework or any of the indoor activities she usually found solace in, for whenever she had a spare moment she found herself thinking uncomfortably of Lord Redding's arms upon her, and his deep, hazel green eyes regarding her with more seriousness than she was used to and oh, her tingling nerves as he smiled. . . .

Then she would think what a ninnyhammer she was being, and of Martha's spiteful remark, which, whilst mean-spirited, was nevertheless unfortunately true. She had been no more than Lord Redding's token wallflower. She must not lose herself in nonsensical contemplation.

She did her very best not to, for she rode vigorously every day and reveled in her discovery of the upper stacks at the Temple of the Muses. She was accompanied to Albany, of course, by her maid and very often by Lila Trewellyn, who was also a bookworm and delighted in finding some of the cheaper bargains above stairs.

Somehow, though, her thoughts were not on Shakespeare—whom she admired enormously and had obtained a collection of his first editions at a lucky price. No, they were more in the way of a *Midsummer Night's Dream* and she had to keep pinching herself to remember that she was in a bookstore, not a certain earl's residence in Mayfair.

Unfortunately, her thoughts, when they were contained, kept straying to Clementine and Vicky, and she could not help but wonder if they had enjoyed their repast undiscovered, and whether a new deportment master had ever been appointed.

"Amaryllis, I could swear you are in a dream world of your own!" Lila's voice had a slight edge to it, for she had been quoting Addington and Steele to her friend for nearly a minute without so much as a chuckle in response.

"I am sorry, Lila, I am such a scatterbrain lately! Shall we get out of here?"

Lila agreed, though she regarded her friend sharply and nearly said something teasing, then determined to hold her peace. It was perfectly obvious to her that Amaryllis was suffering the first pangs of love, and she had a very compassionate idea that they could not be comfortable when there was no hope of reciprocation.

Even as they wended their way down the winding stairs, past the various lounging rooms until they were at last at the huge circular counter that was almost as famous as the shop itself, Amaryllis seemed to be casting anxious glances at the gentlemen lounging behind newspapers and *Morning Gazettes*. But if she hoped to see a certain Lord Stephen Redding, Earl of Devonport, she was doomed most utterly to disappointment.

Lord Redding was not in so sorry a state himself. He was carefully perusing a list that had been placed in his elegant hands by his mama, the dowager countess Devonport. He adored his mama, who had been very kind indeed to him as a child, though she herself had lost her heart to his father and been treated rather offhandedly in return.

He was determined not to cause any woman that pain, nor himself be subjected to the type of agonies his mother had been. His marriage, he was certain, would be warm, but not tender, respectful but not dependent.

More and more, he was yearning not just for an heir—which naturally was his duty to provide—but a child of his heart. Perhaps he was being fanciful, but the time he had spent with his nieces had been so warm and uplifting, so funny and tender that he'd been moved to contemplate the notion of becoming a father himself.

Vicky and Clem were like tonics, but there was always that nagging feeling that they were not his—they belonged, in truth, to his sister, and the moments he had with them, though precious, were ephemeral. He wanted to lavish love on someone who was entirely his own, the product of his dreams and hopes and love. Somewhere vaguely in the background he acknowledged the role of the mother in all of this, but it was an odd and misty notion. All his focus was on fatherhood, and the joys he might bring to a small person, boy or girl.

But heirs did not materialize without suitable mothers. He was not impractical! Indeed, he was pragmatism himself, for he had enlisted his own mother's aid to sort the suitable from the unsuitable, the wheat from the chaff.

Certain names on the list had been circled, others had had neat deletions penned through them with short comments in indigo in the margins. These were often edifying, for the countess had a sharp wit—and my lord smiled as he read.

He himself held a quill and every so often appended his own comments and deletions. Miss Martha Caddington had already been deleted by the countess, but her bosom bow, Miss Camilla Ingles, had not. His lordship, his memory fresh from the tedious quadrille, now corrected this obvious omission with a firm deletion of his own. He could tolerate hauteur, but not archness. Miss Ingles, he felt certain, was not only arch, she was mean.

At one name, however, he stopped, and his hazel eyes grew slightly softer. When the girls crept up on him, his hand was just hovering to append a question mark to the crisp margins.

"What are you doing, Uncle?"

"Gracious, girls, I think I have told you a dozen times not to creep up on me like that!"

"Sorry!" But from certain merry giggles my lord inferred they were not very sorry at all. He smiled.

"Are you satisfied with your new deportment master?"

"He is perfect."

"Good. I shall await with interest your evolution from a parcel of monkeys to two elegant young ladies."

Vicky grinned. "Won't Mama and Papa be surprised? They shall hardly recognize us when they return from Rome, so decorous we shall be!"

My lord smiled. "I am not placing my trust in miracles. Mr. Darrington may be handsome, but I don't think he is omnipotent! So long as you girls behave just a *fraction* more becomingly, I shall be well pleased."

Clem looked indignant. "You wrong us, sir! We have been perfect angels ever since the unfortunate ink incident."

"The . . . er . . . unfortunate ink incident, as you put it, has cost me a small fortune. I was obliged to pay Mr. Petersham a term's fees and replace his confounded hat besides. Do you know he uses Renfrew and Grogan hatters? It was no small expense, I assure you."

"Tsha! I'll bet he never set foot in their premises in his life. Renfrew and Grogan indeed! You were hoodwinked, Uncle."

"Again? Dear, dear. I thought once might be enough."

"What do you mean?"

"I mean, you little scamps, that you did not suffer your due punishment for that particular crime. I noticed a certain Miss Amaryllis Hastings coming to your rescue."

The girls stared at one another guiltily.

"Oh, Uncle, *pray* do not be displeased! Punish us again, if you like, only don't, don't delete Miss Hastings from your list."

"My list? By thunder, I should take my whip to you girls! Do you mean you have been reading my correspondence?"

"Only that one, Uncle, it was on your desk and we could not help but notice . . . have you danced with Miss Hastings? She really has the prettiest of ankles. We noticed, for she nearly tripped over our spy glasses . . ."

"Out! Both of you out before I lose my temper!"

Clementine held her ground. "Uncle, please, please consider Miss Hastings! Miss Ingles is a simpleton and Lady Wimberley is patronizing and Miss Caddington is nothing but a witch in woman's clothing . . ."

"Out!"

There was no denying that tone of voice. The girls withdrew at once, but not before catching a glimpse, once more, of his lordship's piece of parchment. It was entitled, rather crisply, "Suitable brides."

Miss Hastings attended a number of soirées and balls in the following few weeks. They were all bittersweet, for though she glowed with anticipation, and was the prettier for it, she could not help but notice that his lordship paid her precious little attention at all, and that the prized offer of the waltz that she cherished so deeply in her memory was not repeated.

Lady Hastings, her mama, tried not to show her disappointment at this, but pushed Amaryllis even harder to find partners for every set. To Amaryllis's extreme discomfort she gave up even her cards to do so, so now there was simply no respite and dozens of young gentlemen were forced by common civility to make their bows.

Amaryllis found this process excruciating and withdrew

more than ever into her shyness. As a result, any suitors she might have had soon gave up, and only Mr. Ratchins kept making sly remarks about matrimony and the "honor he might imminently bestow a certain young lady."

Amaryllis had now ceased to hope that the earl might call, and lived in constant dread that Mr. Ratchins might live up to his promises and do so instead. As far as possible she hid in the herbarium, and what comfort she got was in the delicious scents of lemongrass that pervaded the area, for the propagation had taken very well indeed, and the transformation of rose petals to essences was worth the effort.

She had almost forgotten her strange malady—for such she had come to think of those nonsensical pangs of hope and tenderness that overcame her at times—when she heard the crunch of carriage wheels across the cobbled entrance to Melville House—the town residence they rented for the summer. Her heart sank into her slippers, for they were expecting no guests, and she was still haunted by the notion that Mr. Ratchins might come up to scratch.

She glanced at her gown. It was an old one, for there was no sense in wearing her best silks when she was pottering about the garden—and her hair was all about her face instead of neatly pinned. She fixed this detail, and waited, her heart beating erratically in her chest.

After half an hour or so of suspense, the carriage moved on—she could just see it from the high window of the herbarium, but not any of its details. She heaved a tiny sigh of relief. It could not, after all, have been anyone of consequence.

Chapter Four

How wrong she was proven! It was someone of great consequence indeed, and had she but known it, those few quiet moments in the herbarium were to be her last.

Just as she was trimming some dead leaves off a small tree of Valencia oranges, her mama whirled into the room and positively crushed her to her bosom in an embrace that practically squeezed all the air from her lungs. When she was released, Amaryllis was astounded to note that Lady Hastings was crying, and that the tears were staining her India silk shawl. Lady Hastings did not seem to care.

"Oh, Amaryllis! It is like a dream come true! I knew it would happen, oh, I knew it! Oh, my dear, I am so terribly, terribly happy for you! "

Amaryllis felt a strange lurching in her stomach. Her mama's happiness could surely mean only one thing, and that one thing was something she had been perfectly dreading for weeks.

"Mama?"

"Yes, my angel?"

"Have I received a proposal of marriage?"

"Yes, yes, yes, my poppet! And didn't I tell you it would be so? Oh, how I could ever have doubted . . . oh, Amaryllis I am so happy for you, but you must change at once. That old muslin won't do, you know, not anymore . . ."

"Mama, I have not been consulted!"

"Very proper too, for naturally your papa and my consent had to be obtained first. You surely would not think he would be so improper as to approach you before speaking to us, do you? Now run along, dear, and ask Mattie to dress you in that white fichu with perhaps the string of pearls . . ."

"Mama! Am I not to have a say in this matter?"

Lady Hastings looked suddenly flustered.

"Now, Amaryllis, you are not to create a fuss! In matters as important as this you really must trust your parents. Have we not always had your best interests at heart?"

"Yes, but . . ."

"So then? You are not going to let your silly shyness stand in the way of matrimony, Amaryllis! I won't allow it, I simply won't!"

"Does it not matter whether my affections are engaged?"

"No, Amaryllis, it does not! Such romantical notions are for writers and poets. You shall do very well, my dear, and if you are a trifle shy at first, well, you will grow in confidence as every year passes. That is how it was with your father and myself, and you know how happy and comfortable we have been together!"

"Mama, you can't compare Papa to Mr. Ratchins!"

Lady Hastings stared at her daughter. Then, with a little tremble of laughter, she drew her closer.

"Good Lord, Amaryllis, for an intelligent girl you are really rather slow! We gave Mr. Ratchins his comeuppance about a week ago. I would prefer you remain a spinster forever than marry that odious, pompous creature! Gracious, do you realize he actually expected us to be relieved? Inquired after your dowry too, which is nobody's business but your father's and the man you actually have permission to marry. The effrontery of it, can you imagine? I enjoyed sending him packing, which I shouldn't say, for I do aspire to be a peaceable kind of person, but that man could try the patience of saints!"

Amaryllis felt her legs weaken in relief. Then, as the next obvious question occurred to her, she felt her chest constrict, and she would really have been very close to a faint if she did not have such a remarkable, resolute character.

"Then, Mama . . . ?"

"Oh, Amaryllis, can you not guess? It is the Earl of Devonport who has offered for you and in such charming form, too—you cannot imagine. You are to be a countess, my dear, and my only hope is that I can be present when the likes of Martha Caddington open their *Morning Gazettes*."

The residence was in more of an uproar than Amaryllis had ever known it to be before. From cupboards and stairwells maids and underbutlers and even Cook from the kitchens were taking the opportunity of popping out and staring at her as she made her bewildered progress from the herbarium to her bedchamber above stairs.

Apparently, the secret was less of a secret than she had imagined, for here and there maidservants grinned and bobbed shyly, and even Charlie, hired for his skill with a team of matched bays, whistled as she caught sight of him from the windows.

Amaryllis was shaking and hardly knew what to think, never mind respond, as the servants paid their respects. Even her bedchamber was not private, for her dresser was waiting, and had laid out three of her favorite gowns, not to mention all her mother's jewels upon her bed. Amaryllis politely asked her to leave, and ignored the woman's disappointment as she put her head in her hands and tried so very hard to think.

It all seemed so impossible! The earl had not looked at her once in a fortnight! Oh, he had made his bow to her and exchanged a few civil words, but nothing to suggest . . . nothing to suggest such a step as this! She wondered, for a moment, whether it might all be some cruel joke, then shook her head.

The earl would not behave so wickedly. If he had spoken to her parents, then he was in earnest, though she was still no clearer as to why. When he made his formal proposal, she would ask him. She would overcome her stupid shyness and ask him outright. That, she thought, was the very least she could do.

Thus decided, Amaryllis invited her dresser back and determined to choose the prettiest gown possible. The diamonds she waved away, but a necklet of roses she kept, and a circlet of amethysts for her soft, golden hair. She looked the closest thing to a princess that she had ever done before and viewing her image in the glass, she felt, for once, almost satisfied.

The interview with his lordship was arranged for two o'clock precisely. At that moment—and not a second before—the Earl of Davenport was announced in ringing tones by Carthews, the resident butler. Amaryllis stood up to greet him, as did Lady Hastings, and Lord Hastings, too, who had taken time out from Boodles to accord the earl this civility.

The earl, Amaryllis noted with a sinking heart, was immaculate beyond compare. He was not a dandy, but his elegance was tangible, and his ease with that elegance seemed enviable. He did not stare uncomfortably out of his shirt points as Lord Hastings did, nor did he seem too starched to move, though his doeskins fit every muscle like a glove, and Amaryllis felt the heat pouring into her cheeks as her eyes lingered too long upon this interesting fact.

Lady Hastings smiled indulgently, and after pointedly removing Lord Hastings from his Heppelwhite mahogany shield-back chair, of which he was very fond (and into which he had just thankfully sunk), she announced that under the circumstances it would be perfectly proper for the couple to engage in some moments of private conversation.

As the door closed behind them, Amaryllis felt more nervous than ever, and that marvelous feeling of looking almost princesslike had evaporated. Her circlet of amethysts now sat heavily upon her brow and she found she could hardly dare look up.

Lord Devonport removed the awkwardness of the moment by taking Amaryllis's hand in his and looking deeply into her eyes. They were a lovely color, her truest asset, especially as they were surrounded by those dark, lustrous lashes that seemed to frame her face.

Stephen was not merry, or flirtatious, or even for a moment unsure of himself. He merely took her hand, ungloved it, and slipped upon her finger a gold band sparkling with gems of a deep, and rather unusual hue.

"Amaryllis, will you do me the honor of becoming my bride?"

Amaryllis did not know what had happened to her tongue. It simply wouldn't speak, and as the moments ticked by they seemed more like hours than a few hesitant seconds. The ring felt heavy on her finger, but sparkled with an intensity Amaryllis could not help but find intriguing. Or perhaps that was because Stephen had still not let go of her hand, and she had never felt such an impropriety before, or not for so very long, and her skin tingled with pleasure and apprehension and a million other sensations she could hardly analyze or understand.

After a moment, the sound of the ormolu clock on the mantel became embarrassing, and Stephen found his interest arrested. So! Miss Hastings was not the type of maiden he had latterly encountered. The type who would do anything— anything—to get his ring on her grasping little finger. This lady was the only one who had ever had the honor, yet she seemed to be battling against some inner demon. He admired her for it, though he felt slight exasperation on his own account.

"You hesitate?"

Amaryllis flushed. "You must think me so ill-mannered! I

am sorry, my lord, there can naturally be no question that the answer is yes."

"And yet, I think, there *is* such a question. Your eyes speak volumes and you tremble, my dear."

"It is just so . . . so . . . sudden."

"It must seem so to you. For me it is not sudden at all. I have been thinking of matrimony for a long while."

"With me?"

Stephen smiled gently. "No, not necessarily with you, for I have long known that my succession must be secured. Indeed, I find myself wishing more and more for that happy state known as fatherhood. My own father, you see, was rather distant. I would like to reverse that cycle, if I can. You are not the first I have contemplated marriage with, but you are eminently suitable and I feel we shall deal handsomely together."

He hesitated as he saw the crushed expression on Amaryllis's face. His tone grew gentle.

"You may know that there are several ladies I would not even contemplate marrying no matter what their dowry or lineage. I may not be in love with you—indeed, it would be foolish to pretend so—but I am nevertheless glad that you are the one I have chosen. I feel certain I shall not be disappointed in my choice."

For an instant, Amaryllis wanted to take the ring back and throw it in his face. He was not offering for her out of affection, merely out of calculation! It is tremendously lowering to think one is to be joined in wedlock because the matter is convenient, because an heir is required, because one's bloodlines are appropriate . . . she felt ready to burst with chagrin.

Then, as the moment grew as dangerous as it was ever likely to be, she noticed that the earl's eyes were kind. Though they might be slightly ironic, they were laughing as much at himself as at her.

"It is strange, is it not, how society never seems satisfied until it has thrust every last bachelor and every last spinster into wedlock?"

Amaryllis, recovering her composure, nodded.

"It seems a consuming passion, my lord."

"Indeed, and we are doubtless going to be grist for the gossip mills."

"My lord . . ."

"If we are going to be betrothed, you might just as well call me by my given name. It is Stephen, in case you were unaware."

Amaryllis blushed, for naturally in her first throes of love she had discovered all she could about the noble Stephen Redding, and his earldom of Devonport. She did not say as much, however, but murmured that "Stephen" sounded too . . .

"Familiar?"

She blushed again, if this was possible. My lord thought it a pity that she usually wore her hair braided so severely, or that her bonnets always hid half her face. She looked so much prettier with her honey-colored locks flowing softly about her face. When she blushed, her eyes grew round and misty.

She nodded. "Yes. It is too familiar. We hardly know each other, after all."

"That can be rectified. I am not an ogre, and though I might be some eight years older than you, I fancy I am not yet in my dotage. Come, call me Stephen, for I shall certainly call you Amaryllis!"

"Stephen . . ." Amaryllis hesitated, for though it was difficult, now was the time for plain speaking. Now, whilst the door was shut between them and the prying ears beyond. Now, before she was chaperoned to the alter or married, when the question would be too late to be asked.

He waited, not prompting her, or making the matter any easier. The ormolu clocked ticked on the mantel. Amaryllis took a deep breath. Then she raised her eyes to Stephen's and smiled.

Chapter Five

Lord Redding needed to catch his breath. Her smile was more devastating than he had noticed before. He folded his arms behind his back. Nothing could be so intemperate as kissing her now. He had seen what became of relationships that began as love matches.

His own mama's had been a case in point and the matter had been disastrous. His father—long deceased—had trampled all over her feelings, dominated the household, and reduced her to many hours of tears.

As a little boy this had made the greatest impression upon him, and he'd resolved long ago not to make the same mistake himself. He did not wish to see any wife of his hanging upon his shirtsleeves, her happiness dependent on his smiles. Neither, of course, did he wish to be the silly fellow whose heart burnt every time his wife breathed, and whose every moment was caught up in trifling jealousies or infelicitous calf love. He cursed himself for a fool to be so taken by Amaryllis's smile.

He bent his mind, instead, to the question.

"My lord . . . Stephen . . . may I ask . . . that is . . . I cannot help wondering why *I* am your choice. You are not in love with me—how could you be?—and I cannot believe the nonsense put about by my mama that our land marches close together. Hastings land is but a garden meadow compared with yours! There must be some other reason for your offer and I believe I have the right to know it before taking this . . . this . . . step."

A faint gleam hovered about Stephen's eyes.

"This horrible step?"

"No. Oh, no!" Amaryllis's answer was speaking. "This . . . *significant* step. Marriage is a very final thing."

"So is spinsterhood."

"You are saving me from spinsterhood?"

Amaryllis's tone was panicked. This must surely be the most humiliating reason ever given for a marriage offer!

"I would not be so unmannerly as to say such a thing, but I overheard one or two remarks about you which were both absurd and . . . and . . . downright nonsensical. I could not take up the cudgels in your defense—that would have been improper—but I did think that if I made you an offer it would silence a good few tongues."

Silence a good few tongues! Amaryllis felt the color rise to her cheeks in mortification. This betrothal would not silence tongues! It would set them wagging like she was a nine-day wonder, no less!

Still, the thought of the likes of Martha Caddington being forced to give her precedence was pleasant, but more like a silly daydream than any kind of reality. It was not the best basis for a marriage, though Amaryllis felt absurdly grateful that someone of Stephen's caliber should put himself to such pains on her behalf. She brushed back a tear and hoped Lord Redding would think it was merely sunshine in her eyes.

"My dear, I have expressed myself badly! I would not have offered for you for that reason alone, for there are many young ladies who suffer from spiteful tongues and I cannot be expected to rescue all of them! No, let us just say, Amaryllis, that *you* are saving me from bachelorhood."

Amaryllis laughed, and the most delightful dimples appeared on her cheeks. Stephen wondered why he had never noticed them before. Perhaps because she was always so earnest in company!

"You talk in riddles, sir. You need no saving, for there must be a hundred young ladies at least dangling after you."

"Indeed. Dangling after my title, you mean. I shall be perfectly direct, Amaryllis. I need an heir—preferably, though not necessarily—in the immediate future. I would very much like to be a father. My estimable mama is also badgering me like a bloodhound to marry.

"Whilst there are several suitable young candidates—I shall not hide this from you—you seem to me to be the most sensible and the kindest. I cannot say I will make a good husband, for I almost certainly shall not. In matters of—shall we say the heart?—I shall tread my own way and expect you to be complacent. I shall always, however, accord you respect, for though I may not love you, I *do* admire and like you."

Stephen took a breath and noted, with a frown, the high flush on Amaryllis's cheeks. His tone was gentler as he continued. "I do not expect you to care for me, Amaryllis—not in the traditional way—but I do think you might grow to hold me in esteem and that is as good a basis I know of for such a union."

Amaryllis hardly knew how to respond. He continued with a wry smile.

"Do not, I pray you, look so terribly forlorn! I do not offer you love in the conventional sense, but I am not an ogre! You will be compensated by a title, such as it is worth, all the pin money you could desire, and the company of my young nieces whose acquaintances you have already made. In due course, of course, you shall have a child of your own. We shall hope it is an heir, for nothing will make me—or, indeed, my mother—happier than this felicitous outcome.'

Amaryllis blushed, but dared not speak of this time, for fear of appearing either ignorant or worse, eager. He, she noted, did not appear to be suffering from any degree of overeagerness. As for ignorance, she knew perfectly well he was not afflicted with that malady! News of his paramours was almost legendary.

She questioned, him, therefore, on the safer topic.

"Your nieces. You say I have met them. I cannot think when . . . ?"

A grin almost crossed his stern, attractive features. It made him look human and charming. Amaryllis told herself not to be a fool.

"Can you not? The night of my sister—Lady Charlotte's—ball at Devonport. Lady Charlotte is abroad and I, for my pains, stand as ward to the two young scamps."

"You mean . . ."

"Yes, the iced gateaux and the . . . sugar plums, was it? But we digress."

Amaryllis thought she could detect a twinkle lurking in my lord's eye, but she could not be certain.

For a good ten minutes more the discussion became rather more earnest. The earl, in an effort to be perfectly honest from the outset—made it abundantly—but politely—plain he was not interested in Amaryllis personally, though he liked her a good deal and thought she would make an excellent countess.

He had, however, no intention of altering his bachelor way of life or removing to his considerable estates in the country. He required an heir, a chatelaine, and an escape from the insufferable debutantes who seemed more and more inventive in their attempts to snare him.

He did not mention that he found himself drawn to Amaryllis, that it had taken a great deal of resolution not to dance with her in the last two weeks, that he found her more charming than he cared to admit, and that, even as he spoke, he was yearning foolishly to kiss her pretty lips.

No! He omitted such matters as unimportant to the contract before them. In truth, he felt uncomfortable with the matter, for he had no wish to allow Amaryllis false hopes and his amorous adventuring had been extensive enough for him to realize that such burning attractions often did not endure more than a sennight.

So he continued on in a cool and collected manner, outlining all the advantages that would accrue to her if she became his betrothed.

Amaryllis was informed that as countess she could do precisely as she pleased within the bounds of propriety, she might command an ample supply of pin money, and she might escape the indignity of dwindling into unwed loneliness. It was a crushing proposal, not the type of Amaryllis's dreams, but she accepted quietly, if not joyfully.

Stephen had done her the justice of being truthful and for that she was grateful. It gave her the space to hide her budding feelings for him—no, to *crush* her feelings for him—without exposing all the pain of her longing. There was no question of her refusing such an offer. Her parents expected her to accept, and she had no reason not to, save for some foolish bit of daydreaming.

Hundreds of arranged marriages were made each morning and if her own was not quite out of a storybook, she was no worse off than dozens of girls before her. After all, Lord Redding was no Mr. Ratchins! Her mouth tilted upward at the comparison and the earl, unbeknownst to her, almost groaned in anguish.

He had never wanted to kiss someone so much in all of his life, but he knew perfectly well he must remain controlled.

Amaryllis, having accepted the proposal, did not leave the drawing room without a few victories of her own. In exchange for such a convenient marriage, she asked that her judgment be respected. She shyly demanded that she be seen harmoniously in the company of the earl on such occasions as was necessary to avoid speculation. She also asked, with a little catch to her throat, that she be permitted free rein with the earl's nieces.

The earl, surprised at this show of independence, but not unduly alarmed, agreed affably. Miss Hastings, after all, was a sensible young woman, if not a diamond of the first water. He did not wish to be disturbed on every small matter relating to his nieces, and basic manners was not an unduly stressful demand.

He had already resolved be kind to her both in private and in public, and to accord her the respect she deserved as his wife, as the mother of a future earl, and as a peeress of the realm. On all other issues, he would go his own way. He bowed magnanimously, white teeth gleaming, and acquiesced, with a faint smile, to her terms.

Miss Hastings, who did not know, until that moment, that she had been holding her breath, released it and afforded him one of her rare and excessively beautiful smiles. She held out her hand to shake on the agreement but was disconcerted to find it taken from her and kissed, gently, lightly, slightly ironically.

Such was the effect of his lordship's touch that Amaryllis felt light-headed. It was all she could do not to snatch her hand away, but the moment passed before she disgraced herself in such a ridiculous manner. It was just that she had not expected the earl's touch to be so . . . she could not find the correct adjective, even in her secret thoughts.

She curtsied, and he bowed gravely, but he looked troubled. The last thing he wanted was to be saddled with a wife who suffered a *tendre* for him! He would be roasted by his friends and feel a cad himself for not being able to amply reciprocate the sentiments.

He was in no doubt that despite his troublesome stirring of passion he would be unable to feel remotely drawn to Miss Hastings, who did not resemble his first love or his string of subsequent paramours in the slightest. They, of course, were

all beauties of the first order, raven-haired, curvaceous, selfish . . . he did not know where that particular thought came
from, but he supposed it was true.

Still, when one is beautiful and can command all eyes, a
certain degree of self orientation is forgivable. Expected,
even. Stephen shifted uncomfortably with the concept, which
did not sit true. His thoughts moved on to Amaryllis, with her
shy smile and her impulsive kindness.

There was no doubt that with her demure looks and fair,
understated coloring, she was gentleness itself. He had noted
this on several different occasions, though he doubted
whether the recipients of her warm spirit were ever even
aware of her benevolence.

Yes, there was no denying a generous nature behind the
limpid, somewhat insipid looks. Lord Redding, accustomed
to thinking of Amaryllis in such terms, put aside his sudden
fancies, and the fact that Amaryllis, today, looked anything
but insipid. She was beautiful, but he, lost in his reverie,
would not admit as much to himself.

In want of a wife, he had chosen the enduring quality of
kindness over beauty, generosity over passion. Not that he
ever intended to forsake beauty or passion, but his liaisons
were discreet, and they had the indubitable advantage of
being expendable.

Wives were different again. Wives were to be mothers and
he wanted his offspring to have someone kind and caring to
turn to in times of trouble. Miss Hastings, he thought with a
slight sigh, was eminently suitable.

Lady Hastings was in high alt, and Lord Hastings, who
knew little of Amaryllis's previous failure to "take" was
nonetheless gravely pleased. He enjoyed the round of con-
gratulations at Boodle's when the announcement appeared in
the *Gazette*, and Lady Hastings's home had never been so full
of morning visitors.

As for Amaryllis, she had mixed feelings. It would be impossible to say she did not feel a certain exhilaration when my lord danced attendance on her, or when he gazed deeply into her eyes at the exact moment that Martha Caddington's sour gaze alighted upon them.

Indeed, he went out of his way to ensure that she was seated beside him at dinner, that her glass was never empty, that their hands touched for a flicker of an instant (but long enough for certain debutantes to notice), and that he commented, in general terms, about his great good fortune in securing such a beautiful and noble bride.

Unfortunately, this kindness was too much for Amaryllis, who felt certain he was only being compassionate. She realized he was wreaking his revenge on the Martha Caddingtons of the world, but it was not exacted without expense.

Chapter Six

Each time he smiled at her, each time he complimented her, touched her, and hovered over her made her feel more beautiful or breathless than she had ever felt before, she had to remind herself that it was all a sham, that Lord Redding was rescuing her from spinsterhood, that he was simply teaching uncivil debutantes a rather pointed lesson. He was being kind to a wallflower. She must remember that, and learn to live with it.

His lordship, on the other hand, was rather amusing himself. The gossip columns had run a funny cartoon which figured a certain Miss M.C. colored all over in green, for envy. She was curtsying to a certain Miss A.H. and swallowing a drink labeled "gall." He told himself it was this revenge that was causing him to hover at Amaryllis's side.

In truth, it was more than that. He had not known, before they were thrown continually in each other's company, that she was bright, intelligent, and showed flashes of the ironic humor that very nearly matched his own. He had known she was kind, but not that she was inventive, conversant in the classics and interested in horse breeding. Not a fit conversation for a lady, perhaps, but Miss Hastings became animated when she spoke of it, which led Stephen to speak about his stables, which in turn caused her to forget her shyness. When Amaryllis forgot to be shy, her eyes—her finest feature—lit up with animation and her cheeks glowed with vitality.

He found himself wondering why he had always thought her so insipid, then reasoned it must have been her gowns. They were always of a pale shade (untrue, for the one she had worn for Lady Charlotte's ball had glittered becomingly), but Stephen, at a loss for any other explanation, was convinced. Also, she had now been coaxed to loosen her braids and wear her fair hair loose, a very advantageous move, for though his lordship admired brunettes, the softness of Amaryllis's locks, and the paleness of her skin against the honey gold was alluring.

Stephen decided she needed a set of diamond pins to scatter about her. When he had bought her these, and enjoyed her exclamations of soft delight, he could not seem to help himself. He found himself spending his days dreaming up little objects that might delight her, or little treats like a visit to Hamilton Palace, where the duke's interest in horse breeding was matched only by his interest in art, both of which were favorites with Amaryllis.

During this time, however, he had to catch himself up short, for the stupid penchant he seemed to have developed kept making him want to do something he might later regret. Almost, almost he kissed her at Asham, where the grounds were so sweet and the waterfall nearby trickled appealingly.

Miss Hastings's maid was safely stowed in the chaise and the moment had seemed ripe, oh, far too ripe . . . then at Vauxhall, where the displays of fireworks could hardly have been brighter than the sparks he felt between them, he had taken her in his arms and succumbed to the moment.

Miss Hastings's mouth was sweeter than he had dreamed of, and softer. He could have drowned in that moment, only her arms crept about him timidly, and he cursed himself for a damn, idiotic, foolish fool. He must not allow her to have expectations, he must not expect her tender emotions to settle into anything deeper than affection for her husband.

If she loved him, he'd be lost, marooned in guilt, incapable of offering her more than she needed . . . he would, in fact, be a veritable cad. He must set his distance from the start. He must be firm about it, else this marriage would have no hope.

He set her from him sternly and apologized shortly. Amaryllis, sensing the mood change, was puzzled, and the raging pulses she was experiencing now slowed miserably. The fireworks seemed discordant and the night darker than a moment before.

The earl had coldly helped Amaryllis into the chaise and hardly murmured a word to her on the return trip, partly because his heart was racing, partly because he felt a fool, and partly because he was angry his little wallflower was looking far too delectable for his peace of mind.

Amaryllis, sure she had offended, could nevertheless not work out where her mistake lay. Miserably, she sat with her fingers clenched, watching the sparkle on her betrothal ring against the cozy flame of the interior gas lamp. Her own inner sparkle seemed to have vanished.

After that, Lord Redding kept his distance and Amaryllis saw him only at those engagements to which they had mutually been invited. The days flew by, though, as Lady Hastings planned the wedding feast, and the bridal breakfast, the floral arrangements, the displays, the accommodation of guests from as far afield as Paris and even Rome. Then, of course, there was the wedding gown to consider, a shimmering confection in organdy with pearls stitched into every seam and diamonds (provided by the earl) interlaced subtly with every swirl of broidery Anglaise.

Dressers arrived, and milliners, and seamstresses from every corner of London. Merchants with bolts of silk, morning callers of every description, florists, oh, the list was endless, and Amaryllis barely had time to take a breath, never mind to think. When she saw Stephen, he was everything that was civil—indeed, she could hardly fault him on that score—but the intimacy that seemed to have developed between them was dimmed. And though her pulses still raced uncontrollably when their eyes met, and she still shivered, a little at his touch, these touches were rarer, as if Stephen himself were conscious of the matter and rationing them accordingly.

If Amaryllis only knew how much he burned for her! He steeled himself, now, to see her, for even her smile affected him in a manner he found salutary, and her gowns, increasingly modish, revealed delicate areas of flesh he had not previously been aware of, never mind been permitted to glimpse.

Worse, other gentlemen seemed to have noticed these advantages, for she now seemed to have a court about her, and he sometimes had to wait to greet her or scribble his name on her card or reserve her for the supper dance. Once, he had taken the matter for granted and positively seethed when he found Staunton Reynolds had beaten him to it. He nearly demanded his rights as her betrothed, then considered how foolish he would look.

He had retired, but in a black sulk, something wholly alien to him and therefore even more tiresome. Sometimes he wished he had never set eyes on Amaryllis, nor never chanced to see her hide sweets for his nieces in her reticule. Even now, his lips curved at the memory and a twinkle appeared in his deep, hazel-green eyes. He could not complain, however, for every time she saw him her eyes softened and her cheeks glowed with color.

There was never a time she did not prefer to be in his company, a fact he both loved and abhorred, for though she did not precisely wear her heart on his sleeve, he knew she felt a *tendre* for him and this was against everything he had so carefully planned.

His one consolation was that Martha Caddington looked alternately green with envy and red with rage, neither of which color suited her sultry looks. For a devilment he invited her to dance, but he held her at such a formal distance and

Amaryllis at such a tender one that Miss Caddington had no time to gloat; indeed, she seethed all the more.

Amaryllis, confused by my lord's strange whimsies—first tender, then cold, blushed uncertainly but could not resist Stephen's smile, or the firm arms that held her closer than they strictly should.

The marriage took place with all the pomp Lady Hastings had wished for, and the dowager Countess of Devonport considered fitting. She liked Amaryllis very much, though wished there was not so much distance between her and her son. On closer observation, however, she seemed satisfied, a small smile playing about her regal cheeks.

It was the object of her heart to see a grandson born before another year was out, not only for the succession, as she had mentioned time and time again to Stephen, but also because she thought her son would benefit greatly from being a papa. She felt certain that unlike his father before him, all his more tender emotions would surface with a baby to delight in.

She was tired of reading reports about his exploits in *The Tattler*, she was bored with the succession of opera dancers he paraded and that dreadful Lady Luttlow, who all the world knew to be his established mistress in Honeydew Street.

No, she was wise enough not to speak of any of these concerns to her son, but glancing at Amaryllis through her lorgnette, she laughed to herself. She considered she had done very well indeed with that little list of hers. Amaryllis Hastings, who would have thought it? But she would serve, certainly she would serve!

Miss Hastings became Lady Amaryllis Redding, Countess of Devonport before the morning was out. Her mama shed several happy tears and her papa whispered that he was very proud indeed of her. Misses Clementine and Victoria Farnstone disobeyed all orders by rushing out and hugging

Amaryllis, so that her gown was crushed and her veil—a delicate gossamer silk of the palest pink—had to be adjusted.

Amaryllis did not care, for the girls' laughing welcome was like the freshest of wild breezes to her, and her spirits lifted unaccountably. At her request, they were flower girls, and looked as pretty as pictures in gowns of shimmering pearl with snowdrops in their hair. Unfortunately, their mischievous faces were not nearly so demure as their dresses, but since they got up to no more mischief than tugging at Miss Miranda's sash and spilling tea over a violently ill Miss Caddington, no one scolded at all.

Stephen, handsome beyond imagining in his formal dress of velvet knee breeches, clocked stockings, and a jacket that Weston himself had forged from the closest fitting fabric imaginable, took Amaryllis's hand solemnly, but his eyes were hooded, so Amaryllis knew not what he was thinking, or whether he regretted his impulse of kindness.

The day passed as a dream and it was not long before Amaryllis was being tucked into a traveling chaise, bound for her new home in her husband's country seat. There were cheers and bells pealing and a thousand—surely it must have been a thousand at least?—well-wishers wishing them all happy.

For an instant, Amaryllis's eyes rested on Lady Luttlow, who had not been invited to the wedding, but who nevertheless was present as the coach set off. She was startled by the hostility in her eyes, but had no time to question the matter, for the horses were off and she was alone, at last, with her husband.

Shyness fought with longing and the desire to appear conformable and sophisticated. Stephen, had he but been thinking straight, might have laughed aloud at Amaryllis's attempts to be engaging. She alternated between languor and extreme timidity, but succeeded in doing nothing more than arousing Stephen's senses.

She was so soft, and her hair smelled so natural, so unlike the heady perfumes he was accustomed to . . . he wondered, for the hundredth time that day whether he ought to kiss her, to cradle her in his arms, to murmur the sweet nonsenses that he longed to. Gracious, he should push aside, for heaven's sakes, those voluminous skirts with their shimmering jewels. He should cover her mouth with his own, make her his in truth. He wanted, he discovered with a pang, to be her husband in more than just name, for more reasons than he had promised.

He wondered what she would say to such a change of sentiments. How pompous he had been, laying down the rules of their betrothal! He could cringe when he remembered some of the things he had said . . . worse, what he had omitted. He had practically told her he meant to be no husband to her, that she was simply a practical means to fatherhood.

He was not a fool, he knew perfectly well she would know of Lady Luttlow and his other paramours. It was he, after all, who had invited the woman if not to the wedding, than at least to the breakfast. He sank back into the squabs and tried his level best to ignore his annoying desires. For once, he would have been grateful for a chaperone.

Chapter Seven

Amaryllis, Countess of Devonport, only nibbled on her dinner. The servants were all very kind, and discreet. She had had a wonderful scented bath and rose petals were strewn about her chamber, in deference to her wedded state. Her maid, appointed by the earl himself, had had her gowns unpacked and pressed in record time, so that she had a considerable choice to agonize over when her bath was at an end and the time had come, at last, to change for dinner.

She chose something simple, a stark contrast to the grand confection she had been wearing earlier. It was a gown of pastel blue trimmed in silver and embroidered, at the hems, in a darker blue to match her eyes. Lady Hastings had been positively triumphant with the result, but Amaryllis felt strangely nervous and rather shy.

This was to be her first dinner alone with her husband and it was natural that she feel a constriction in her throat as she was led down the main staircase to the dining room below.

Stephen was waiting for her, equally tense, but when he saw his wife he smiled and she felt all that awkward shyness melting away. He seemed resolved to set her at ease, and by the second remove her eyes were shining and she was able to enjoy several of the absurd *on-dits* that were doing their rounds about town.

Between them, though, there was a tension, for it is not every night that is one's wedding night, and not every marriage that begins in such constrained circumstances such as theirs. So Amaryllis nibbled, despite the excellence of the meal, and Stephen poured her some negus, which whilst sweet and hot and somewhat spicy, soothed her nerves.

Presently, conversation faltered. The candles glittered about them, and Lord Redding was regarding his bride with a peculiar sensation of pride mingled with frustrated desire.

"Amaryllis, I . . ."

"Yes?" Amaryllis almost whispered, for she could tell Stephen's tone had changed and her heart was beating so loud she was afraid he would hear it. Indeed, he did, and he reached out and felt it for a moment, so Amaryllis thought she might faint from both embarrassment at her transparency and something more, much more. . . . Her eyes darkened, and Stephen groaned, for he was certainly not in control as he had planned to be.

He had planned to make a little speech about settling into the role, no hurry for heirs . . . gracious, he could not remember the half of it. Then suddenly, he no longer wished to. He pulled Amaryllis into his arms and kissed her the way he wanted to, the way he had resolved not to, the very way in which Amaryllis had tormented herself with forbidden dreams.

The candles had long burned down before he had finished exploring her delightful mouth, with those expressive curves that tilted so sweetly upward when she was not remembering to be shy.

He had long since pulled out all the diamond pins and the posy of snowdrops she had adopted with her simple evening gown. Her hair, as he imagined, was soft and fresh and sweet, unscented with powders but no less alluring for their lack. He twisted her hair about her, then pulled her toward him again so that she had no choice but to draw closer and laugh softly as he kissed her.

As the last flames flickered in the grate, he raised his brows

expressively and asked her whether she wished to explore her
own pretty bed or his own. Amaryllis swallowed hard, for she
feared that if she threw herself at Stephen, the nature of their
relationship would change forever.

She doubted whether she could hold on to her heart, steady
her feelings, smile blithely as he became remote . . . then she
stopped doubting as she saw the wry smile that twisted his
features, almost as if he himself were hesitant, hanging anxiously upon her decision.

"Yours, Stephen," she breathed.

His lordship nodded and lifted her gently from her formal
seat. Her gown trailed the floor dramatically as he carried her
up the stairs, past the marble sculptures of Venus and An-
dromedes, past the portraits of earls and countesses past, past
several candelabras with wicks of varying lengths and lumi-
nous flames of orange gold, past everything, in fact, except
the mahogany door to his own sumptuous chamber. This he
opened with his elegant tasseled boot and closed, again, with
a firm and feverish click.

That night, Lady Amaryllis Redding forgot all her troubled
anxieties. Her ignorance was more than compensated for by
Stephen's worldliness, and though she was still young and
youthfully innocent, she nevertheless became countess in
far more than just name.

The days that followed were probably the loveliest Amaryllis had ever experienced. The girls were back from their
convenient holiday in London—not for the world would he
have them anywhere near his home on his wedding night—
and there were lively games and a great deal of truancy and
much laughter. Time and time again Amaryllis thought what
a good father he would be, for he was not too pompous to
play hide-and-seek, or bob for apples, or remember what it
was like to muddy one's clothes or pinch pies from the
kitchen. He was a master of charades, and kept them in fits
of laughter, save for the odd moments of tenderness.

Stephen still felt uncomfortable about these——he wished he could preserve the boundaries he had set, but every morning his resolve became less and by evening had evaporated completely, so that the new countess had not, as yet, had the pleasure of sleeping in her own pretty bed or waking to the chocolate her maid promised her each morning.

Instead, it was Stephen's bed that drew her, and Stephen's pot of hot coffee that scalded her tongue each new day and filled her heart with pride and secret delight.

In the mornings they would ride, or open letters together, or crack chestnuts or fish (though without any great measure of success, save for a single trout which Amaryllis swore had been her catch, and Stephen swore was his). In the afternoons, Amaryllis would play the flute, or the harpsichord, or stab at some needlework, which she hated but felt she really ought to improve upon. The earl laughed at this, and would more often than not throw the horrible thing away, but Amaryllis would always smilingly fetch it out of the bin. They would read together, for their tastes were remarkably similar, though Stephen found Pope too stern and Amaryllis found his penchant for Byron amusing, though she loved to hear his deep, velvety voice read certain passages aloud.

But she was still naturally shy, and she could feel the earl's restraint at times. She reminded herself firmly that she must not complain or grieve when this brief idyll came to an end, as it must.

The end came far quicker for her than she had imagined, for Stephen received two letters one morning, one from Lord Diggory, his best friend, and one from Lady Luttlow. It could not have been a worse juxtaposition, and when he excused himself shortly to peruse them in his study, Amaryllis felt a deep sense of foreboding that lasted the whole morning and a good part into the afternoon, too, despite a vigorous ride and several games of charades.

Stephen did not join them, though her eyes searched the

horizons for him anxiously. She was too timid to enter his study uninvited, so she did not know that he sat there with a wry expression on his countenance, and his hands clasped bitterly across his brow. She did not know that he poured himself two glasses of brandy, nor that he scrawled and carefully franked two return missives.

Lady Luttlow, of course, was begging him to return to London "for it is so tedious without you, my dear," but there were also veiled hints that if he did not immediately restore their previous amicable situation she might be forced to bestow her pleasures elsewhere. This note, heavily scented and underlined in purple ink, quickly found a place in his lordship's fire.

The second, however, stung, for it contained laughing jibes about being caught in a parson's mousetrap. There was even an enclosure from the *Gazette* about "a certain Lord R. who was in increasing danger of falling in love with his wife." The *ton* apparently found the notion amusing and Stephen, who should have scorned both messages, fell instead into the trap of scorning himself.

He had been weak, and selfish, and oh, so stupid. He had not only *not* kept the distance between himself and his wife, he had been as eager to close it as she. As eager as a greenhorn! He could squirm when he thought how careless he had been, how quickly Amaryllis had got under his skin, undermined his resolve, made him husband in deed as well as name.

Well, that was not what he wanted! He wanted his freedom without constraints. He had been at *pains* to tell her so! Indeed, he had only chosen her because she was lonely and an antidote. He had never intended to marry a beauty that held him captivated by her every charm. She was bewitching and he simply refused to be bewitched. He had resolved long before the first stirrings of manhood that his would be a reasonable union, one founded on respect and integrity rather than love.

Love, he knew, could be suffocating. His mama had loved his father and had exposed herself cruelly to a multitude of unkindnesses. If she had not felt so passionate, she would never have been so hurt. Stephen shook his head. The gossips were right! He *was* in danger of falling in love with his wife! He would be a laughingstock if he did not do something drastic.

In this resolute state of mind, the earl sent his missives on to London and prepared himself for the trip back to his Mayfair residence.

He expected tears or pleas and hardened his heart. In essence, he received neither, for Amaryllis had been expecting such from the start. It made it no easier for her, though, but she resolutely nodded and smiled and agreed that of course he must return.

The girls pleaded with him to stay, but Amaryllis hushed them, and Stephen frowned, though in truth he had never spent a more delightful time than with these scamps and his own—had he but admitted it!—very dear wife.

Again, that terrible yearning for children like Vicky and Clem, to start a family with Amaryllis, to have a child of his own . . . he closed his eyes firmly to such wishful visions. Amaryllis was becoming more part of his dreams than his own flesh and blood. He was placing more importance on her presence as a mother than on dreams of the heir himself.

He was not a fatherly type. He didn't know why he had ever thought he was. Foolishness! When his heir was born, he would be brought up properly in the nursery and presented to him on such occasions as were appropriate. But something in his heart mocked him. He got up from the table abruptly and disappeared into the house. Two days later, he was gone.

Amaryllis determined not to be forlorn. She threw herself into her new home and family. She took to teaching the girls herself when they played truant, so in the end, they were not truant at all, and, indeed, they had learned more in the few months since Amaryllis's arrival than they had learned in a year of deportment classes.

The governess, a kindly woman, but pale and of ill health, was only too grateful to the new countess, so the regime remained unchallenged.

The Countess of Redding also took a keen interest in the stables and in the bloodstock of her nearest neighbor, Sir Hugh Finlay-Orb, an easygoing country gentleman who happened to share her passion for bloodstock. When she was not consulting Sir Hugh, she was doing the rounds of the district, for a positive heap of calling cards had arrived for her, and there was simply no end to the amount of invitations she received.

Amaryllis was still reserved in company, but there was no doubt that her new rank helped a great deal—it gave her confidence, and no one would have believed that the shy little mouse who had sat out most of the dances at Lady Coverford's ball was now the poised young lady who honored the neighborhood with her wit and occasional bright and dazzling smile.

At night, however. Amaryllis felt the loneliest, for without Stephen the residence seemed very large and cavernous, and though there was much to read in the library, and much to discover in the various drawing and music rooms, she could not settle her thoughts, or devote her attention to the well-cared-for tomes as she should.

She found herself staring out of windows, dreaming of those first magical nights of her marriage. Oh, if only Stephen felt the same way about her as she did about him!

But she must not be maudlin, nor should she complain. The situation had been plain to her from the outset, and she had no reason to regret matters now. She wondered, for the hundredth time, what Stephen was doing, and she blushed when she re-

membered that house on Honeydew Street. She stood up rest-
lessly and took up her embroidery frame. If she concentrated
on the complicated pattern, she would not be able to torment
herself with improper—and decidedly unpleasant—thoughts.

Chapter Eight

Improper thoughts were exactly on Lord Redding's mind as he sent up his card to Lady Luttlow. It was a mere courtesy really, for he expected her to be within and he had already divested himself of his jacket and cane when she made her appearance. Very fetching it was, too, in a gown that could hardly be called modest, so low-cut as it was. Her skirts were dampened and Lord Redding noted that she had applied an alluring patch to her slightly rouged cheeks. Well, doubtless *she* thought it alluring. He did not, though he was not so unmannerly as to say so.

Indeed, he wanted no conversation at all, for Lady Luttlow's finest points lay not in speech, but in the seductiveness of her touch. Unfortunately, though she hovered close to him, in a manner he had always regarded as inviting, she also seemed desirous of verbal reassurances.

Perhaps she was threatened by his lordship's marriage, though such inconveniences were commonplace to the *demimonde* and should really have affected nothing at all. Perhaps the sight of Amaryllis in her wedding gown had come as a shock.

Lady Luttlow, who had come by her title by a scandalous marriage to the Baron Westenbury, who had thankfully not survived the Peninsular wars to know how many times he had been cuckolded, was annoyed. She had been perfectly reconciled to a simpering little wallflower becoming Stephen's bride. Indeed, she had laughed at the matter, for even those who are not admitted to the illustrious venues of the *haute ton* know something of what takes place within their hallowed walls.

Amaryllis, as far as she had been aware, was one of those unfortunate young ladies who simply did not "take." For all her acceptable lineage, she was an antidote.

No one—*no one*—had said anything about her being an entrancing beauty with lashes that she, Eugenia Ponteforth Luttlow, would have personally killed for. She might have scratched Amaryllis's eyes out if she'd had the opportunity. Since she had not, she had spent the first weeks of this annoying marriage endeavoring to make the new countess a laughingstock. Now, she made her first grave mistake. She passed an uncomplimentary comment about Amaryllis to Stephen's face, never dreaming that he would be offended.

"How is your little wallflower? How terribly dreary for you to have to marry such a creature!" Lady Luttlow tittered seductively and fanned herself with an ivory creation topped with seven curling plumes in seven dashing colors. Stephen, who had been about to explore Lady Luttlow's scant bodice, now straightened himself up coldly.

"I will not have you speak that way of my wife."

A trilling laugh greeted this comment.

"Oh, but how perfectly sweet! The . . . *countess* . . . has a gallant at her disposal. So medieval, don't you think?"

The earl, who had not missed the hesitation over "countess" nor the veiled hint that Amaryllis needed a defender, closed his eyes.

He was unused to such waves of anger as he was experiencing. It had obviously not for a moment struck Lady Luttlow that he might actually *like* his wife. That his paramour should feel patronizing was simply too much for him. Suddenly, he found her scent more than just overpowering—it was nauseating, and he could not help but notice the fine lines that creased her forehead and eyelids, but were penciled over in alabaster paint. None of these details had ever concerned him, but even her buxom advantages seemed to have lost their thrall.

Perhaps because he was comparing them with soft, shy, rounded curves . . . but he must not think thus! He opened his eyes and stood up coldly.

"My lady, I think you and I have reached the end of our acquaintance. You will find I am not ungenerous if you call upon my banker, Hargreaves and Fireston on the morrow."

Lady Luttlow paled. Her veiled threats had been meant as a taunt, not to be taken at face value! Stephen was every courtesan's dream—generous, handsome and seasoned enough not to be a tiresome greenhorn. There was every advantage to maintaining the alliance,

The only other men on her horizon was Lord Fortesque, who no one—simply no one—could compare with Stephen, and Mr. Gregory Dacks, who was a skinflint. She seethed, but was careful enough not to show Stephen her extreme displeasure. Instead, she leaned over very calculatedly, so his view of her charms was really first-rate. She tried a childish giggle at his silly humor, but when that wouldn't fadge, she became cloyingly seductive so that Stephen had to literally hold her at arm's length, his masculine strength obvious with every tensed muscle.

This galvanized Lady Luttlow into even more panic at her loss. Unfortunately, it also caused her to forget that jealousy was not a particularly enticing trait. She fought to narrow the gap between them challengingly. Then, in a low voice, she spat out her fury.

"What? So leg-shackled to that . . . that . . . creature that you cannot see the advantages of experience over youth? It is not as if she is a diamond of the first water! Far from it! She failed to take this Season and if it were not for your intervention she would very likely be packed off to Bath with no more hope of a match than . . ."

"Than yourself?" Stephen's tone was smooth and belied his sudden desire to catch Lady Luttlow at her jeweled throat and throttle her. He did not, of course, but Eugenia was in no doubt about his restraint.

Seething at the insult, she threw a pot at Stephen. It was made of the finest porcelain from Sevres and inlaid with delicate colors that were gilded at the edges. It had been one of Stephen's presents: an expensive knickknack that now narrowly missed his head.

Stephen said nothing. He took up his jacket and cane and let himself quietly out the door. The next day, Lady Luttlow received a bracelet of diamonds from Rundell and Bridge. Though it sparkled deliciously upon her wrist, it afforded her no satisfaction at all. The Earl of Davenport was notoriously generous with his farewells. The bracelet—particularly its price—spoke not of conciliation, but of endings. Lady Luttlow slammed the door in the face of Mr. Gregory Dacks. She was so consumed with fury, she could hardly speak.

The only good thing about London was the rain. It matched Stephen's mood as he waved away his carriage and trudged the fashionable streets of Mayfair on foot. The fact that he was making a spectacle of himself seemed to have eluded him, for he was lost in a series of unpleasant thoughts and had the devil of a headache besides.

This, not unnaturally, was the result of several nights of fitful sleep and three decanters of smuggled port bought at a premium. None of these decoctions seemed to have helped in the slightest, hence the earl's desperate attempt to take the air. When his butler confronted him with a salver full of invitations, he waved him away testily, announcing that whilst the countess was not in residence, there was no reason for him to attend any functions whatsoever.

Naturally, such a strange start could not go unnoticed, especially as the butler's niece was a particular friend of the second under maid to Lady Charing, who was the greatest gossipmonger in all of England. Stephen found he could not go to so much as his tailor's without being quizzed most damnably, and as for his greatest friend, Lord Diggory, he was the worst of the lot.

So smitten with mirth was he that he soon found himself sporting a bloody nose, a fact that had Stephen shaken out of his daze of moroseness and apologizing profusely.

"Think nothing of it, Stephen! I've suffered worse than a bloody nose before, I assure you! Only . . . if your wife causes you to behave in such a manner, your feelings for her must be deeper than you would have the world think."

"What if they are?" Stephen's tone was still fierce, despite his shock at his behavior. "Here, have my handkerchief—there is blood all over your lip."

"Thanks. Precisely. What if they are? Is it really so terrible, Stephen, to be in love with your wife? She is a pretty little thing, if I recall, and she looked ravishing at your wedding."

"Yes, I distinctly recall your ogling."

"Then I am lucky to be alive, never mind sporting a bloody nose! She is fetching, Stephen, and now that she is out of her shell, she is lovelier yet."

"And how would you know?"

"I don't. Not personally, so you can take that growl out of your tone, but Hugh Finlay-Orb thinks she is perfection itself and . . ."

"Hugh? What has *he* to say to it?"

"He is only your nearest neighbor, Stephen! It is natural they should meet! What is more, if her ladyship's eye for horseflesh is as unerring as Hugh thinks it is . . ."

"That's it! Confound it, I am going back to Devonport! Hugh Finlay-Orb indeed, jumped-up old popinjay!"

Lord Diggory laughed. "He is actually a pleasant chap . . ."

"Pleasant! He is a meddlesome, troublesome old geezer . . ."

". . . Who you would like to pummel the living daylights out of! Stephen, go and mend things with your wife. I don't think society can bear much more of your tetchiness."

"There is nothing wrong between me and my wife!"

"There is everything wrong, Stephen! You love her and you are too much of a gapseed to tell her so!"

"I've loved a hundred times before! It never lasts!"

"Stephen, you are not your father. Trust yourself. It will last."

Then Lord Diggory, the earl's dearest and most trusted confidant, took himself off. He had said what he had come to say. He counted himself thankful that he had come off so lightly. In the greater scheme of things, a bloodied nose was better than pistols at dawn. In Stephen's current state, pistols were a decided possibility.

It was no more than a day later that Stephen was ready to make his journey home. He'd had much time to contemplate Lord Diggory's parting remarks to him, but in spite of everything, he fooled himself.

He simply was not—could not—be such a sapskull as to have fallen in love with his wife! He needed to take the upper hand, that was all. He would be stern but dignified. He would ignore her soft, appealing eyes and the whisper of the smile that lingered, so often, upon her lips.

He would endeavor to forget how sweet those lips were, for whilst Lady Luttlow had palled, there would surely be some equally ravishing creature to take his carnal fancy.

He would return to Devonport simply to inform Amaryllis that her conduct was displeasing to him. She was interfering with his stables, spoiling his wards, striking up unsuitable friendships with eligible gentlemen . . . oh, there was an endless list of complaints. All unreasonable, of course, but Lord Redding was not in a reasonable mood.

He was *still* not in a reasonable mood when he finally reached Devonport, and noticed that the cottagers had all been given a holiday, and that the children had set up games and shies, and that chestnuts from his avenues of trees were being cooked and conked with varying degrees of mirth and greed. There was laughter in the air, and though Stephen was cross, he was not so cross that he could not smile when he was saluted smartly by a small urchin on his estate, or stop when an old woman wanted to bless him.

It would have been churlish to refuse one of his own roasted chestnuts, or not to take a swing at the shy—and successfully, too, much to the applause of his cottagers. Nevertheless, his heart remained heavy, for it was unpleasant to have to scold, and he felt if he did not do so his whole world would soon be turned completely upside down.

He was just wondering what attitude he should take in his confrontation with Amaryllis—he did not want to crush her, merely resume his masterful control—when his heart almost missed a beat.

In an instant, all his well-prepared speeches flew out of his head. His anger was so absolute and devastating that he ground his nails into his palm. If he had not been wearing riding gloves, he would have done himself an injury.

There, at the top of his avenue, at the main entrance, at the very site where his own horses were meant to stop, was a fashionable barouche. It was painted in gold and emerald green and had cost no less than a small fortune.

He knew, for he had procured the item himself, from two of the best carriage makers in all the land. It was not the carriage he objected to—indeed, it was very fine and extremely well sprung—it was the owner. Unless he was mistaken, Lady Luttlow had had the audacity to darken the very doors of his estate.

Chapter Nine

The ensuing scene was not one Stephen wished to remember. Lady Luttlow was genteelly sipping a dish of tea whilst Amaryllis, pale and stony-faced, helped her to some slices of seedcake.

Too stunned to make an entrance, the earl watched as Lady Luttlow skillfully set about poisoning his wife's mind. Her bracelet sparkled upon her wrist, and when Amaryllis's eyes fell upon it she trilled self-consciously that "Dear Stephen is always so generous."

Amaryllis said nothing, but Lady Luttlow, observing that her hands trembled, pushed home her advantage sweetly.

"It was only last week that he gave me this, though I have told him a dozen times or more that there is really no need. Still, I don't think he can help himself. He is very épris, as I am sure you are aware, such a modern couple as you are! Oh, my dear, *dear* . . . countess. You have spilled your tea! And on such a becoming gown, too, though perhaps a little too . . . sweet for our Stephen's tastes! Still, you hardly know him after all, so perhaps I may advise you—"

"There will be no need to advise, Eugenia! My wife wears every gown to perfection and she seems to have a profound understanding of my tastes."

Stephen entered the room in a cold fury he hardly thought possible. He hardly dared look at Amaryllis's face, so he walked over to Lady Luttlow, whose own tea had now spilled in her surprise.

"Stephen! What brings you here?"

"What brings me to my own home? My wife brings me, if you wish to know! Did you happen to mention to the countess that your little . . . trinket was a parting gift? No? Somehow, I thought not. Amaryllis, I am sorry you have been so imposed upon. It does not fall within your duties to entertain my ex-mistresses, however kindhearted you might be."

Stephen's voice was stern, but Amaryllis thought it had never sounded more wonderful. She wondered if she was in a dream, then saw she was not, for Stephen's top boots were muddy, and such a thing would have been unthinkable in a dream.

As a matter of fact, Stephen had been so incensed by the notion of Lady Luttlow cutting up Amaryllis's peace that he'd had no thought for such matters. He had not even waited for his chaise to halt in an appropriate place before leaping into the dirt of his orderly flower beds.

Now, looking immaculate but for this slight imperfection, Amaryllis was engulfed in so much love she thought it must surely show upon her countenance, though she tried hard to remain cool and collected. Stephen was merely being kind. She should have known he would be too courteous to expect her to entertain his mistresses! She was glad Lady Luttlow had been discarded, for she was mean beneath her studied elegance. Amaryllis thought she might prefer someone who was sweeter tempered, even if a little more vulgar.

She must accustom herself to such thoughts. She must not think that just because Stephen was giving Lady Luttlow her marching papers he would not replace her. He had made the matter plain to her from the outset.

She smiled, and Stephen smiled back. It was not the smile of someone who was thinking of his next paramour, but Amaryllis could not be expected to know that. She did, however, feel insensibly warmed and hardly noticed Lady Luttlow make her exit.

Eugenia Luttlow was defeated at last, not by Stephen's words but by the way he looked at his wife. Worldly-wise, she knew there was no competing with the repressed passion she read in his immobile features. Lord Fortesque, she reasoned with the ruthlessness of her kind, had the advantages of being rich, if not handsome or even young. She had her horses turned round and rapped out the address of Portman Close, Lord Fortesque's residence at Albany.

The Countess of Devonport felt breathless. She always did, when Stephen was near, but now his eyes bored into her own and she really thought if he did not say something she might disgrace herself by swooning or worse, throwing herself into his arms.

She did neither of these dramatic actions, however, but fluttered those lashes a little, for her eyes felt misty and she was determined not to give herself away by wiping her threatening tears.

She need not have worried, for Stephen closed the distance between them almost artlessly, and it was he who offered her a handkerchief—indeed, it was he who carefully dried her eyes. He would have kissed her, too, had she not blurted out the first thing that came to her mind.

"Stephen . . . could . . . would . . . can you tell your mistresses to remain at Honeydew Street? I know it is very wrong of me, but it is really such a . . . such a shock to see them in the country. I hope you understand."

Stephen did not understand. He had just publicly flayed his mistress in front of his wife, and she seemed not to care! Amaryllis was speaking to him as if he had dozens of such creatures—as indeed once he *had* had, if one were to count them year by year rather than all at once as *she* seemed to be doing.

Ironically, he was shocked. His wife was not supposed to know of such matters, much less about his house in Honeydew Street. She spoke about it so composedly, as if she did not care that he was carrying on liaisons when he should be devoting his time to her. Perhaps he had misread her feelings. He had thought . . . oh, he had suspected . . . oh, what a coxcomb he was! He had taken it for granted that she loved him.

Now he was not certain. He knew that if *she* spoke of lovers he would not blink casually and ask her to conduct her affaires more discreetly. But she was doing no such thing. She was not raging like a banshee, she was not as jealous as a vixen, she was not slapping his face as she ought to be doing.

Good heavens, she was simply asking him to break his vows elsewhere. Perhaps she did not care after all. Perhaps his own twisted views of marriage had distorted hers. Perhaps he had been too careful a tutor in preparing her for a marriage based on reason.

He stared at her, trying to read her thoughts. Amaryllis's eyes faltered under that stare. It was too intense for her, too probing. She did not want Stephen to read the secrets of her heart and be embarrassed by them. She forced a gay, slightly false laugh.

"Gracious, is that the time? I am due at the stables in half an hour. There is a stud foal I am particularly desirous of viewing. I had best change, for I am not exactly dressed for mud! Will you come? Sir Hugh will be there, he has been very instructive . . ." Her voice trailed off. Her husband was looking like a thundercloud.

The foal was as promising as Amaryllis had hoped. She purchased it from Sir Hugh, but her heart was not in the transaction, though good manners bade her chat peaceably with her neighbor before turning back for home. She had her groom with her, of course, but he was keeping a respectful distance, so Amaryllis could be alone with her thoughts and her secret longing to rush into the house and throw herself about Stephen's neck.

She dared not think of the evening, when she might have the choice of her own cozily furnished chamber or his. She must not be so shallow as to think of such carnal matters! But Stephen made it very hard, when he was so damnably handsome and persisted in wearing unmentionables that seemed to emphasize every muscle of his lean body.

But no! It was his smile, so heart-stopping, and the sudden blaze in those hypnotic eyes of his. . . . She would not think of it, she must not! All her resolve seemed to melt to custard, which was very foolish of her. But it was not just those intimate nights she was thinking of . . . indeed, it was not.

She wished even more for the pleasures of the day, for laughter shared and humor understood in sudden flashes of quizzical glances across the heads of other more sober individuals. She wanted to ride with Stephen, and read with him, she wanted to be part of his life, involved in his decisions. She wanted to be able to tease him, to not feel shy or anxious . . . to have his baby with joy and pride. . . . Oh, she was asking for the moon! She pulled her horse up short.

"'Rilla!" It was the children. Their high voices could be heard a mile away, and she smiled at their unconscious nickname for her. She slid off her mount and handed the reigns to her groom.

"Where are you?" She put her hands to her mouth to call. It was unladylike, but she felt unladylike with her disheveled hair and the wind at her back

"Up in the gardens by the gazebo. Come help us! There is a cat stuck up a tree!"

Amaryllis smiled as she covered the distance quickly. Doubtless the poor creature had run up there to escape Clem's fond attentions. In this she was more right than she knew, for Clem had taken the notion into her head that the cat was cold and was doing her level best to dress it in a jacket from the charades box.

"It won't come down."

"Nor would I, if I were forced to wear that hideous garment!"

The girls laughed.

"Can you get her?"

"She will come down if we leave her."

"What if she can't? What if she is frightened? She is only a snip of a thing, you know. "

"Oh, very well, give me a leg up, will you, and don't— I repeat—don't—tell your governess I have been teaching you such tricks!" The girls laughed.

Amaryllis was faster up the tree than her gentle upbringing ought to have allowed. Very soon, she was cradling the kitten, who gave her a very satisfactory purr before snuggling into the side of her face. The only snag was that looking down, Amaryllis suddenly felt dizzy.

This sensation was compounded by the fact that she now had one hand, not two, at her disposal. The kitten could not be expected to cling on unaided. She could place it in her pocket, but she was not sure it would stay there while she was looking for suitable footholds.

Amaryllis remained calm, for there were worse things, after all, than being stuck up a pear tree with a kitten nibbling at one's ear. If she remained perfectly still, there was no danger of falling. She refused to be beaten by a wave of silly dizziness.

"Girls, I'm afraid you are going to be shocked," she called without looking down.

"What is it? Is it safe? Is it shivering? Is it . . . is it sick?"

"None of those things. The problem, I am afraid, lies entirely with me. Would you think me very shimble-shambled if I tell you I am stuck?"

"*You* are stuck?"

The girls, some way below, did not look worried at all. If Amaryllis did not know better, she would have thought they looked gleeful. On second thought, they *were* gleeful. Cheeky little devils! But they had a point. It was not often one could boast of a live grown-up ignominiously stuck up a pear tree. Worse, one that was swathed in skirts and billowing petticoats that seemed to tangle into every wretched twig.

"I am afraid so!" Amaryllis was almost cheerful, for the kitten was sweeter than she expected, and softer. It felt good—immensely good—to have something to feel tender about, no matter how absurd one's current condition. For a letting moment she thought of motherhood then smiled mistily.

"Call Rivers. Ask him to bring a ladder."

"Yes, but the kitten . . ."

"See, she is safe. If I had a ladder I could tuck her in my pocket and make a smooth descent. As it is, I cannot! What is she called?"

"She hasn't got a name! We were just deciding."

"How about we call her . . ." Amaryllis blushed. Fortunately, the children could not see her face, for it was obscured by branches.

"Well, how about we call her Stephanie, after your uncle?"

The children agreed doubtfully, unaware that their uncle himself was now interestedly watching the spectacle. He had been thinking of Amaryllis all day, and had responded immediately when he heard his nieces call

As interested as the children, he'd watched as a tiny scrap of a thing was held aloft for inspection. It was, he thought, with a sudden lifting of his spirits, a singularly unworthy specimen for his namesake. It mewed.

"May we keep it?"

"I daresay you might, if I ever manage to climb down this

tree. It is a shocking thing, is it not, that I have forgotten how to do so? My spirits are quite overset! Now do me a favor, Vicky, fetch Rivers before we both fall out."

But neither Victoria nor Clementine ever got to fetch Rivers. Instead, they turned about and squealed with delight at the sight of their uncle, who was not nearly so stuffy as he liked everyone to think.

Amaryllis, her heart beating wildly—as it always did when she caught sight of her husband, a most annoying trait, she did pray it would pass—gasped a little in surprise.

The kitten wriggled. Amaryllis, caught off guard, threw her weight forward to catch it. She lost her grip on the topmost branch and the one just beneath it cracked from the sudden weight. Or something like that—Amaryllis could never perfectly remember the exact order of the proceedings.

Suffice it to say she did not land on the hard, root-riddled land as she had feared. Instead, she found herself being caught, gallantly, by the very person she'd been trying her level best to rid from her mind.

Never, never, had she wanted to be kissed more. She turned her face away so that Stephen would not understand the yearning in her eyes and be embarrassed by her stupid longing.

His lordship, suddenly suffering no such qualms, turned it right back. What he read in those eyes removed all the last vestiges of his waning doubts. She loved him, of a certainty she did. There was no longer any question about what he felt either, or whether it was right or appropriate or proper. It was the most perfect thing in the world, and he would be damned if he would fight against it another minute of his life!

He teased her with the softest of feather-light kisses. Just one, as naturally he had to endure the hoots and shouts and good-natured teasing of his nieces. He set Amaryllis down and frowned upon the truant duo. He ruined his effect, however, for the kitten found her courage and sprung down, to land helter-skelter upon his head.

His smart town beaver was almost entirely squashed, but since his arms now crept about Amaryllis's waist, he did not appear to mind. It must have been her christening the cat Stephanie that had removed his last doubts. Or perhaps it had been a day spent in contemplation, regret, remorse, musing, remembering. . . . Whatever it was, the nagging doubts seemed to have evaporated like dew on a spring morning.

The children, sensing something intriguing and exciting afoot, were inclined to stay, but they were sent packing by Stephen himself in the lordliest of terms.

"And take this . . . this creature with you. I cannot think Stephanie a good name for it. It is far too scrawny. Ask Nurse Rowlings to fatten her up, will you? And don't come back till after tea. The countess and I have some . . . well, we have some talking to do."

At which, when they were safely out of harm's way, the naughty young scamps resumed their improper giggles. . . .

The earl and his lady were reconciled, at last, to their marriage. Under that fateful pear tree they discovered that it was no longer a matter of convenience, or pity or kindness.

Amaryllis, conscious, from the start, of the latter two, was at pains to discover what it was that had changed Stephen's outlook.

He was silent for a moment, unable to say anything, except that love had crept up on him, that Amaryllis's freshness was a welcome change from the cloying affectations he had become accustomed to.

Studied beauty compared poorly with her speaking eyes and the joy that emanated from her heart rather than from the painted red lips he was more familiar with. Her question was difficult to answer, but he gave it the thought that was its due. Plainly—for he resolved always to be plain with her—he told her that he had come to celebrate the very qualities he once pitied her for.

"Generosity and openness of spirit, kindness, calmness . . .

subtle beauty over overt sensuality . . . But I am a fool! Your subtle beauty is inspiring me with prodigious lust! Come, spare your blushes, young lady! You are a siren, Amaryllis, and you shall suffer the forfeit!"

Amaryllis did not seem to mind in the least. A few teasing kisses and Stephen was convinced that an heir for Devonport was now a priority of the highest order.

He said as much, whispering that he did not know how he might possibly tolerate another year without the promised delights of fatherhood.

"I promised no such thing!"

"Indeed you did when you consented to marry me! I told you specifically that I needed an heir."

"Yes, but you said not necessarily immediately."

"I've changed my mind. I want one at once."

"What if we have a girl?"

"I would be delighted. Now do stop talking and let me begin the business forthwith."

But for once, Amaryllis was firm. She set Stephen aside and asked, with a rather more serious note to her tone, "Do you really want to be a father?"

"Indeed I do! That is why I went to all the trouble of marrying you, after all."

Amaryllis smiled. "Too bad I had to be part of the bargain."

"Nonsense! I couldn't imagine a nicer way to become a parent. Amaryllis, loving you has been my first and most vital lesson in fatherhood. I was selfish and arrogant before, not good qualities, I am afraid, in a father. I hope to do better with our son—or, yes, with our daughter! Now do stop talking and allow me to kiss you or we shall never have this paragon . . ."

Amaryllis shyly informed him there was no such need. She was with child, but he was neither to fuss nor to forbid her to climb trees.

His lordship stared. Then a slow, unequivocal smile of delight crossed his features so that Amaryllis was left in no doubt whatsoever about his feelings.

"Minx! When did you know?"

"The knowledge has just crept up on me and I saw Dr. Adams yesterday morning."

"And you had to entertain that . . . that . . . creature today! Oh, Amaryllis, I am so sorry!"

Amaryllis smiled through sudden tears. "No need, Stephen, you have made me happier than you will ever know."

"Have I? Then I shall have to rectify that at once. I forbid you to climb trees!"

"I will not be cosseted!"

His lordship, arguing the point, kissed her nose.

Then, of course, he progressed to her belly, for he could not exclude his heir in such amiable matters. Then, feeling that the pear tree, though a delightful refuge, was not quite so cozy as his bed, he took Amaryllis up in his arms and strode with her into the house.

Two housemaids and a gardener giggled, but the earl did not care in the least. Neither did Amaryllis, for she was shedding her shyness with each increasing second.

By the time his lordship had kicked his door closed—a shocking way of treating such costly wood—he was more than reconciled to the astonishing notions of becoming a father and loving his wife.

Amaryllis, content with his next masterful series of actions, was similarly reconciled, though the heir to Devonport was not. Snug in his womb, Amaryllis could have sworn he kicked in indignation. The countess smiled and blithely ignored his protests. For once, she had other matters upon her mind. . . .

Historical Romance from
Jo Ann Ferguson